BRIGHT YOUNG THINGS

ALSO BY ANNA GODBERSEN

THE LUXE
RUMORS
ENVY
SPLENDOR

BRIGHT YOUNG THINGS

ANNA GODBERSEN

HARPER
An Imprint of HarperCollins*Publishers*

Bright Young Things

 For information address HarperCollins Children's Books, a division of HarperCollins Publishers, 10 East 53rd Street, New York, NY 10022.
www.harperteen.com

Produced by Alloy Entertainment
151 West 26th Street, New York, NY 10001

Library of Congress Cataloging-in-Publication Data is available.

ISBN 978-0-06-196266-0 (trade bdg.)
ISBN 978-0-06-201529-7 (int. edition)

Design by Liz Dresner

10 11 12 13 14 CG/BV 10 9 8 7 6 5 4 3 2 1

First Edition

For the Coven

Something bright and alien flashed across the sky . . . and for a moment people set down their glasses in country clubs and speakeasies and thought of their old best dreams. Maybe there was a way out by flying, maybe our restless blood could find frontiers in the illimitable air. But by that time we were all pretty well committed; and the Jazz Age continued; we would all have one more.

—F. Scott Fitzgerald, "Echoes of the Jazz Age," *The Crack-Up*

PROLOGUE

IT IS EASY TO FORGET NOW, HOW EFFERVESCENT AND free we all felt that summer. Everything fades: the shimmer of gold over White Cove; the laughter in the night air; the lavender early morning light on the faces of skyscrapers, which had suddenly become so heroically tall. Every dawn seemed to promise fresh miracles, among other joys that are in short supply these days. And so I will try to tell you, while I still remember, how it was then, before everything changed—that final season of an era that roared.

By the summer of 1929, when the weather was just getting warm enough that girls could exhibit exactly how high hemlines had risen, Prohibition had been in effect for so long it had ceased to bother anyone much. The city had a speakeasy per every fifty souls, or so the preachers liked to exclaim on Sundays, and sweet-faced girls from the hinterlands were no longer blinded by wood alcohol, for the real stuff had become plenty easy to get. The Eighteenth Amendment had converted us all to grateful outlaws.

We did whatever we liked and dressed in whatever we thought smart and broke rules for the sport of it—diving into public fountains, mixing social classes as casually as we mixed cocktails. There were no longer exclusive balls given for a few people with old money and good names, and even if there were, no one would have cared to go. Nice girls wore the kind of makeup that thirty years before would only have been seen on actresses, and actresses were escorted publicly by the scions of shipping fortunes, and some of them did not even bother to disguise their Bronx accents. Girls took to dressing like boys, and though women had obtained the vote, we had swiftly moved on to pursuing flashier freedoms: necking in cars and smoking cigarettes and walking down city streets in flesh-colored stockings.

New York was the capital of commerce and joy, and young people sought us from every direction. They came in droves, to join the kind of party only a great metropolis can host. They came from wealthy families and farming families, from the north and south and west. They came to avoid kitchens and marriages, to a place where they could reasonably claim to be eighteen forever. Or for the foreseeable future, anyway, which seemed to us the same thing. They came, mostly, for the fun—especially the young things, especially the girls.

I can't remember very many now—although there are three, from that last incandescent summer, whom I resist forgetting. They were all marching toward their own secret fates, and long before the next decade rolled around, each would escape in her own way—one would be famous, one would be married, and one would be dead.

That is what I want to tell you about: the girls with their short skirts and bright eyes and big-city dreams.

The girls of 1929.

1

THE HANDFUL OF WEDDING GUESTS WERE ALREADY assembled in the clapboard Lutheran church on Main Street, and though they had been waiting for a quarter hour, any stray passerby might have noticed a lone girl still loitering outside. It was past four o'clock on that sleepy Union, Ohio, Sunday, and the dappled afternoon sun played on her high, fine cheekbones and on the strands of her loosely braided honey-and-bark-colored hair. The girl was just eighteen, and had graduated from Union's one-room high school two weeks earlier. If that passerby had bothered to ponder her eyes—which were the sweet, translucent brown of Coca-Cola in a glass—he might have recognized in them a brewing agitation.

She let those eyes drift to the glaze of sun between the tree branches overhead; her lips parted, and she let out a breath. The homemade dress she wore was of simple white cotton, and though the style was not entirely appropriate for the event—she had tried, but mostly failed, to sew it in the shorter, sportier fashion now worn in cities—the color marked her as the bride.

Through the narrow windows she could see the guests in their pews and the tall figure of the only boy in Union who had ever paid her any attention, standing patiently at the altar. He was wearing his father's black suit, and his sand-colored hair was a little overgrown and rough around his face, which was big and pleasing but not yet a man's. The sight of him made her agitation worse, and she drew back a little and closed her eyes. Everything had happened so quickly. She hadn't really believed there would be a wedding until that morning, when she woke up and it suddenly dawned on her that her situation was quite real.

"Cordelia!"

She turned at the sound of her name and saw her best friend, Letty Haubstadt, whose eyes stood out like two pure blue planets against the white oval of her face. Her dark hair was parted down the middle and pinned back, and her petite body was clothed in the same black dress and black tights and black shoes her father always insisted she wear. The sight of

Letty reassured Cordelia some, even if her garb was a little funereal for a wedding, and she managed to almost smile.

"I'm sorry it took me so long," Letty told her, smiling more broadly. Then she untucked the folded yards of mosquito netting that she'd been carrying under her arm, shook it out, and stood on her tiptoes to arrange it over the taller girl's head. "I know your aunt says you don't deserve one, but I just think it wouldn't be a wedding if the bride wasn't wearing a veil."

There was a sharp rapping on the windowpane, and both girls looked up to see Cordelia's aunt Ida, her thin lips set in a hard grimace, looking down at them expectantly. Cordelia gave her aunt a curt nod and turned back to her friend.

Letty handed her a bouquet of yellow wildflowers, which she must have picked on the way there, and then asked, "Are you ready?"

Cordelia glanced up to make sure her aunt had returned to her seat, and then pulled the netting away from her face so that she could look directly at her friend. She swallowed hard, and said, "Let's go tonight."

Letty's smile fell, and her face grew pale. "Tonight?"

"You'll never be a star if you stay here." Cordelia fixed her friend with an intense gaze. She was merely saying out loud what they both knew to be true. "The train leaves at six fifty-two from the Defiance Station."

There was only one train a day in that part of the state that would carry you all the way to New York City—a fact Cordelia had known for years. She knew the timetable by heart, for running away was an obsessive fantasy that had carried no special urgency until the dawning hours of that particular day, when the notion that she was to be married had ceased to seem absurd and faraway, and she had begun to apprehend it with a kind of dread. By the time she'd risen to help her aunt with breakfast, the plot to leave had taken on a decided shape, and though her mind had pulsed with it all morning, Cordelia had not imagined she might be brave enough to go until she said it out loud to Letty.

There was no discussion. Letty repeated the train's departure time and nodded. Then Cordelia replaced the netting over her face and followed her friend up the creaking wooden steps to the church. She glanced back once, at the little gabled structures—houses and storefronts and churches—that constituted Union, where she knew everyone by name, and everyone knew her as the parentless girl with the perpetually scraped knees. In a few hours she would be on a train, and all this would be lost to her. By then the dusk would have settled in and the darkness would be soon to follow—and in that part of the world the darkness could go on and on forever, as though there would never be light again. She hadn't ever been able to tolerate that very well.

Moving up the aisle, toward the head of the church, she

could barely feel her own feet. It was almost as though she were floating; her movements had become automatic, beyond her control. A greenish light filtered in through the narrow windows along the sidewalls, beneath the high, peaked ceiling with its unfinished wood beams. John's parents and younger brothers were situated on one side of the aisle, and on the other sat her aunt, with that same grimace, in an old flowered dress with a large white lace collar, and Uncle Jeb, in his overalls, with her cousin, Michael, between them. In the pew behind her aunt and uncle sat Letty's two sisters, Louisa and Laura, wearing the same tight, old-fashioned bun.

In Union, the Haubstadt family was known for their dairy farm, for their austerity and religious reverence, and for having worn all black since the death of Mrs. Haubstadt, during the birth of Letty's youngest sister, six years ago. She was remembered by her children as a saint, and Cordelia couldn't argue: Any woman who withstood the tempers and severe expectations of old man Haubstadt deserved some kind of deification, although it seemed to Cordelia like a dubious achievement, not to mention a questionable use of one's time on this Earth. In the family photographs, Mrs. Haubstadt appeared almost comically small when situated beside her husband. Of the five siblings, only Letty was petite like her mother. "The little one," the others called her, and they treated her as though her size made her invisible.

The faces of each guest turned toward the bride, and though some of them tried to smile, their eyes seemed to say, *I know what you've done.*

Lest their looks cut her, Cordelia reminded herself that she was only half one of them. While her mother had been raised in Union, the other half of Cordelia came from some glittering, far-off place, and like Letty, she was too big for the town she'd grown up in. Letty was right, Cordelia now realized with some relief, to have insisted on a veil. Not only to protect her from the guests' stares and the judgment in their expressions, but also because of John, who was now reaching for her hands. His eyes were shining, but she could not meet them. She didn't want any memory of the happy, expectant way he was gazing at her.

She wanted to remember John Field the way he had been on the day after graduation, when they'd gone down to the place where the creek gets deep, and she had declared she wasn't going to ruin a perfectly good slip by swimming in it, and that if she went naked, he was going to have to, too. John had swallowed hard and watched her as he pulled his own clothes over his head and followed her lead into the swimming hole, running in to the knees, diving headfirst after that. Later they had crawled onto the pebbly bank, shivering and breathless from the cold. In the sunshine it had been so hot, you might have burned the bottoms of your feet, but in the shadows there was a chill. Then she'd kissed him, burrowing against him for warmth, and when she'd gotten bored of that, she had told him not to hold back the way they usually did. At first he'd insisted they shouldn't, but eventually he couldn't resist her. His eyes were green, and they had gazed into hers, impressed, a little fearful, full of wonder. What he'd done hurt at first, but then it was over, too quickly, and she'd wanted to go on feeling that new sweet, searing pain all over again.

And she might have too, without any real consequence, had her cousin Michael not been peeping and run all the way home to tell Aunt Ida. When Cordelia had returned to help prepare the evening meal, there was blood on her slip and her hair was a mess, so it was impossible to lie about what she'd done. Not that she wanted to.

"Just like your mother," Aunt Ida had said, pressing her furious lips together so that the deep, vertical wrinkles below her nose emerged.

Just like your mother was what Aunt Ida always said, even when Cordelia was a little girl, whenever she was late for church or slow fetching water from the well, or when she became too happy or too sullen. *Just like your mother,* until young Cordelia began to wear the admonishment like a badge of pride. *Just like your mother,* Aunt Ida had repeated over and again as she bullied John, and Dr. and Mrs. Field, and Cordelia herself into agreeing to a private ceremony in the Lutheran church on

Main, on the next convenient Sunday afternoon. Thus Aunt Ida secured two things she had always wanted in one fell swoop: her trouble-seeking niece out of her hair forever and the whole transaction sanctified in her favorite place, God's house.

Even standing with John now, at the front of the mostly empty church, all Cordelia could think of was escape. For though he was handsome and good, he would never be enough for her, and she could not help but anticipate the next fifty years of bleak winters and church picnics and screaming babies as no more than dreary distractions on the way to the grave. Not when she had that burning curiosity to see what lay beyond the straight-laid streets of Union, with its church spires and few lone telephone wires and its surrounding farms. Not when she knew for sure that her curiosity would scorch her if she didn't heed it. No, she wanted to see the world, and even as she promised to be John's forever, in her head she was planning how to steal away long enough to grab her case—already packed with the few things she would be taking to the Fields'—and slip out the back window onto the alley, and make her way to the station for the 6:52 train that went all night to New York City, where she had been born.

When she heard her aunt clearing her throat, Cordelia realized that she had missed everything Father Andersen had said, including his prompting to her one and only line.

"I do," she said, closing her eyes so John wouldn't see the dishonesty in them, and hoping he'd forgive her someday.

Then Father Andersen pronounced them man and wife, and John moved toward her and folded the netting back over the crown of her head. She was almost shocked to look at him straight on, with no barrier between them, but when he put his mouth to hers, it was in the same soft, intentional way he'd always kissed her before. Someone—probably her aunt—let out an audible sigh of relief. It was not until the newly married couple had turned to walk back down the aisle that Cordelia realized it was the last kiss John would ever give her.

2

THEY HEARD THE TRAIN A WHILE BEFORE THEY SAW IT, just as they passed out of the woods that separated Union, Ohio, from the next town over, and it was about that time that both girls broke into a run. Letty was shocked by how rapidly the train's noise approached, the screech of steel wheels against steel tracks. She looked over her shoulder to see how it towered over them, but Cordelia, her long legs moving as fast as possible, did not turn her head once. The cars shot by them, rearranging the sun-touched strands around Cordelia's face. Letty's bun was too firmly in place for that, but her old peacoat flapped open as she tried to keep up.

Cordelia was a year ahead of her in school and always

spoke with an enviable sureness. As long as they'd been friends, she'd told Letty that they were both too good for Union, that someday they'd find a way out. But Letty had always known it. She'd known since she was a little girl that there was something special about her. The way she moved, the purity of her voice—she had an attention-drawing quality that her mother used to call her "magic." And Mother had been a true beauty who'd danced with the Cleveland ballet when she was young, before she'd met Father. She used to whisper that Letty was her favorite, the most gifted of her children, when they'd had their dance lessons on the first-floor parlor of the big house on Main Street—back when they were a happy family, before Mother was taken from them and Father decreed that dancing was one of the devil's tricks and that there would be no nicknames in the Haubstadt clan and began calling her Letitia, her given name.

Up ahead, at the Defiance Station, the waiting passengers stepped forward across the platform in anticipation. There was a flurry of activity—everyone shouting, luggage being thrust upward, boys who'd been raised on farms saying good-bye to their mothers for a long time. They probably wore new coats over humble denim, which would of course give them away. But then, the dour quality of Letty's own dress and her strait-laced bun also gave her away, too, as the product of a very backward place. In the city, she used to like to tell herself before she fell asleep, all her most brilliant qualities would be instantly recognized and celebrated. For years, she had dreamed of going there—only, she could scarcely believe that dream was now about to become real, on this summer evening in mid-May of the year 1929.

That is, if she could keep her pace up. She had become breathless, and her legs were tired, and the duffel she carried over her narrow shoulders must have grown in size since they'd left Union. It seemed to weigh almost as much as her younger sister Laura, who still demanded piggyback rides even though she was tall for her age, and even though their father frowned upon that sort of thing.

Up ahead the conductor yelled, "All aboard!"

"Wait!" Cordelia tried to yell, but her lungs were working hard already.

The porters had finished loading the crates of red berries and milk onto the freight car down the line, and all the passengers had disappeared behind the high glass windows. The family and friends who had come from miles around to wish them good-bye had stepped back. Beyond the station, the land stretched out, revealing clusters of clapboard houses and farms.

"All aboard!" the conductor bellowed, and then turned and took hold of the iron handle to pull himself up.

The girls were still a good way down the tracks, and in a moment of horror, Letty saw that they were going to miss the train. Then she would have no place to go home to. For once Father realized she was gone, he would never permit her to return. Father did not tolerate disloyalty or what he would deem frivolous daydreams. Summoning all the power her voice was capable of, Letty lifted her free arm and sang out, "Wait! Wait for us!"

The conductor paused, holding on to the side of the train, and squinted in their direction.

"Please, wait!" Letty's voice rang out.

"All aboard!" the conductor yelled.

They kept up their pace as they climbed the steps at the edge of the platform, and by the time they reached the conductor, their cheeks were rosy with exertion.

"Two more," Cordelia managed once they were just in front of him.

"I can see that." The conductor jumped down so the girls could go ahead of him into the car. Cordelia reached back for Letty's hand, and they ascended the ladder together. Letty barely noticed the rungs—they were only moving up into the train, and then down the car, along the aisle between green felt-covered seats. The bells began to clang, and the doors slammed shut, sealing the passengers in.

"I can't believe it." Letty's voice was musical with wonder. "I can't believe we're really leaving!"

"I thought we wouldn't make it," Cordelia returned in the

same awestruck tone, as her breath slowed to normal.

Letty nodded in agreement. The terror of having to go back to the Haubstadt home ebbed, and in her relief she began to laugh. The laughter became contagious as they located their seats and fell into them. Cordelia went first, sitting close to the window, and Letty followed, slumping against her shoulder in giggles.

"Tickets?"

It had not occurred to Letty, in all the furious excitement of leaving, that it would cost anything to ride a train. But before she could reply, Cordelia had taken a worn notebook from the inside pocket of the old trench she wore, and from the middle pages she removed an envelope stuffed with bills.

"Names?" the conductor demanded, as he positioned his pencil over two soft red booklets.

"Cordelia Grey and Letitia Haubstadt," Cordelia announced, handing over the fare.

"Actually, it's just Letty now," she corrected brightly, twisting to face the conductor. She plucked the ticket back from his hand, and then taking his pencil, carefully began to rewrite the name he'd entered for her. "Letty Larkspur."

There was a touch of knowing disdain in the way he punched their tickets, but Letty decided to ignore the contortion at the corner of his mouth. "To the end of the line?" he concluded.

"Yes," said Cordelia. "To New York City."

"We'll get there sometime tomorrow afternoon."

"Yes, I know," she replied, in that crisp voice that brushed aside any criticism or doubt. That voice had been used over the years to protect herself and Letty both—from cruel classmates and bullying siblings and Letty's own doubts. Even now, Letty shuddered at the idea of bearing Union alone, without her friend's protection.

As the conductor moved down the aisle, greeting the other passengers, Cordelia put her feet up against the back of the next row of seats, stretching her long legs, turning the scuffed, narrow toes of her boots in toward each other. She slouched into her seat, sinking until they were the same height; when she turned her face to her left, her eyes just met Letty's.

"So what do you think?" Letty whispered, almost afraid to hear the opinion she nonetheless badly wanted.

"What do I think of what?"

"My new name." She paused and widened her eyes. "Letty Larkspur!"

"I *like* it."

"You do?" Letty whispered, relieved, even though she'd known in her heart that the name she had chosen was incomparably pretty. She'd been turning over those four syllables in her mind for a long time now, to make herself feel better during a long workday, or almost humming them just before she went to sleep, telling herself that everything would be different once she was known by them. That then, finally, her life would be buoyant and shiny and worthy of notice.

Cordelia pressed the back of her head into the seat and smiled wide. "I think it's perfect for you."

"Isn't it?" Letty squeezed her eyes closed. "Doesn't it sound like the kind of girl who steps off the train into a big city and stumbles into a series of lucky breaks, each new one more glorious than the last, until she is known all around town and her name is up in lights?" The sun outside was fading, but what was left of it was playing in Letty's blue eyes. Cordelia reached over and drew the pins from Letty's hair so that it fell in straight, dark strands around her shoulders. "Doesn't it sound like the kind of name that almost guarantees I'll be a famous singer? Doesn't it sound like *me*?"

"Yes, it sounds just like you. Except—you in the big city, far away from drab parlors and the small-minded people who occupy them, and their itsy-bitsy idea of the world."

"The version of me wearing fur coats, with a puppy under my arm, and a retinue."

"A retinue?"

"Yes, a *retinue*. A chauffeur and a maid and a cook—"

"—a chef."

"Yes!" Letty sighed and shook her hair loose around the prim collar of her black dress.

Besides the three Haubstadt girls, there were two boys who wore their hair with military brevity and the same black trousers and shirts every day, even in the late-summer heat, even when they worked twelve-hour days on the family dairy farm. It hadn't always been like that—her father had been a joyful person once, but that was a long time ago, when Mother was still there to show him how. He must have been happy when they were married, because people were always happy when they got married.

But then Letty remembered the events of the day, and realized that was perhaps not always true. "How John must be crying," she said softly, thinking what a tender person was at the core of that tall, strong boy and how sincere he had sounded when he'd said, *I do*. There was to have been a celebration at the Fields' that evening, and Letty thought of all those uneaten pies with pity, for surely no one in their house was in a festive mood now. John had been a worse one than Letty for following Cordelia around, hanging on her words, trusting in whatever she thought was interesting or correct, and it pained her to imagine him alone back in Union and yearning terribly. But that pain gave way to another melancholy realization: Letty's own flesh and blood probably had not heeded her absence with even half so much woe.

"John isn't the kind to cry." Cordelia spoke with a sad certainty as she pulled the skirt of her dress down over her knees.

"I can't believe we made it," Letty marveled again, because she could see her friend didn't want to pursue the topic. But some of the glitter had gone out of her voice now, and there was a tightness in her throat.

"Well, we haven't made it yet," Cordelia corrected.

But as if in response, the train lurched into motion. And though Letty was afraid of what she had done, she was relieved, too, that she wouldn't have to sit around that sad, silent dinner table anymore, always doing as her father told her, and her tender ears would no longer be exposed to his shouting when he was in one of his foul moods. She leaned forward and began to undo the tight lacing of her boots. Once she had shucked them, she folded her black stockinged feet under her thighs and put her head against her friend's shoulder.

"We haven't made it yet, but we did make it out of Union." Letty closed her eyes and tried to dwell only on the audaciousness, and not the sadness, of their feat.

"Yes!" Cordelia replied, and then she turned to gaze a final time at the only world she'd ever known. It was a landscape Cordelia felt no love for: Dull and repetitive, any beauty in the greenery only reminding her how bare and brown everything would soon enough become, before the harsh winter. That monotonous and familiar brown that infused everything as seasons stacked up into years. And yet as Cordelia placed a palm against the window, what she saw outside did cause her to feel something like surprise.

The tallest boy in Union High School's class of '29 sat on a pile of railroad ties east of the station, watching her. His legs too long, bent upwards, elbows rested on knees, the boyishness of his features suddenly effaced by sorrow. The cuffs of the white dress shirt he had worn to the ceremony were rolled up, and his tie had been removed, so that his Adam's apple created a poignant shadow in the dying light. His feet were too large for his lean limbs, and they looked especially ridiculous in the fancy borrowed shoes he wore. As the train went past, Cordelia's eyes met his, but he didn't raise a hand to make even the slightest wave. It was as though he had been sitting there a while, waiting to see her pass. He must have realized she had left some time before, and then guessed where she'd be going.

But a train travels faster than she could ever have imagined, and with cruel concision, he was gone.

Cordelia gazed out at the cabins on the horizon line, with their kerosene lanterns in the windows. The sky was heavily curtained with purple now, and the small towns and the great spaces in between passed by at a speed that she had known was possible but had never experienced. It was all receding into their past just as quickly as they could have hoped, framed neatly by the train's rectangular, black-rimmed windows.

"I walked right out the front door," Letty murmured. The lids of her eyes were falling shut, each word following the last more slowly now as the haziness of sleep settled around her. No doubt her day had been long already—she must have been up with the dawn, milking cows, finishing her chores so as to be on time for the wedding—and when she started talking of sad things, she often became tired and withdrawn. "None of them even noticed."

Cordelia watched her friend's face, which was as quiet and white as the moon, though it glowed with the full vibrancy of the life beneath the skin.

"Louisa was making dinner, I guess, and the boys must've still been on the farm . . ."

Despite her family's long history of insensibility, Cordelia knew her friend was wounded by their final indifference, by their failure to recognize that she was leaving forever. It was obvious in the way Letty had gone limp against her shoulder.

"They probably won't even realize until, one day, they open the newspaper and find the name *Letty Larkspur* . . . which I suppose won't mean anything to them. But they *will* recognize the picture next to it . . . maybe a picture of me onstage, during a standing ovation, heaps of roses at my feet . . ."

By the time Letty trailed off, her eyes were sealed shut and her lips had parted just slightly so she could exhale the soft, warm breaths of the unconscious.

Cordelia was relieved she didn't have to respond. Escaping Union for the big city was the idea that had bonded Letty and Cordelia to one another, but Cordelia was an altogether more durable creature than her friend, and she knew nothing came so easily as all that—especially fame and fortune and all those treasures that everyone desires.

Perhaps it was this sharper sense of the realities of life that made Cordelia tight-lipped about her own dream. She had allowed her best friend—her only friend, really—to believe she was simply running for the fun of it. But the real reason was the kind of story an orphan girl can feed on for years, and she knew in some buried way that if anyone had questioned or doubted it, she might have had to curl up and die.

Outside, Ohio fell away in the night; she was traveling at unprecedented speed toward the place she had always dreamed of going back to. The other passengers in the car had stopped talking. It was quiet, and the lights above had dimmed. If she could have foreseen everything that was to happen in the next couple of weeks, how sleepless and manic and full they would be, she might have tried to get some rest, too. But her eyes were wild, and there was so much electricity in every corner of her head and heart—she was too alive with awake dreams to try to have any of the other variety. She wanted to see the sun coming up in another state, and everything else the world had been holding just out of her reach.

3

THE MARSH ESTATE WAS DECEPTIVELY NAMED, FOR THE grounds were expertly manicured by a team of ten gardeners so that its appearance would have none of the wildness that name might otherwise conjure. The place was called Marsh only because the man who had built it had been called Marsh. It sat on the lovely finger of land that marked the eastern border of White Cove, on the north shore of Long Island—a short drive to Wall Street and all the money that was made there, but a long way from the city's more sordid quarters.

The impossibly green lawns were populated as far as the eye could see by a hundred varieties of tree, many imported from the English countryside. Beneath the arbor of their branches walked a girl wearing loose-fitting, pale peach silk pajamas, an old tennis visor, and a mink jacket that was short enough to reveal the fast cadence of her slim hips, even though it was late enough in the day that somewhere, people were already dressing for dinner, and a season when fur is hardly necessary.

Her name was Astrid Donal. She had a full head of egg yolk yellow hair, cut so that its tips curled against her jaw, and the soft, heart-shaped face of a girl young enough to still have a taste for sweets but old enough to have been quite frequently kissed. If she had been asked the time, she might have guessed from recent experience that it was no longer morning, but it would have been impossible for her to name the exact hour. As for the coat, it was merely an aberration of Astrid's temperament that she often felt cold when no one else did. But now, as she wandered across the lawns, she began to feel truly warm, and let the mink slip from her shoulders and fall onto the ground.

"Miss Donal!"

Astrid squinted in the bright sunlight to make out her maid on the stone verandah of the home that belonged to her mother's third husband, Harrison Marsh II.

"Telephone for you!"

Astrid's feet carried her up a gentle slope, ending her meander sooner than she'd really intended. "I lost my jacket somewhere, somehow," she announced a little breathlessly when she reached the maid's side. "Do send someone out to find it, dear?"

"Yes, miss. Telephone for you."

"I heard you," Astrid replied, hurriedly but not unkindly, as she went into the dimly lit first floor and tried to make her eyes adjust. Her bones had that delightful weightless quality of having not been awake very long, and she smiled a little to think that she could simply skip over the hours when one wore daytime clothes. Was it only one week ago she had returned from her all-girls boarding school in Connecticut, arriving by a private ferry that carried her and her fourteen pieces of luggage across the sound? She had another year at Miss Porter's, but somewhere over the course of the last seven days she had acquired the fatalistic notion that she would not be returning there. She wasn't exactly sure why, for she could be a very good student when she bothered to concentrate. Perhaps it was that her life here seemed to swallow her so completely, and then everything outside it began to seem vague and unimportant.

Crossing through the library with its leaded glass windows on either side, she arrived in the main hall at the front of the house. No lamps had been turned on yet, and there was only the bluish natural light coming in from the great windows that flanked the door. The receiver of the telephone lay on its side atop a little polished rosewood table. She paused a moment before picking it up, noticing that her pajama pants had become slightly muddied at the hems.

"Hello?" she finally said, resting the receiver next to her face.

"Hello, baby."

Astrid's eyelids sank closed, and a small crescent emerged at the left corner of her lips. The sound of his voice always made her feel like a precious doll. His voice was like him, big and impressive, and it immediately brought to mind the various places they had been last night and the many things they had done. "Morning, Charlie. Are you just waking up?"

"No, baby, I can't lounge around like you all day." In the background, she could hear the voices of men speaking in three-word sentences.

"No . . . you've been up for hours, I suppose, seeing to very important things," she teased. Her eyes were still closed, and she swayed in the cool quiet of Marsh Hall's foyer. It had been more than a year now that she'd been calling Charlie her boyfriend, since the beginning of the previous summer. "Not me. Me, I have been exquisitely lazy, until I got very ambitious and went to see what the grass felt like between my toes."

"Good. You're getting some beauty sleep. I want my girl to be the best-looking girlie at the party tomorrow."

"What party?"

"The party my father is throwing. It's his birthday."

Everyone in White Cove knew that Charlie's father was one of the biggest dealers of illegal liquor in New York, and he used his nearby estate as a kind of advertisement for the lifestyle his wares made possible. "I told you last night. Don't you remember?"

"Did you? I guess I forgot," she replied, not because she truly had no recollection but because she hated ever doing anything according to a plan.

"Wear the silver I sent you when you were at school. I'll have a car come round to pick you up."

Astrid tilted her head dreamily to the side. The silver dress he was referring to didn't fit her, of course. Charlie always bought things two sizes too large, as though he couldn't quite comprehend how much smaller than him she was. But she could have it taken in by tomorrow, she supposed—one of the maids would do the work that night.

Astrid opened her eyes then and realized that she was not alone in the room. "Are you lost?" she said to a young man wearing a denim shirt tucked into worker's pants. He was long and ropey, and his skin was brown from the sun. He had pretty, sad eyes.

"Who's there?" said Charlie on the other end of the telephone line, suddenly at greater attention.

"No one. Never mind. Send a car round tomorrow, cocktail time. Good-bye." Then she put the receiver back in its ornate cradle. "Don't I know you?" she purred, though knowing the handsome, decidedly unrefined boy seemed unlikely.

To her surprise, he nodded. His black hair was falling in his eyes, and he pushed it back a little shyly before answering. "Yes, ma'am. My name's Luke. We rode together a few times when we were young. My pa ran the stables at Count de Gruyter's place over in Great Neck."

"Aha, I knew it!" she lied. "We must have been about eight," she said, because her mother had only been married to the count—her second husband—for a year and a few months, around 1920. "Anyway, what brings you here, Luke? You couldn't possibly be working for us again."

"No . . ." He paused awkwardly and looked at his feet. "I work over at the White Cove Country Club now."

For some reason this made her smile, and when he saw it, he smiled, too. Then she decided she didn't want to know anything about the series of events that preceded his arrival in her foyer on that particular afternoon—it was one of her virtues that she was often content to know little—and shrugged happily. "I'm suddenly so hungry, aren't you?"

"Actually, yes."

She moved breezily to his side and took him by the hand, and they hurried together through the quiet rooms of the house to the kitchen, where the cook and her assistant were busy making bread. The cook glanced up—she had a kind, fat face, just as all cooks should—and there was only a brief moment where a little scandal lingered in her eyes at seeing the young miss wearing pajamas in the late afternoon and holding the hand of a strange boy in work clothes. She had been employed by old, rich families a long time, and could remember the days when a girl's reputation was ruined over much less. But all the rules had changed in the last decade, and in Marsh Hall, as on many of the surrounding estates, people with fine names were always having meals at unusual hours with people who were not at all like them.

These days one might enter a Fifth Avenue parlor or a pool hall and encounter socialites in feather boas and reporters just off the crime beat, Princeton sophomores and heiresses wearing men's trousers, gold diggers and gamblers, bankers and bootleggers (what was the difference, really?)—and occasionally a few stray, incorruptible innocents. One might encounter three generations of debutantes, each wearing her heirloom jewels, shoulder to shoulder with a known racketeer at a boxing match, all heckling with equal gusto the hulking, sweating, bleeding men in the ring, and all manner of fine people frequenting the kind of joint where brandy was served out of chipped coffee cups. And so, the sight of Astrid Donal with a stable boy was unlikely to shock the cook.

"Martha, we're hungry," said Astrid, showing her lips in their full poutiness. Of course she did not mean to pout, and in fact she was comforted by the smell of rising flour and the simple quality of that part of the house, with the copper hoods over the stoves and the brick-sized white tile everywhere. She let go of Luke's hand, with its rough skin and firm grip, and crossed the room. "Won't you make us some eggs?"

"'Course, dearie," Cook answered, as Astrid draped her arms around the older woman's neck, happily receiving a kiss at the hairline. "Only, sit down and don't be in my way. There's coffee on the stove."

Astrid winked at her new friend. He was fussing with his belt and lingering on the margins of the kitchen. No doubt he felt a little funny being her guest there, since he himself was more or less the help, too. She poured them each a cup of coffee in delicate china cups and beckoned for him to come sit next to her on the high stools at the worktable in the center of the kitchen, so that they could watch as Cook scrambled their eggs.

He took a tentative sip and glanced at her as though he were unsure whether or not it was his place to speak.

"You work at the club, you said?" He smelled like cut grass and sweat, and sitting so close to him gave her a pleasant, easy feeling.

He nodded. "Training the horses."

"I never have time for that kind of thing anymore," she replied with a careless wave of her hand. "But maybe I should take it up again, now I know *you're* there." She rested her elbows on the table and leaned toward him, pausing long enough that his dark eyes were forced to meet hers. "Would you help me?"

He nodded, but was prevented from replying by the cook noisily putting two bowls in front of them. Into each she shoveled a pile of scrambled eggs, topping them with a slab of bacon.

"Thank you," he said to the cook, with a sincere bob of his head.

"Yes, thank you," said Astrid, as she picked up the bacon with her fingers and nibbled thoughtfully at the end. "I remember you now," she mused, forgetting that a moment ago she had pretended to know him for sure. There *was* something familiar about him, she saw it now: a quiet boy in a plaid flannel jacket who used to lead her pony for her. "There were three of you, weren't there?"

"My older brothers, John and Peter." His eyes were shining, and she realized that it pleased him to be remembered.

"And you used to walk my pony Arabella around the corral for me. You and I were the same height then . . ." A mischievous smile crept onto her lips. "You used to look back at me sometimes," she whispered sweetly.

His own smile fell at this, and his face colored. Then she knew that his childhood self had had a crush on her childhood self. She was perfectly aware that the cook was giving her a disapproving look, but she didn't care. That was Astrid's way—she loved Charlie, of course, but she was an incorrigible flirt, and anyway it was glorious, making a man blush like that.

"Oh, *there* you are."

The cook's eyes darted up first, and then Astrid and Luke glanced over. There, framed in the hall doorway, was her mother, Virginia Donal de Gruyter Marsh, whose strong features conveyed any displeasure that her tone might have left in doubt. Her physical presence was composed of brittle parts, but the overall effect was one of fierceness. It was very generally known that the lady of the house enjoyed a party as much as—and maybe more than—her daughter did, a fact that always made the latter wince.

Indeed, Astrid's mother was in full evening dress now, but it was apparent, especially in the natural light streaming through the large windows, that she was still wearing what she had gone out in the evening before. The quality of her pale skin was dull, and her sleeveless black dress, with the black sash tight at her narrow waist, hung off her in limp, wrinkled tiers. Her hair had surely been done up for whatever fete she had abandoned her husband for last night, but now it sat around her shoulders like weeds. The buckles of her high-heeled shoes, which involved diamonds and emeralds, were the only part of her that shone.

It was only after several seconds that Astrid realized it

was not she, but Luke, her mother had misplaced. "I have been looking everywhere," Virginia added unnecessarily.

The exact circumstances under which Luke had met her mother and been invited into Marsh Hall would never be fully explained to Astrid, but a vague outline of what must have occurred had now taken form in her mind—after all, her mother was very frequently at the White Cove Country Club, and people on their third marriages are rarely sentimental about fidelity—and the idea of it disgusted her. Although Astrid had inherited her mother's flirtatiousness, she was not nearly so cavalier. She gave Cook as true a smile as possible before standing up.

"Thank you, Martha, but it's just occurred to me how late it is, and I must have my dress fitted for the party tomorrow night at Charlie's," she announced. Without meeting the eyes of anyone in the room, she advanced toward the hall; on the threshold, her mother grasped her wrist.

For a moment Astrid imagined she was about to be admonished for having slept so late, for so clearly planning to skip dinner in the formal Marsh dining room, for ruining a very expensive pair of pajamas, or for announcing so casually that she was going to socialize at a house that belonged to a known bootlegger. But instead her mother parted her thin lips, caught her daughter's gaze, and asked: "What time is the party?"

4

DESPITE HER FEVERISH LATE-NIGHT INTENTIONS, CORDELIA must have slept, because in one moment she was watching the suburbs go by, lulled by the stutter of the train, and in the next everyone around her was pushing forward down the aisle to exit.

"Letty," she whispered. Her friend shifted in the seat beside her. Cordelia swallowed. "We're here."

Letty's eyes opened and darted right and left. "In New York?"

At the sound of the city's name, Cordelia's lips sprang into a smile. "Yes." Then she stood, tightened the belt of her coat, and reached for Letty's hand so that they could join the mass of bodies.

It was possible that neither girl drew breath from the time they stepped down onto the platform until they ascended the metal staircase into the giant main space of the station. *Space* was the only word that Cordelia could think to describe it, for it did not resemble any lobby or entryway she had ever seen. The floor was of some shining stone, which hundreds of pairs of shoes crisscrossed in a single-minded rush, heads down, as though the iron and glass ceiling high above them was not strung aloft by some set of miracles.

"Oh," Letty whispered, her petal pink mouth hanging open as she gazed up. The hands of an enormous clock, suspended over the tracks, ticked between Roman numerals. It was almost four o'clock; their first day in the city was half over.

"Here we are." Cordelia's voice had become soft and amazed. But they had only a moment to pause and take it in, for the crowd was pushing every which way, and the only rule seemed to be that one was not to stand still.

So they went on, through the warm concourse and out into the brisk day.

The sky was cloudless, and the sunshine forced them to squint as they came onto the grand marble portico of a building that appeared large enough that it might have squatted over all downtown Union. The clamor of voices around them was so constant they could scarcely make out a word, and the horns of automobiles blended with the screech of tires as drivers pulled their vehicles off the wide avenue in front of the station and back into the stream of traffic. The air was heady with exhaust and the smell of food frying and men's cologne. Beyond all that rose a city like a painted set, buildings jutting up with geometric assertiveness to dissect the sky, one blocking out another, all of them festooned with turrets and Gothic spires, repeating over and over until they grew hazy in the distance.

Letty's palm was cold against Cordelia's; she appeared perhaps too shocked to speak, and they both slowed a little as they reached the sidewalk. This was at least in part because of the crowd that had formed there—mostly women, their feet inert despite all the movement around them, and their necks craned to look up.

"What is it?" Cordelia asked a woman in a geometric-patterned dress that hung loosely over her long frame. On the woman's head was a soft gray felted hat shaped like a helmet.

"Don't you know?" The woman turned to Cordelia and Letty with an air of irritated surprise. She blinked at them for a moment, but it was clear that it pained her to remove her gaze from the sky even for a moment. "It's Max Darby, the famous aviator, performing one of his tricks . . ."

Who? was the question on Cordelia's lips, but the woman had already gone back to doing what everyone else was doing, her hat tipped back and her nose pointed upward. Cordelia's eyes traveled in the same direction, and she saw—in a field of perfect blue, higher even than the skyscrapers—a small silver capsule, twisting about and emitting a white smoke. She flattened her palm and put her index finger to her brow to soften the glare.

"Oh, no!" Letty gasped. "His plane is on fire."

"No, it's not," said the woman in the gray hat impatiently. "The smoke is for skywriting."

"Oh," both girls replied in quiet unison, faces turned heavenward.

A glittering sensation passed through Cordelia's body as she gazed at the daredevil spinning white letters over Manhattan. A curling *P* followed by an *A* and then an *R* . . . she hadn't the faintest notion what it would come to spell, but the spectacle had nonetheless stolen her breath. It confirmed for her, with its breezy beauty, that she had not been wrong—that New York was more extraordinary than a girl from Ohio could possibly have imagined, that it was a place of wonders where the citizens used the sky as their tablet and airplanes for pens. And to think—the city was not yet even an hour old to her.

"Should we see what it feels like to ride in a taxicab?" Cordelia asked after a while, once the aviator's message—PARK ROYALE NOW OPEN, whatever that meant—became enlarged and blurry against the blue sky. Then she took several long steps toward the traffic, holding her old suitcase against her hip, and raised her arm in the air.

With a blast of its horn, a square black car careened across two lanes and toward Cordelia, coming to a halt just in front of her. For a moment Letty thought the man was going to drive right through her and onto the sidewalk, and it took several seconds for her breathing to become normal again. Then Cordelia gave a gleeful little bow, opened the cab's back door, and with a flourish of her hand shepherded Letty into the backseat.

Impressive was one word that had been used in Union to describe her friend, because of Cordelia's swift, impatient walk and the high, sharp planes of her face and her ability to hold a stare. And of course, there was the way she'd stolen John, the handsomest boy in town, from Reverend Wallace's daughter, without ever seeming to lift a finger to draw his attention. That was the way Cordelia always did things—with a coolheaded stealth that never failed to catch her detractors unawares.

Letty's hands moved from her lap to the leather seat, and she had trouble lifting her gaze much higher than her knees. What one did in a taxicab was a mystery to her, but she hoped Cordelia, who had placed the two pieces of luggage between them and was closing the door behind her, had some inkling.

"You girls actresses?"

Letty's eyes darted up, and she saw the reflection of the driver in the rearview mirror. He might have been poking fun, she knew, but there was something likable about his weak chin and soft cap and the way his blue eyes stood out against his drab, worn face. A face like that wouldn't make fun. Anyway, she knew she had that indescribable quality—the same one Cordelia saw, the reason they both knew they had to try their luck in a big city—and perhaps people in New York were just more adept at recognizing that kind of thing.

"I am," Letty said brightly, leaning forward. "A singer, too, and I dance. That's one of the reasons I moved here. My friend Cordelia Grey isn't really anything of that kind—she's just made for this city."

"Well, you certainly have a nice enough face, miss."

A blush crossed Letty's cheeks at that, and she had to avert her eyes. She looked to her right and saw that Cordelia had taken the notebook out of her coat pocket, and was studying a page scrawled with her own handwriting:

> *Love is all right, as things go, but lovers can be a terrible waste of a girl's time.*
>
> —*Cara Gatling*

It took Letty a moment to remember why that name sounded familiar to her, and then she realized it belonged to a character in a radio play they'd listened to during the winter, but which she hadn't thought Cordelia was interested in particularly. Below that was a list of what appeared to be addresses, some written in pencil and some in ink, as though the list had accumulated over a good stretch of time.

"Do you know the Washborne Residence for Unmarried Women?" Cordelia asked, glancing up and closing the book.

"Sure," the driver replied, starting up the motor. "Down in Greenwich Village?"

"Oh, I don't think we want to live in a village," Letty cut in, trying not to sound rude but having to speak more loudly than before on account of the noise the car made. "You see, we came all this way because we want to live in the city."

The driver's eyes met hers again in his rearview mirror. He seemed to be assessing whether or not she was joking. When he'd made up his mind, he said, "Greenwich Village, I mean. Believe me, it is the city." Then he winked.

Letty nodded, blushing again, and the car rumbled into motion. They watched the city pass as they traveled downtown. Men in hats thronged either side of the street, marching past store windows or perhaps strolling with women who wore artificial flowers pinned to their brims. Girls breezed by, their skirts swishing a little, the seams of their stockings straight as arrows, their pert noses pointed upward. By comparison, Letty and Cordelia appeared rather shabby, she supposed, although no one was glancing in the windows of their cab. And anyway, all really interesting girls invent themselves, or so Letty's mother used to say.

For a long time they traveled on the broad avenue, stopping and starting, lurching forward and coming to sudden halts. The noise of the city came in waves. On every street corner something was for sale—flowers or magazines or fruit arranged in colorful pyramids. Another few blocks passed, and then they turned onto a twisting, narrow street of trees and low structures that were nonetheless taller and more tightly placed than any downtown she had ever seen.

"Here we are: the Washborne Residence for Unmarried Women." The driver indicated a four-story redbrick building set a little farther back from the street than those on either side.

Carefully, Cordelia removed a bill from the envelope in her book and paid the man. Then she and Letty heaved their luggage up the steps and entered the spare, clean lobby of the Washborne. Their heels clicked on floors made of old planks. Through a large doorway on their right they spied six or so women of varying ages in a sitting room, drinking coffee from mismatched cups and speaking in low voices.

The housemother wore her gray hair in a Victorian pincushion of a bun, and though she was situated behind the desk, Letty felt it was fair to assume that her dress was long enough to protect even her ankles from lascivious eyes. Cordelia strode up to her, and asked how much a room cost.

"Twelve dollars a week for a room with two beds," replied the old woman matter-of-factly.

"Twelve dollars a week?" Cordelia repeated, closing her eyes.

Letty had stepped up behind Cordelia, and glanced over at the open page of her notebook where she had written THE WASHBORNE RESIDENCE, 2 BEDS PER ROOM, CLEAN, $7 A WEEK. Letty had barely any savings, because her father kept all his daughters' earnings to give to their husbands when they got married. She felt badly that it was all up to Cordelia to pay their expenses, at least for a short while. But they would have jobs soon, which would pay them much more than they could have made back home—or perhaps Letty really would get famous overnight, and then they would have nothing to worry about.

"The room comes with a washbasin and a chest of drawers. The rest of the facilities are at the end of the hall, shared." The lady cast her eyes down her own long nose at the newspaper she had been reading before the girls walked in. After a moment she folded the front page back, closing the newspaper as though to say the matter was already settled, before continuing. "You won't find anything cheaper anywhere close by, my dears, not without risking your necks—or your reputations."

For a moment, Letty wondered if Cordelia would want to leave—after all, she never had taken well to that kind of sermonizing—but by then something else had stolen her friend's attention: Cordelia was staring fixedly at the old woman's newspaper.

"May I read that?" Cordelia said as she reached for the paper, and turned it around so that she and Letty could read the headline. Sprawled in large letters across the top of the page was FROM HIS LONG ISLAND RETREAT, BOOTLEGGER GREY DENOUNCES ACTS OF VIOLENCE.

"How funny! He has the same name as you!" Letty gasped, taking hold of her friend's arm.

"Isn't it strange?" Cordelia replied a little faintly.

> *Meanwhile, Darius Grey continues to throw lavish parties at Dogwood, his White Cove property, and to laugh off any accusations of nefarious doings. "My business is legitimate," he insisted, during an unusual lull in his guests' demands, as he lit this reporter's cigarette. "My business is good times, and the people of Long Island and New York and indeed the whole country love me for it."*

There was more, but Letty didn't get to read any because Cordelia handed the paper back to the housemother rather suddenly.

"Our first day in New York, and your name is on the front page of the newspaper," Letty said excitedly. It felt to her like a sign that leaving Union had been the right thing to do—that this was their destiny. "Ma'am, when you're finished, do you think we could have that paper?" She smiled at the housemother. "Then we'll have it forever, as a keepsake of our arrival!"

Behind them, a redhead smothered a laugh in her palm.

For a moment, both girls' attention flickered toward the sitting room. Letty's spirits flagged, and the triumph of the previous moment dimmed, when she realized that she had been too eager and too simple. The girls in the next room were wearing smart clothes and were posed languidly over their magazines, and they certainly did not have any dirt on their shoes—which Cordelia and Letty still did, from their dash through the woods.

If Cordelia had heard the slight, she did not acknowledge it. She turned sharply, with all the confidence of a girl who has the means to pay for what she wants, and began counting out the twelve dollars from the envelope in her notebook. "We'll take it," she said as she placed the money on the desk.

The housemother took the bills, slowly recounted them, and tucked them away in her skirt. Without smiling, she rose and beckoned for them to follow her up the flight of stairs. She picked up her long skirts as she walked to avoid tripping.

"Curfew is at ten," she admonished. "There is no drinking, no smoking, and no men allowed at the Washborne." Then she turned on the stairs and focused her gaze on Letty's blue eyes. "No exceptions."

"Oh, we don't do any of that," Letty replied quickly.

For a moment they lingered on the second-floor landing in silence, until the housemother cleared her throat and continued. "You say that now, but I know girls like you—you come here pretending one thing, and then you do another."

The harshness of the housemother's tone, and the intensity with which she continued leading them down the hall, made Letty tremble. She supposed all the Washborne girls had impeccable manners and followed the house rules scrupulously—but of course, she only believed that because she was new.

At just that moment, though she could not have known it, a young divorceé named Lilly whispered to her parrot, Lulu (whose presence in her room was absolutely prohibited by the rules of the Washborne), while her artificially black hair sat in curlers. On the third floor, two girls who had spent their day in the typing pool of an advertising firm made themselves pretty in anticipation of being taken out by two gentlemen from the accounting department. One wore a lemon yellow beaded dress, and the other wore black satin; they were going to a far-off land called Harlem and intended to dance the Charleston, and if they returned home by curfew, it would not be by choice.

"Here we are," the housemother announced, opening a door onto a small room with one window, two wire-frame beds, and a single bureau with an old cracked mirror hanging over it. The walls had once been pink, but they had since faded and chipped to a shade less identifiable.

Cordelia went in first and looked around. She twirled back toward the housemother, raised her chin as though she had been expecting better, and made her voice rather neutral and cool. "It will do," she announced.

"I should think so." The housemother regarded them haughtily.

Letty slipped past her into the room and sat down on the nearest bed. When she put her weight on the mattress, it let out a croak that almost made her jump up in fright. "Thank you," she said in a small voice.

The housemother did not acknowledge her thanks. She only puffed her chest a little, and said, "Remember, curfew at ten. And don't try anything funny. I can smell bad behavior a mile away."

As the housemother withdrew, Letty gulped and nodded. The door clicked closed, and Cordelia stuck her tongue out at the place where the old lady had been. Her eyes popped, theatrical and silly. Once Letty saw that her friend could make fun of the situation, she began to feel not quite as intimidated by her new surroundings. Then Cordelia threw herself down, next to her friend on the first bed, and they both let their laughter out.

Eventually Cordelia and Letty's giggles subsided, and

they put their clothes away, shook out the blankets on the bed, and opened the window, which looked down into a dismal air-shaft. On the floor above them, someone walked across the room in high heels.

Just as they were beginning to wonder what else they could do with themselves, there came a knock at the door, and before either Letty or Cordelia could say anything, a girl with bobbed brass-colored hair popped her head in the room.

"Oh, hello, new girls," she said. Her lips were painted with cardinal red lipstick, and her eyes shone as she assessed them. She looked like a magazine illustration of what they called "flappers."

"Hello," the new girls replied in unison, although Letty's voice was quieter than her friend's.

"Well." The girl rested her hand on her hip and issued a saucy wink. "Are you coming out with us or not?"

So Cordelia and Letty used what they had to do what girls on all four floors of the Washborne Residence for Young Women were doing—blackening eyelashes and winnowing brows—with fewer resources, but also with that anticipation of a first night in the big city that always brings a special hue to feminine cheeks. They had each brought two pairs of stockings and all the dresses and skirts they owned—which is to say, not many. But when they paused in front of the warped old mirror on the second-floor hall, Letty saw what she had often seen before the country dances in Union: two girls who were unlike the others. The taller one, with her wide lips and strong, sun-touched face, setting off the best features of her petite friend: those large blue eyes which overwhelmed her dot of a nose and button of a mouth, and the pale skin made dramatic by her nearly black hair.

When it was time to go, Letty still felt flutters of trepidation over what it meant to go out into a city at night. But she could not be so nervous—for after all she had Cordelia, whose every gesture was full of ready excitement, to follow.

5

BY THE TIME THEY STEPPED DOWN ONTO THE STREET with Norma, the brass-haired girl, and three others, the night had already begun to swing. They could hear laughter bubbling up from half-cracked car windows or from invisible gatherings on rooftops, and Letty, arm in arm with her best friend, began to see that the hilarity might have less to do with her own backwardness, and more with something very gay in the atmosphere. The girls glided forward, their eyes gemlike and sparkling.

"Where are we going?" Cordelia called out to Norma, who twirled and walked backward for a few strides, as though she needed to look them over before giving a full answer.

At that time of year, in that particular town, they might have knocked on any number of doors and stumbled into a party in progress. Speakeasies of every imaginable variety lined the streets; speakeasies for the right kind of people and speakeasies for the wrong. There were private clubs, where rich men kept their own store of illegal liquor; sordid clip joints for suckers; places to watch a water ballet while sipping juleps; rooms done up in the style of Louis XV; basement spots with dark red walls where no one said much and a lone trumpet wailed mournfully from a shadowy corner, expressing for all those people just what it looked like inside their souls. But the newest girls to alight in Manhattan could not possibly have known yet how pregnant with possibility every closed door should appear to them.

"To Seventh Heaven, of course," Norma said at last, and pointed straight ahead, to the speakeasy most Washborne girls experience first, perhaps because of its proximity but also because it was, in May of 1929, the place everyone wanted to be.

Letty followed Norma's gaze and saw a stone structure with a bell tower several stories high at the front and arched stained glass windows along the sides of the main building. "The church?" she asked, incredulous.

"Well, I suppose drink is a kind of religion for some," Cordelia quipped.

Norma's reply was no more than a silvery laugh. Soon enough the big church with the bell tower was looming over them. The street was quiet, and there was no sign that the building housed a nightclub. But then Norma knocked against the wooden door exactly four times, and it popped open.

"We're here for the wedding," she informed the slick-haired man whose head appeared in the doorway.

"Which wedding?"

"The Murphy wedding," Norma replied, with supreme confidence. After the passing of a few seconds, Letty realized there was no wedding, and that this must be some kind of password. It reminded her of her younger sister Laura, and how she would sometimes hide behind the sheets hanging on the clothesline and demand to hear the magic word before showing herself again. But before Letty could get lost in melancholy thoughts, the girls were being swept inside the archway.

People were out walking along the sidewalks at that hour, but even so, Letty felt as though they had stepped in from some quiet graveyard; for inside the old church on Seventh Avenue were a hundred people to look at and a thousand things to see. They stood for a minute on the homely stone floor of the entry, taking in the busy spectacle of what had once been a house of worship. Most of the pews had been removed, and the open space under the high ceiling was now occupied by round tables and people in shimmering clothes. Cigarette girls, dressed in outfits that some women might have been shy to bathe in, trotted across the floor, offering colorful packages from trays strapped to their narrow torsos. Waiters in black suits dodged them, ferrying full cocktails as though gravity were just some fiction they did not personally subscribe to. On every table in the room sat glasses of all shapes, stuffed with festive green leaves and bright straws. A ten-piece band played on the altar.

"Oh," said Letty, realizing that her mouth had been open for some time.

"Five of us," Norma said to a small man in a tuxedo, brushing past a crowd of people loitering in the entryway, with the rest of the girls following close behind.

The crowd, which was mostly male, made grumbling noises, but the man in the tuxedo must have known Norma already, because he whisked the girls through the room to two round tables near the bar. Letty didn't know where a girl learned to talk that way, but she was relieved Norma could do it for all of them. Before they had settled in, a waiter appeared demanding to know what they would drink. Letty hadn't the faintest idea—she had never taken a drink in her life.

"Beers for all of us," Norma said brightly. When he was gone, she leaned in toward Letty and said, "Don't worry, doll, we'll get something more exciting once we meet some fellows to buy them for us."

"So this is a speakeasy," Cordelia whispered reverently

on Letty's other side.

Their eyes roved across the spectacle, darting from women with bare shoulders draping themselves over men in sharp suits, to girls not so much better dressed than themselves, wearing no jewels but sparkling with laughter at whatever jokes their escorts told. Even so, Letty felt a little self-conscious about her red cotton dress with the square collar—it was cinched at her natural waist, unlike nearly every other dress in the room. When she'd worn it to country dances, she used to think it was pretty. Cordelia was wearing the white dress she had married John in, and Letty couldn't help wondering if her old friend hadn't been thinking more of a place like this than of him when she had stitched its low waist and high, scalloped hem.

"Five beers," the waiter announced, plunking them down on the table.

Letty contemplated the tall glass in front of her, the bubbles rising up through the pretty amber liquid, before lifting it to her lips. The first sip was sour in her mouth, and she swallowed it quickly so that she wouldn't have to taste it any longer. Then everything in the room around her became a little too vivid, and she found that the only thing that might steady her was another sip. But she must have made some kind of noise, of disgust or surprise, because over her shoulder, a male voice commented: "Five bucks says her friends have to carry her out of here."

The white skin of Letty's cheeks grew pink, and she cast her eyes down at her toes.

Beside her, Cordelia felt that old fury, familiar from when the Haubstadts would accuse Letty of being too scrawny to do as many chores as the rest of them, or when other girls in Union would call Letty's legs skinny. She swiveled in her chair and saw a man not much older than she was, with a great square jaw and light hair darkened with the grease that held it back from his face. He leaned against the black lacquered bar that curved below a wall of stained glass windows with a superior air that made Cordelia bristle. His eyes were brown and unkind and spaced wide apart under a low brow. The strong arc of his shoulders reminded her of a snake coiled, loaded with ready aggression.

"What makes you an expert?" Cordelia said, coolly but loud enough that he wouldn't miss it.

The man smirked and lit a cigarette. "You'll find out."

"Doubt I'll care much, if in fact I ever do," she drawled. Then she picked up her beer and drank it in one long, theatrical gulp. The bitter liquid fizzed in her belly and up in her head, but she placed the glass back on the table so that it made a decided thud, and raised one controlled eyebrow at the man who'd mocked Letty.

Disgustedly he turned to the bar, so that his back faced the girls. His friend, who had been standing close by and wore a similar dark-colored suit, but whose slouching posture and unfocused gaze made him appear far drunker, came toward them, leering at Letty. "Hey, little lady," the man slurred. "Come on, and I'll show you we didn't mean no harm."

Then he practically lifted Letty up from her seat and danced her across the floor, up toward the band, where Cordelia could just glimpse him knocking into couples and causing a scene. She wanted to go help her friend—after all, it was her fault they'd drawn that fellow's attention—but she was afraid that if she stood up, everyone would see how unsteady she was after downing her drink like that. Norma and the other girls were involved in a conversation with a table of sailors and were no longer paying attention to their new friends. Anyway, the dance didn't last long—one of the cigarette girls cut in, and began dancing Letty to safety, away from the man who'd accosted her. The girl was wearing a cream jumper, and her dark hair was marcelled into wide waves. She was a good deal taller than Letty, her long legs accentuated by the heeled shoes she wore. Cordelia decided she looked like a good sort, and she closed her eyes, willing the dizziness away.

From over her other shoulder she heard a faint chuckle, and turned to see who was milking a laugh out of the two girls from Ohio now. She tried to put on a prideful expression—but she soon realized that it was going to be impossible to maintain. The boy who had laughed was sitting at a table just behind her, and though his body was facing away, he had twisted his torso around to look at her. His coppery hair was parted and combed from the side, and he had an angular quality to his face, as though a sculptor had carved out slabs from either side of a strong nose. One of his legs was crossed over the other in an easy, careless way that suggested he had never known worry or want. His deep blue suit fit his long limbs somewhat loosely; from the chest of his mauve dress shirt, he produced a gold object that, cupping his hands, he used to light a cigarette.

"Hello," she said.

"Hello," he answered, his moody green eyes flicking up to hers.

The air was thick with fast music and chatter, and every atom of her body was suddenly full of a ticking boldness. All that day had been a process of transformation. What fun it would be to meet someone as her new self, she thought, just after she had. And how lucky that he happened to be someone who looked just like the personification of everything bright and urbane she'd been seeking when she left home. "I hope you weren't laughing at me."

"Not you—that man," he answered, gesturing at the fellow with the broad shoulders who'd first insulted Letty.

"Oh." A smile played at the edges of Cordelia's lips. "But I don't find him interesting at all."

"I like the way you shot him down. Anyway, don't I know

you?" He pushed back his chair so that he could more fully face her. "Are you some kind of actress or something?"

Cordelia made a scoffing noise and tried not to glance down self-consciously at her homely white dress. White, she had noticed while glancing around, was not a color to wear to a nightclub. But the taxi driver had asked them a similar question—perhaps that was a line all pretty girls in New York heard sooner or later.

"An aviatrix?" His voice was what she would imagine an educated man's voice was like, especially when he used words she'd never heard before.

"What's that?"

"I've got it . . . You're a moral crusader, here to shame us for our law-breaking, bourbon-drinking ways!"

"*Lord,* no."

"Three strikes." He shrugged and sighed. "Excuse me, I've been very rude, you have no drink. Can I get you one?"

Cordelia pretended to waver a moment and then gave a little nod. He gestured to a passing waiter, who seemed to require no more than a flourish of a pinkie finger to take the order. Sitting so close to this boy, the backs of their chairs almost touching, it was obvious how alike in size and presence they were. Then she became exquisitely aware of how near their hands, idling on the backs of their chairs, had crept.

"Cigarette?"

"No, thank you."

"Don't smoke?" He turned down the corners of his mouth.

"No . . ." She rolled her eyes upward. "I don't smoke or not smoke as a rule . . . only it sounds like a lot of distraction just now."

"Ah." A ghostly white spiraled up from between his index and middle fingers, where he rested his cigarette, and for a moment it obscured her view of him. "This much I am sure of: I haven't met you before, because a girl like you I surely would have done everything in my power to keep on knowing."

"You do say pretty things, don't you?" she replied, leaning away from him and narrowing her eyes, as though he were not to be trusted. And perhaps he wasn't to be trusted. In this city, how was she to know? But talking to him was thrilling, and she wanted to go on doing so regardless of the consequences.

"So—you take offense at the innocent suggestion of moral crusading . . ." He paused, contemplating her. It was a long, searching look, as though he could see the pulsing of her heart or somehow read the transmissions of her thoughts. "Perhaps your living is robbing banks or holding up unlucky pharmacists and the like?"

A wry smile spread across Cordelia's face. "That would take some style—committing crimes by daylight and then spending your nights in a busy joint like this."

"True. But, in my humble opinion, style is one thing

you've got plenty of."

The flattery almost overwhelmed her. And it had come so quickly. She couldn't help but think, briefly, of John, who was always so gentle but could never quite keep up with her. Resting her cheek against her palm, she let her eyes drift across the room, taking in the movement all around and the glint of the table candles reflecting on white teeth when people laughed.

"Oh, dear," he said. "Compliments make you sad, don't they?"

She pushed the image of John from her mind—she didn't see any logic in dwelling on those she'd left behind—and smiled wide. "Now what kind of girl doesn't like compliments?"

"I hope you like old-fashioneds, too."

"Is that what the waiter is bringing us?" she asked. "I've never had one."

"How unfortunate!" he replied. "Rest assured: They are delicious. If you find I'm in error, we'll see to it that you get something that truly pleases you. The bartender is a friend."

Both her eyebrows rose. "You have a lot of friends, don't you?"

"What makes you say that?"

"It's the way you carry yourself." She paused, considering, and took a breath of smoky air. Everyone around them was jittery and excitable and chatting at high speed, and she was amazed to realize that, despite the crowded room, she had perhaps never had a conversation that felt quite so private as this one. "And also the fact that you don't mind sitting alone amongst all these people."

He smiled faintly. "But how do you know I am not waiting for someone?"

"*Are* you waiting for someone?" she asked, a hint of flirtatious challenge wavering in her voice. There was something about the way he said it that made her believe him and suspect one of the well-heeled ladies seated at the bar of biding her time until she left. But before he could answer, the waiter returned. Whatever they had been saying was lost among the placing of glasses on napkins, the administering of soda water, the relighting of his cigarette.

"To you, whoever you are," he said, raising his glass once the waiter had departed.

She raised her glass just the way he'd done, and touched his so that it made a sound.

"To a perfect moment. May it never end," he concluded, and drank.

She drank, too, but not with his assurance. The sensation on her tongue was sweet and scorching at once, and when she swallowed the mouthful of thick, sugary liquid, she felt dizzy and had to close her eyes. The glass was still cool against her palm, but then she felt the warm sensation of his fingertips on her wrist.

"Do you like it?" he asked.

"Yes," she replied and opened her eyes. It seemed remarkable that only yesterday she'd woken up in a very far-off place and now she was here, and then she heard herself say: "I grew up in Ohio, but in fact I was born here in New York. It's my first night back in town. I'm here to find my father."

All of that ought to be followed by a great deal of explanation, she supposed. Yet she was in no particular hurry. He had said he hoped the moment would never end, and indeed she felt that she might go on contentedly like this forever. The air was rich, and the drinks were cold. In every corner of the room, a gentleman or lady was watching or being watched, and Cordelia paused, taking in the crowd, until she realized that she was in fact one of the ladies being observed.

"Your father?"

Letty was standing over her, wearing a new shade of lipstick.

"But I thought we were here because . . ." The room had grown blurry, and Letty found she couldn't finish her sentence. Already tonight she had been accosted and then saved by a cigarette girl named Paulette, who had taken Letty aside and cleaned her up and made sure she understood that that kind of thing happened to everybody, and she needn't go to confession over it or quit the city before she even got a real taste. Paulette had then given her a swipe of red lipstick and a shot of brandy to calm her nerves. After that Letty began to see that good people could be found anywhere.

But that new sense of calm waned when she came to stand beside her old friend and overheard her saying something that didn't make any kind of sense. "I thought we came because I was meant to be a star," she finally said, though it sounded foolish to her now.

Cordelia's cheeks had grown rosy, and her eyes were dark and mysterious. She sat up straight and then paused. The other Washborne girls had been absorbed by the crowd. Everything in the vast room swam toward Letty and away.

"My father—he's here." The dim light accentuated Cordelia's cheekbones, as well as the haughtiness of which she was sometimes capable. She glanced back at the man she'd been talking to, as if they shared something, though he'd already looked away and begun to recede into the background. Then she turned the glass of amber liquid in a circle across the table and went on in a nonchalant tone. "Not here at the club, here in New York. I'm going to find him."

Letty's red mouth stood open, and the whites of her eyes expanded. Up until that moment she had believed she'd known everything about Cordelia; now she wondered if she knew anything. She wanted to ask why her oldest friend had never told her of this suspicion before, or how she had come by it, and if it was the whole reason they had left everything they'd ever known for a vast and fearsome city, or if Letty's hopes and dreams had played even a small role in the decision. But she was afraid that if she spoke again, she would begin to cry. Then she'd have to be taken aside a second time and cleaned up again, and she already felt sufficiently humiliated.

Letty turned and hurried toward the exit.

"Letty, wait!" Cordelia yelled after her.

But Letty was pushing through clots of people, all straining in the opposite direction to be in the spot she had just vacated. Even in the entryway a raucous good time was being had, and she probably should not have been surprised that with all the shouting and revelry, her stricken expression went entirely unnoticed.

"Letty!" She heard Cordelia yell again once she had traveled halfway down the block. There were fewer people outside now, and the warm windows of a few brick houses illuminated the darkened street below.

Although Letty did not turn around, Cordelia's long strides soon brought the two girls side by side.

"Don't be angry," she said.

Letty did not at first glance up as they continued at a furious pace back toward the Washborne. "I didn't even know you had a father," she said eventually. "You never told me. I tell you everything, and you never even—"

"Well, I don't know for sure," Cordelia went on, in a

placating tone, as they turned off the avenue and onto their own twisting street. Then she sighed as though she had stumbled upon an irritating but simple misunderstanding. "I know where he is, because he's famous. At least, I think he is. He's that bootlegger, Darius Grey. It's not coincidental that we have the same name. Aunt Ida always said that I should keep my father's name as a reminder of the sinful life that had begot me . . . And I've read the papers: It would have been right around the time Mr. Grey had to leave Chicago for New York. He was small-time then, and that's what Aunt Ida always implied my daddy was: small-time and crooked. Of course, she doesn't keep up with the news. She doesn't know what he's become."

"We came all this way because you think Darius Grey is your father?" Letty shrieked. Her body had gone cold, and the great distance between her and everything she'd ever known felt suddenly more real and more painful than before. "You really believe he'll just take you in? He's a criminal. You think a man like that wants a daughter to take care of? You think he doesn't have a dozen forgotten children all over the country?" For a moment, Letty thought she might cry. Instead she heard herself wail: "You're deluded!"

"Me? You're the one who's deluded," Cordelia shot back, just as quickly. "You think you can just show up in Manhattan, and instantly you'll be a star? There are thousands of girls trying to make it in this city."

The night air was cooler than it had been during the day, but both girls had grown hot by now. They had ceased to notice anything about their surroundings, or whether any of the old men on stoops watched them. By the time they spotted the Washborne, Letty's throat was sore and all logic had gone out of her sentences.

"You're a liar!" Letty shrieked, her tiny mouth like a balled fist as she looked up at the girl who had once been her best friend. She placed a hand on the railing of the Washborne's steps.

"I am not." Cordelia stared back, her eyes wide open and full of fire.

"What's this?"

They both turned, startled, and saw the housemother through the crack of the doorway, her hair in the same ornate arrangement, her body covered in a full-length dressing gown. The blood drained from Letty's face.

"What's what?" Letty asked, drawing herself up innocently. Overhead, the leaves of the trees rustled, but everything else was quiet.

The housemother's long fingers clung to the doorway, and she put her head forward to sniff the air dramatically. "Alcohol," she said.

"Excuse me?" Cordelia replied.

But their faces were flushed, and there would be no

convincing the housemother now. Her eyes had grown narrow, her mind hardened with conviction. "There is no drinking and no carousing in this house." The old lady's nose pointed upward and the corners of her mouth turned down. "I thought you were good girls, but I was wrong. You'll have to be going now, before you corrupt the others."

Of course, it was not their malignant natures that had gotten them in trouble, only their newness; had they lived in the city a few more days, they would have known how to fool the housemother. As it was, they were escorted to their room and watched as they packed their few things.

"But we've paid for the whole week," Cordelia protested, once they were back in the lobby.

"Perhaps God saw that and will take it as partial penance for what you've done," the housemother answered coldly, before slamming the front door against their faces.

Outside, the moon dressed the cobblestones in pools of white, and the air felt damp. Letty was so shocked and ashamed to have been put out on the street that she almost ceased to remember her rage. Almost. She stood watching Cordelia in the moonlight; her features and her stance were the same as always, but there was something strange about her. She had been cruel to Letty for the first time, and Letty found she wanted to be cruel back. "I don't know that I like you anymore," she managed finally.

If Cordelia flinched, it was subtle. "I suppose you're on your own, then," was all she said, and then she turned and walked alone into the night, her suitcase bouncing against her hip.

The city howled all around, and a chill settled into Letty's bones. She wanted to call out to Cordelia and beg her to stay, to tell her that she couldn't possibly survive alone. But over the course of that day, she had already felt her heart swell and sink, and then she'd shouted with a fury she had not known herself capable of, and at that late hour, it seemed her voice was no longer up to the task.

6

THE TOWN OF WHITE COVE HAD BEEN FOR SOME generations unyieldingly small and outrageously expensive; it was close enough to the city to attract a great deal of wealth, but offered enough natural beauty and quiet that one could go there with his secrets and count on seclusion. The grand houses were surrounded by buffers of hedges or high gates or arboretums, and were either completely invisible to their neighbors or only willing to reveal themselves in coy parts: a few white columns here, a tiled roof there, a lap pool reflecting the orange and pink glow of sunset above. To Astrid, reclining in the spacious backseat of a Daimler that did not belong to her, it was a sky deliciously reminiscent of sherbet.

So, she thought, as they proceeded through the gates and up the long gravel path, *it is not to be a small party after all.* The narrow public road that connected the estates did not look like much—pine trees and intermittent pavement—and the whole stretch on either side of the Greys' place was lined with automobiles, pulled to the side so that their right tires were in the ditch. Guests in willowy dresses and lightweight suits strolled through the gates, where they were observed by discreetly out-of-view gunmen, before venturing up the lawn. They did not have to be told that only known vehicles were allowed on the property.

"Mr. Charlie says I should bring you 'round the side," the driver announced when they had almost reached the house.

Astrid smiled and said nothing.

Her forehead was mostly covered by the band of a turquoise and silver beaded headpiece, which skimmed over her ears and was fastened at the back of her skull under a curve of rich yellow hair. Her lips were very red, and the skin of her eyelids was shaded deep purple; the dress she wore was made up of exquisite diamond-shaped pieces of silver-colored silk, with a rather low neckline supported by whisper-thin straps. Charlie had given it to her on her seventeenth birthday; he had delivered it to her at school himself, along with a hundred white roses. Only girls were allowed on the campus, of course—it was still a mystery how he had managed it without getting caught.

The fading day had cast the grass the color of straw, and the guests were trailed by their own long shadows as they ascended toward the vast white tent, strung up with tiny lights, where a band had already begun to play. But Charlie wanted Astrid to be dropped not at the tent or even on the grand stone steps of the house, but around the side, and she couldn't help but wonder, as she often did with Charlie, if it wasn't because there was some treat in it for her: a bracelet he wanted to slip on her wrist before the party, or a room filled with the smell of hyacinth, or baskets laden with pink grapefruit shipped all the way from Texas. So she went on smiling, and once they'd come to a stop, she let the driver help her out of the backseat and up to the side entrance. She shivered—it was almost a premonition of the chill that would really come only late at night—and wondered if Charlie hadn't chosen a new fur for her. It was hardly the right time of year for it, but that would be just like him.

She went through a darkened spare room and then into the gothic library with its showy, uncut books. When she saw Charlie, she stopped. His back was to her, the broad expanse of it crossed by dark suspenders that held up light brown pin-striped pants. As often happened when she entered a room and saw him for the first time after a matter of hours or weeks, she found that she had forgotten how unusually tall he was, and had to let her heart calm a few seconds. She loved the size of him.

She wondered if it was possible to love someone as much as she loved Charlie.

Beyond him, in a stuffed leather chair by the window, was Elias Jones, who always seemed to be in Charlie's father's wake, doing him some discreet and loyal service. He was probably in his late thirties, and he had a long horse's face capable of only a few expressions. His gaze rose slowly to assess Astrid, and then Charlie turned. When she saw his eyes, she knew there was no gift for her.

"Thank you, Elias," Charlie said. There was fury in his tone.

Elias rose and gave Astrid a gentlemanly nod. When he opened the door, the twinkling voices of a few women and men—particular guests of the Greys who mingled in the glass-enclosed west porch, having a first cocktail of the evening—carried in the air. He left the room.

"Hello, mister." Astrid put a flirtatious hand on her hip and smiled at Charlie with one corner of her mouth.

"Don't try that with me," Charlie snapped as he took several long steps toward her.

"Try what?" Astrid asked innocently.

A moment ago she had felt such expectation and excitement over being Charlie's special guest, but now she wanted nothing so much as to be with those others down the hall.

"Acting sweet to cover up the things you done."

Astrid's smile dissolved. "What things?"

"You know exactly what things," Charlie replied hotly.

Now it was her turn to speak angrily. "I certainly don't, and if you think I enjoy playing silly guessing games with you, then you are sorely mistaken."

"That tack may work with your teachers at your fancy school. But it ain't gonna work with me. I know you been flirting with strange men in your own home, eating breakfast in the kitchen with 'em and God knows what else."

Astrid returned his accusation with a cool stare. Honesty had never been a point of sentimentality with her. "You're crazy," she said. Then she brushed past. She was almost to the door when she felt his grip on her arm.

"I see everything you do." His breath was on her ear—unpleasant with whatever he'd eaten for lunch, and she disliked him irrationally for it.

She glanced back at his face, at its high, taut plains, at the constrictions of his neck. His fingertips were pressing into the white skin of her pale, soft arm; her eyes darted from the red irritation growing there and back to meet his.

"Your jealousy tires me," she announced, allowing a decided lightness to creep back into her tone, before shaking him off and striding on, in the direction of the voices, toward the safe clinking of glasses and excited murmurings.

Astrid moved through the crowd in the enclosed porch, ahead of Charlie, toward the edge of the room, where she could look down at the girls in slinky dresses on the lawn below and the men trying to get up the courage to talk to them. She knew Charlie had followed her, but she was still jarred when he put his mouth near her ear and spoke again.

"Well, if you weren't flirting with him"—his voice had now grown a little plaintive—"who was he, and what did you want with him anyway?"

"If you are so determined to bore me, I may just have to go home." Astrid sighed carelessly. "What a shame, when I am wearing such a pretty dress."

"It's only that I'd hate to rough up a man who doesn't deserve it," Charlie—becoming gruff again—shot back.

Down below, Astrid noticed a boy, who would have been handsome except for his unfortunately large ears, whisper something to a long, thin girl with straight blond hair, which made her blush. Astrid's heart softened, remembering how involuntarily pink a girl could become. When they were first in love, Charlie used to make *her* blush all the time. Suddenly she was sick of always being this way with Charlie—of adoring him and hating him, of promising each other everything one moment and tearing each other down the next. She twirled to face him.

"Oh, let's not be quarrelsome!"

But by the time the words had lifted off her tongue, Charlie had already turned, his attention caught by something near the door, and before she could help it, the softening in her heart had ceased. A moment ago, she would have done anything to win back his goodwill, but his distraction angered her, and she drew herself up, hard and proud, and decided not to give him any more of her attention.

Some minutes before Astrid and Charlie's hushed altercation, a dusty pickup slowed to a stop down on the main road, in front of Dogwood.

"Right here is fine, sir," a very different sort of girl announced.

"Here?" The farmer looked away from her, toward the wrought-iron fence and the row of cars along the side of the road. His brow was rippled with misgiving. "Are you sure, honey?"

Cordelia took a deep breath and smoothed the skirt of her light blue dress. "Yes." It was the only explanation she felt it necessary to give the old man, who wore overalls just like all the old-man farmers where she came from and had the same deep lines in his face.

She was not without trepidation, but she had no intention of showing it. Anyway, whatever doubt she felt was overcome by the strength of her desire to prove that Letty was wrong, that the connection between Cordelia Grey and Darius Grey was not fantastical in the least.

"Thank you," she added, and then she slipped down from the worn green vehicle and slammed shut the door. For a moment she left her hand on the metal side, feeling the warm shaking of the engine.

"You take care, now," the man said, and then he gave the truck gas and went on down the road.

She stood still, her limbs heavy, until the smell of exhaust and dust faded. It had been a long time since she'd slept. She'd moved through the night and the morning with a single purpose. Of course—as she had discovered at about dawn—she had been going about finding her way to White Cove all wrong, and her feet had taken her instead to the southern tip of Manhattan. If her peregrinations had delivered her to some other place, she might have grown angry, but the smell of the sea was new to her, and she had been able to see—through the freight and masts—piers and houses across the water, sparkling at the beginning of the day.

"That's Brooklyn," an old bum had told her.

"Brooklyn," she mouthed to herself. She knew, from the maps she used to collect and study, that Brooklyn was part of the city but also on Long Island. There was something whimsical and genteel about the word—not at all like Manhattan, which had the bravado of a conquering Indian—and it gave her courage. She remembered how, when she and Letty went to the movie theater in Defiance, they would walk along the road with their thumbs extended for a ride, and she figured that New Yorkers might not be such a foreign race that they didn't use that gesture, too. She had hitched with several different people, of all types, and she had walked a good deal of the way, too. It had taken her all day, but now, at dusk, she found herself on the road that snaked by the famous bootlegger's mansion.

The gates stood open, but for a moment she was paralyzed by the notion that she was standing on the threshold of the place she'd been yearning to see for so many years. There remained, ever since the conversation with Letty, a great angry knot inside her. It insisted that with a few graceful hand gestures, she could make logical the strange history of her origins. How her mother, the younger of the two Larson girls of Union, Ohio, had been spotted on the front porch of her parents' Elm Street home during the long, hot summer of '09, by a young man working as a driver for a Chicago gangster who was well known in those days but whose name is now forgotten. Fanny Larson had been sixteen at the time, and the driver knew at a glance that he had to have her. He had told her father as much, but the Larsons were God-loving people and didn't want their daughter mixed up with that unsavory element. But Fanny had never seen a display of romantic feeling like what this young man showed her. She left that same day and went east to live with him.

Sometimes they had a good deal of money, and sometimes they had none, but nothing was ever so perfect as that summer day when they first laid eyes on each other. It was when Fanny realized she was pregnant that she began writing home again and came to regret the choices she had made. This according to Aunt Ida, who burned all the letters. Of course Aunt Ida would never do harm to a Bible, and so when Cordelia was given her mother's copy, she found the love letter buried deep in its pages with the signature D.G. That was the year Cordelia started working in Uncle Jeb's shop, and the legend of Darius Grey was just beginning to spread west, and she began to put the two stories together.

Soon after giving birth to her only daughter, Fanny fell ill, and there was no money for a doctor, and they had run out on their bills when the baby came, so there was no goodwill, either. "The only sensible thing your mother ever did," Aunt Ida used to enjoy telling her niece, "was telegramming me when she knew the end was near. I came immediately and took you away from the bad man who was your father, and brought you back home. And he *was* a bad man, an evil man, even—and I think he would have stopped me by whatever violent means, had he not been so weak with drink when I found him."

Cordelia was certain that he had only been distraught, and if he had not been laid so low by her mother's death, he would certainly have made sure his daughter wasn't taken from him. He wasn't a bad man, she had assured herself in the silence of Aunt Ida's hall closet, where she was made to stand in the darkness when she had broken a rule, or sent to bed when she was not yet tired enough to fall asleep. And now it was plain to her, as she looked across the sprawling lawn at the parallel rows of lindens that ran along either side of a gravel driveway, at the soft curve of a hill that obscured all but the sparkling roof of a grand house—for no one truly evil could live in a place as beautiful as that.

People whose whole bodies were dotted with bright and colorful ornaments, and who seemed already to have drunk in some joy that evening, were moving in twos and threes along the side of the road and through the front gates.

"Darling, have you never been to any of Grey's parties?" said a voluptuous girl in pink flowered chiffon, which at that hour proved see-through.

"Isn't it shaming?" replied another.

"Yes!" cried the first, and afterward the whole lot of them shrieked in laughter.

Cordelia had that itchy sensation as though she were being watched, and her eyes darted to a little guardhouse on the edge of the property. It appeared empty, but she couldn't shake the suspicion of a presence there. Still, she kept close enough to the well-dressed group she was trailing to conceivably be one of them, and she held her old trench folded over her arm, the way she had seen New York women do it.

"They say it's a party for Grey's birthday . . . ," the girl in chiffon continued. She probably believed that referring to him by his last name made her sound jaunty and urbane, but to Cordelia it was exasperating. No matter how country she may have looked, Cordelia could spot a labored gesture.

"The party *is* for his birthday," one of the boys agreed. "But they say Grey grew up a street urchin with no knowledge of his parents and doesn't even know the day he was born, and so he celebrates it whenever he pleases."

"Which is often several times a year!" added a second man.

They all twittered at the audacity of this.

By then the group had walked a good way up the drive, and the house's redbrick face and curving white accents had come into view. All around rolled green land and giant lawns with billowing trees. Just below the house, on one side, stood a large white tent. Music traveled on the breeze, and for a moment Cordelia was exquisitely aware of the leaves touched by that current, their gentle shaking and the playful shadows they created on the grass, as though everything had been placed there, just so, to please her.

The moment ended when she became cognizant of the twittering again, and when she looked up, she realized the big girl in chiffon and the girl who had never been to one of "Grey's" parties were staring back in her direction—that it was now *her* they found funny. Cordelia rolled her shoulders back and met their gaze. By then they had all taken a path across the grass, toward the tent, and when the girls could no longer go on walking straight and staring, they turned away, and Cordelia herself veered in the direction of the house. She knew that in a moment they would all begin watching her again, but she kept her head high, and reminded herself that this was, in a sense, *her* house. Then she found she did not mind them very much.

Cordelia climbed the grand curvature of stone steps ascending from the circular gravel drive toward the house, and then another impressive flight leading to the entrance. The double oak doors stood open, and she stepped tentatively inside. The entryway was more expansive than any church in Union, and it seemed to soar higher, too. On one side, a great staircase of dark wood went one direction and then another, up three flights or more; and to her right, the hall extended in the direction of mild laughter. She turned toward the sound.

"Whoa, there."

Cordelia froze.

"No guests in the house," the voice went on. He was young, though he suffered from a reddening of his face that made his age difficult to determine. His hand rested on a holster, but he did not move to point the gun in her direction.

"Of course not." Cordelia leveled her gaze and locked eyes with the boy. "But I'm not a guest, you see."

"No? Then who are you?"

Cordelia paused a moment, and then began to explain: "I'm the girl who jumps out of the cake." The phrase hung in the air, confident and strange. She didn't know where it had come from, but now she went on: "It's Mr. Grey's birthday, I suppose, and someone thought it'd be a nice touch. That *I* would be a nice touch."

"I know when Mr. Grey's birthday is." He adjusted the angle of his head slightly and assessed her from head to toe. "You don't look like a dancing girl."

Now Cordelia offered him a sly smile. "You don't think we girls walk around giving away what we got for free, do you?" She lifted the suitcase, partially obscured beneath her trench coat, and patted it with her other hand. "My dancing things are in here."

This inspired a goofy grin to overwhelm the young man's face. Then all of him relaxed. It was possible, but doubtful, that Cordelia fully absorbed the lesson of this moment—that when girls use the brightness of their eyes or the softness of their skin, they have an uncommon advantage in getting what they want. Being cleverer than most, she might have counted herself lucky, but it is a lesson that few women truly appreciate until their looks begin to go.

"I see now. Sorry, miss."

"Where's the kitchen?" Cordelia went on breathily, before he could think better of letting her inside.

He inclined his head, indicating a door beyond the stairs, away from the murmuring. A different kind of noise emanated from the kitchen—the low curses of servants, the rushing of water, the clattering of plates. Cordelia headed in that direction, but when she saw that the guard's back was turned, she slipped through another doorway, darting into a series of rooms that must have lined the hall where she had just been apprehended. She passed through an enormous dining room with drawn aubergine drapes and a long, mighty table from which knights of old might have supped, and then through a vast, empty ballroom with a waxed floor and a white grand piano, its lone piece of furniture. The curtains were drawn there, too, but they were of a filmy cloth, and she could see through them to a great stone verandah, another series of stairs, and lawns stretching out to trees for what seemed like miles.

Her feet fell lightly. Breath was almost impossible. She had known from the papers that Darius Grey was rich, but this house and all its objects were beyond anything she could have imagined. Everything was big and everything shone. Here she was, at last. Sneaking through the house, it was true, invisible and silent—but most definitely here.

After the ballroom came a library, with the same dark wood that paneled the hallway, and built-in shelves crammed with every kind of book. Ferns curled from the corners, and the sofas were well stuffed and worn, and she wished for a moment that her aunt Ida could witness just for a second what a collection of books was kept by the man the old lady believed so rough and bad. On the low, squat table at the center of the room, a gold-rimmed glass contained a few melting chips of ice and the dregs of an amber liquid. Someone had been there recently—they might come back. Her heart beat a little faster when she realized she could not stay here very long, either.

Finally, she stepped back into the hall. At the opposite end from the kitchen she could now see the source of light chatter and clinking glasses—the doors were ajar, and she glimpsed the silhouettes of ladies and gentlemen. Behind them great windows framed a sky striated with magenta and gold and every color in between.

Cordelia stepped into the room, which had a heavy, sweet smell—of lilies, perhaps, or else the women there were wearing a great deal of perfume. If this was the case, it would not be their only point of excess, for the ladies wore a truly defiant amount of lipstick and those who smoked did so out of cigarette holders that appeared implausibly long. Cordelia felt as though she were sitting at the back of a darkened theater, watching a beautifully choreographed scene projected large just for her.

But that illusion did not last very long.

"Who let this girl in?"

Everything in the room grew louder and then entirely quiet. Then she saw, through the assembled bodies, a face she recognized: It was the boy with the cruel brown eyes, the one who had made fun of Letty last night at Seventh Heaven.

"*Who let her in?*" he repeated, striding aggressively in her direction.

Now all the faces in the room turned to her—and what a catalogue of amusement and surprise and chagrin and curiosity they wore. On the ladies, the makeup exaggerated whatever it was the sight of this plainly dressed girl, carrying a suitcase and old coat, stirred in them. She knew she would make herself ludicrous if she told any of these people that she was Darius Grey's daughter, and beyond that, what was there to say? She had half decided that she would demand to see the bootlegger himself and hope for the best—when a beautiful, soft-faced thing, wearing a gleaming and exotic band on her forehead, slipped through the crowd smiling. Her skin had an unearthly quality, as though it were made entirely of diamond dust.

"I did," Astrid said in a suave and sparkling voice, and then she hooked her elbow with the girl's.

It was impossible for Astrid to imagine what Charlie might have against this girl, and she hated him for his bullying tone. She was reminded of the time she had accompanied Charlie and his father on a hunting trip and realized that they were going to deal a mortal blow to some defenseless creature. Perhaps that was why she had crossed the room—the silver silk rustling against her legs, her fur stole slipping just slightly from her shoulder—to intervene on a stranger's behalf.

Now that they were close, the girl turned her big brown eyes—which had been fixated on Charlie in cool defiance—to Astrid. Even though her dress was made of the humblest cotton, and her shoes were laced-up boots like some nineteenth-century schoolteacher, there was an elegant quality about her prominent cheekbones and long, strong limbs. She blinked perhaps once, but if she was surprised or confused by what Astrid had said, she did not let it show on her features. Astrid offered the stranger a plush smile, and then turned to face the room.

Charlie was standing before her, legs spread wide and glaring. Behind him guests watched with mouths slightly agape as the very important girl in the elaborately beaded headpiece and five-hundred-dollar dress clung to the unknown girl in plain, wrinkled country cotton. One of the women stifled a giggle, and in the silence of the room everyone could plainly hear a man whispering at her to shut up.

"Come, darling," Astrid said, to the room as much as to the girl, giving her new friend a tug. "Let's get you a drink, shall we?"

7

SEVERAL SECONDS PASSED BEFORE CORDELIA realized that *she* was the darling in question and that they were moving across the room to get *her* a drink. Cordelia liked the way the girl said *darling*—not in the plummy, cloying way that snobby, upper-class women in talkies did, but rather more breezily and naturally, as though the world were full of darlings, as though she'd lived her whole life in an orchard of them. Her skin was unlike anything Cordelia had ever seen, and it glowed as though it had never been exposed to harsh light or dirty air.

"Do you favor juleps?" she said as they approached a uniformed waiter, who kept his eyes inclined in the direction of his small black bow tie even when they were only a few feet from him.

"Doesn't everybody?" replied Cordelia, who hadn't the vaguest idea what a julep was.

"Why, yes! How clever." The girl issued a subtle wink from the left of her great blue-green eyes. "Eddie, will you fetch us two juleps, please?"

The waiter nodded and went out of the room.

"I'm Astrid," the girl continued, her words gaining in velocity as she steered the newcomer through the sparse crowd of men in summer suits and women in shimmering dresses, all engaged in a fierce farce of not glancing in their direction, toward the great glass wall and the view it held. It had never occurred to Cordelia that a wall could be that high—it must have been twenty feet or so—and still made of such a fragile material, and she had to be stern with herself to not go on staring upward. "What do we call you?"

"Cordelia."

"Well, Cordelia, I'm *so* glad you're here. I haven't the faintest idea where you could have come from, but I am terribly relieved that you arrived just when you did. How delightfully contrary of you to wear that dress! You'll have to tell me later where you got it. Anyway, it was looking to be a most dull party, and we are so in need of new blood, and I hope you like dancing as much as you like juleps, because I am planning to drink a lot of juleps and dance a lot of dances, and I don't at all feel like being tied down by a partner tonight, at least not a boy partner, the kind who wants to lead you and hold you and make sure none of the other boys looks at you, don't you know exactly what I mean?"

"Yes," Cordelia replied, and though everything about the scene was very new to her, it was with complete sincerity that she added, "I know exactly."

"Oh, good. You see, I feel so entirely pretty tonight, I think I want everyone to have a chance to look at me, and not have anyone make me feel bad about it, and moreover, I think we're going to be awfully good friends, and also that—"

"My dear Miss Donal."

"Yeessssssssssss?" Astrid trilled, turning.

Cordelia's arm was still hooked in hers, and so she too was forced to turn in the direction of the low, purposeful voice. There, shoulder to shoulder, were the snake from the night before and a man like him in size but older, and without the younger one's restless, agitated quality. The older man's dark tan was especially striking against his white linen suit; it was not unlike the tan people in Ohio had by the end of a summer season—the kind acquired through uneasy living. There was a distinguished white burst in his sandy hair at each temple, however, and he drew the stares of everyone present. His eyes were chestnut brown. Cordelia knew at once that he was Darius Grey, and she felt a sinking disappointment. Until a few seconds ago she had believed that when they at last came face-to-face, there would be an instantaneous flash of recognition, but he only watched her with an intense and inscrutable gaze. No one said anything for several breaths, and for the first time Cordelia considered the possibility that Letty might be right—that her father might just be any ordinary man, lost or gone. That the well-dressed man in front of her was no relation, and would shortly and swiftly dash all hope that she would ever know the truth of her origins.

The famous bootlegger was holding a silver tray with two tall glasses filled to the gold rim with ice and amber liquid and mint leaves, which was somehow incongruous with the power he so clearly exuded in the room. For everyone wavered and regarded him, waiting for his words, and it was indeed he who eventually broke the silence: "Whom have we here, Miss Donal?"

Astrid's arm drew her in. "Mr. Grey, I'd like to introduce my friend Cordelia . . ." She paused, as though her memory might produce a surname. "Cordelia . . . ?"

"Grey." Cordelia could not manage to make her voice louder than a whisper. Her face had gone cold, her eyes bright.

"Cordelia Grey?" A shadow crossed the bootlegger's face for an instant, but he masked it with a smile. "No relation, I assume."

"She's nobody," the boy snorted. "A troublemaker. I saw her at Seventh Heaven last—the other night."

Cordelia swallowed and realized that she was a few minutes from being thrown out. If she wasn't brave, her chance to explain herself would disappear, and she would soon be standing on the side of the road like the foolish girl everyone in Union always believed her to be.

"I'm your daughter," she said, her voice halting and sudden, and she tried not to look afraid.

Darius Grey's eyes moved away from the young man at his side to the interloper, and then his eyebrows slowly rose, moving upward with a multitude of emotion. The tendril-like muscles of his eye sockets were strung with surprise and sympathy and so many other elements, she could not readily identify them all.

"My daughter?" On Darius's tongue, it sounded like an entirely different word from the one she'd just used. The word she'd used had sounded prosaic, almost pleading; his *daughter* was like some rare, possibly fantastical creature.

Astrid's grip loosened a little, and everyone in the room gave up the pretense of not gawking at the scene by the glass window. Cordelia took a breath and spoke in as clear and even a tone as she could manage: "My mother's name was Fanny Larson, and I was born in April of 1911 in New York City. I don't remember it—the city, I mean—because she died when

I was still a baby and I was taken back to Union, Ohio, where she was from. My aunt Ida, who reared me, always said I had to be saved—she talked of my father as though he was a man like you . . . and I wanted to find out if indeed you might be him."

Outside the sky was turning from lavender to a darker shade, and down under the great white tent the music and the celebrating had grown rowdy. But in the glass-enclosed porch, silence prevailed again and every mouth hung open.

Darius Grey pursed his lips, mulling a small mystery. "You found your way onto my property, inside my house, to this intimate little gathering of my most trusted colleagues." He made a flourish with his hand. "We keep this place awfully well guarded. How did you manage that?"

Cordelia admonished herself not to blush. She hadn't found it difficult to tell the guard in the hall that she was a dancing girl, but it was another thing entirely to say so to the man she'd long believed to be her father. "I told the guard at the front door I was the girl who jumps out of the cake," she relayed flatly.

In the corner of the room, a woman laughed through her nose. Cordelia's eyes darted from face to face as laughter spread through the crowd. Soon the snake was laughing, too, and she could feel that Astrid's shoulders shook a little with the humor of this. Even Darius Grey, with his calm demeanor, cracked a smile.

"The girl who jumps out of the cake?" he hooted. "The way, in a movie, a dancing girl might pop up—surprise!—on a gangster's birthday."

Cordelia's heart was beating quickly now, and she turned her eyes to her humble, scuffed shoes, realizing in horror that this was the exact reason she knew that dancing girls sometimes were hired to jump out of cakes—that she and Letty had once seen a moving picture in which it had happened. Only, in the movie, the girl is on a revenge mission, because her sweetheart has been murdered for having been an accidental witness to a crime, and after everyone shouts, "Surprise!" she draws a pistol from her headpiece and shoots the gangster dead.

But contrary to her worst fears, Darius's voice now took on an approving tone. "Only a daughter of mine could convince a man like Danny that she was a dancing girl in a dress like that." He shook his head and stared at Cordelia admiringly. "She must have the Grey eyes—capable of hypnotizing man or beast."

Now all the faces in the room turned slightly to get a better look at the stranger in the unfashionable dress. Cordelia straightened and let her neck lengthen, and cautiously allowed the feeling of elation that this approving statement created to spread from her lungs across her shoulders and down to her fingertips. Meanwhile, Darius's eyelids fell closed.

"Fanny . . . ," he said in a far-off, almost sentimental way.

The twenty-odd bodies in the room leaned closer, and Cordelia became acutely aware that even Astrid, who had so recently come to her defense, was regarding her with bemused detachment. Then Darius opened his eyes, and the whole room waited for what he would say. Eventually, he let out a long sigh. "Your mother had a coat just like that one."

"It was hers." For a moment Cordelia, who hated to cry in public, thought she might be choking up.

But then all of Darius's features rearranged themselves, and his voice grew angry. "Eddie!" he bellowed.

The waiter Astrid had sent off earlier appeared now, skittering toward them. "Yes?" he asked, a touch fearfully.

"Take this," Darius said impatiently, thrusting the tray of drinks toward him in such a way that Cordelia and everyone around trembled a little, thinking they would fall and shatter on the floor. But Eddie proved deft at his job, and soon he had the tray righted in his hands and was turning to go. Darius continued in an exasperated vein. "*Ed* . . . the lady's things?"

Cordelia looked down, remembering her coat and the battered suitcase she'd been trying to hide underneath it. Eddie nodded and hurriedly reached for both while balancing the tray in his left hand.

"Put them in the Calla Lily Suite," Darius commanded. Though Cordelia could scarcely imagine what those three words meant, they made her feel protected, as though she had been wrapped in some rich, clean-smelling blanket and given a cup of tea made from the rarest herbs. "That shall be Cordelia's."

When both were unburdened, Darius stepped forward with open arms. One hand drew her in and the other rested on the crown of her head, gently roughing her hair. In its abatement, she realized that her entire life up until that moment had been marked by an urgent desire to flee wherever and whomever she was. For the first time, in a perfumed room with walls of glass, being taken into the protective arms of the father she'd never known, she experienced a moment of being exactly where, and exactly what, she was supposed to be.

When the embrace ended, Darius stood away from her at arm's length to get another look. "How like Fanny you are." His voice had softened again. "Charlie," he said, addressing the younger man, whose face was still a portrait of irritation, "say hello to your long-lost sister."

Cordelia's eyes grew wide, but she managed to keep herself upright and calm as Charlie leaned forward, took her hand, and gave her a cold kiss on the cheek.

"You're Charlie Grey?" she said, and then regretted it immediately. Embarrassment seeped into the moment, and she felt sure that her tone had betrayed all the many articles she had read about the Grey family of Long Island, hoping from her dusty, provincial home, to meet her real family someday.

Charlie, however, had already looked away from her, and Darius did not seem to have noticed her gaucheness.

"Ah, so you know of him? Good. I'd already had him when I fell in love with Fanny; it was one of the reasons Ida didn't care for me, Lord knows she had the right to feel the way she did. Long time ago, it all was. But now," Darius continued, clasping his hands together, becoming abruptly businesslike, "I am very impressed by all you have accomplished in these sorry clothes, and I understand that they couldn't do any better for you in that godforsaken part of the world, but I will not have my daughter in rags. Miss Donal, dear, will you find Jones and ask him what we have on the premises? Surely there's a good frock that will fit Cordelia. Tomorrow, of course, we will get her her own things, but in the meantime, help her get dressed, would you? There is a party on—I will not have half the world meeting my daughter in anything but the best."

Now Astrid's grip became once again warm and possessive. There was a gentle swishing of expensive fabrics as the women in the room stepped backward to make a path for the two girls, for they had realized over the past minutes that when she returned to the party, Cordelia Grey would be better than any of them.

By '29 it was quite generally known that Grey the bootlegger threw memorable parties. Early on in his career, it was said, he realized that he would sell more liquor if liquor came with a glamorous aura, and since he believed people to be generally dull and useless, he set about living a decadent lifestyle as a kind of demonstration. So there were always parties at his estate, and the parties always produced stories. But the evening on which he appeared under the great white tent—a little late, as usual—not with a showgirl or a socialite of rather outré taste on his arm, but instead with a young girl everyone was calling his daughter, was a particularly unforgettable one.

"This evening is to celebrate my daughter, who Providence has seen fit to return to me!" he bellowed to the crowd, sometime later that evening, and everyone pushed forward to get a better look. "I introduce to you . . . Cordelia Grey!"

There was a fresh quality about her eyes and they moved rapidly over the scene, as though she was eager to miss nothing. After much hushed discussion of what type she was, it was generally agreed that she looked uncompromisingly like nobody but herself. The thin, metallic band that circled her head and almost disappeared against her tawny hair was a very Astrid Donal–style touch. The dress she wore was nothing special—a swath of sleeveless teal silk that showed off strong, speckled calves and trailed a little behind her—but then, her clothing was hardly what made her interesting.

Two A.M. arrived more quickly than it ever had before, and by then the dancing was no longer any good. But the velvet dome of the sky had been punctured a million times over by stars, and the girl whom everyone wanted to meet had traipsed away from the crowd under the tent and into the darkness where she could get a better look. Earlier, when her status in this place had been a matter of minutes and not of hours, Astrid had smoothed Cordelia's wavy hair with a cream that smelled like chemicals and gardenia, and pinned it in a dramatic bun at the nape of her neck. As she stepped forward into the grass, that bun began a beautiful process of unraveling.

In addition to the dress, which was of a smooth, soft material that possessed a magical quality when it brushed against her skin, Astrid had outfitted her in a pair of black suede heels. Cordelia would not have dreamed of ruining them by walking on the lawn, so it was in bare feet that she strode forward. The grass felt like a cool, soft cushion, fresh smelling and not at all damp. Soon enough Astrid, who was having trouble walking in heels on uneven terrain, lost her footing and pulled both girls down in a fit of giggles.

Cordelia's head came to rest against a sprawling pillow of her own hair on the ground. Astrid gripped her arm, her fingernails pressing against the skin. She'd drunk more champagne than Cordelia, who had not yet forgotten the consequences of the previous night, and her movements had become relaxed and floppy.

"Darling, look!" Cordelia pointed at a white burst crossing

the sky. *Darling* was already becoming one of her regular words. "A shooting star."

"Oh," Astrid whispered.

Cordelia had seen plenty of stars falling in her time, but they seemed somehow closer here, with the music still within earshot and the convivial glow beneath the tent emanating across the lawn. It was almost as though she might be able to reach up and grasp the next star brazen enough to pass into her planet's orbit. Before she could help herself, she remembered that it was John who had first explained to her that a shooting star was not a star at all, but a great hunk of something from outer space breaking apart when it came too close to Earth. John's mother was as God-fearing as Aunt Ida and wouldn't have believed in such "nonsense," but his father, perhaps just to spite his wife, read a science magazine every night while he smoked his pipe and had explained this to his son. And then John had related it to Cordelia, one night when they'd crept away from a church picnic. They'd lain on their backs a long time that night, watching little explosions miles and miles above the ground, and John had asked her if she believed in fate. She'd laughed hard and reminded him she wasn't a child anymore and he wasn't, either, and that neither of them should believe in fairy tales. But that field in Ohio was a long way away now, and from her new sky-gazing position, it was difficult not to feel that she was fulfilling a kind of destiny.

"Cordelia, where did you go?" Astrid pushed herself up on her elbows and watched her with round eyes. "You're missing them."

"Where would I possibly go?" Cordelia replied, her voice soft with awe at the turn her life had taken, even as she reminded herself not to let her mind go down that path again.

"Well, I haven't the faintest, but I hope you don't disappear because—because—" Astrid stammered, fighting a yawn. "Because I've already gotten so used to having you here. Please don't leave—ever. But all of a sudden I'm so sleepy, aren't you?"

"No," said Cordelia, and then realized that she was. "Come on, let's go back. I wanted to thank my . . . father"—the word was not yet quite natural to her, but she knew it would be soon—"and say good night."

"Yes." Astrid struggled up onto her coltish legs. "Say good night to Charlie, too. He's not as bad as he seems. You know . . ." Another yawn swallowed up whatever it was she was going to say, and then as they began to walk she added, almost as an afterthought, "I love him."

When the two girls came back to the tent, each with a pair of shoes dangling from her fingers, the party had ebbed from its previous heights. Now the dance floor was again occupied by couples, the girls hanging from their partners' necks with ribbonlike arms. The rest of the crowd had dispersed into quiet groups; some played cards on white tabletops or were already engaged in whispered storytelling about the evening's choicer antics. The armed guards Cordelia had known to be invisibly present from the moment she had entered the Grey estate that afternoon had stepped a little from the shadows, although the people waiting to see where the party was headed next did not seem to pay them particular mind.

"Mr. Jones!" Astrid caroled at the horse-faced man emerging from the tent in their direction. Behind him, Cordelia noticed the wall of curious stares. "Are you here to get me in trouble again?"

"My dear," the man replied, in a tone of perfect equanimity, "my function is to get you *out* of trouble."

"Cordelia, this is Mr. Elias Jones. He sees to things for your daddy," Astrid went on lightly as though the man hadn't said anything at all. "Isn't that right?"

"Yes, that's right." Elias Jones gave Cordelia a curt nod. "Mr. Grey has retired for the evening. He wanted to tell you good night himself, and how relieved he is that you have been restored to the family. But there will be plenty of time for that. Also—he has ordered a car to take you into the city tomorrow to buy new clothes. He was hoping that you would accompany her, Miss Donal, and for convenience' sake, he suggested you stay the night. There is plenty of room in the Calla Lily Suite for both of you, and you know how unsafe the roads can be at this hour. I will have someone call over to Marsh Hall, so your parents don't worry."

"Oh, Mother never does. But thank you, Elias." Astrid's voice had grown dreamy, and she was having trouble keeping her heavy eyelids open. "Where is Charlie, by the way?"

Elias cleared his throat. "He didn't spend much time at the party tonight, Miss Donal."

"Oh, what a bore." Astrid exhaled a sigh of profound indifference and took hold of Cordelia again. "Come on, let's see if the kitchen staff won't bring us ice cream in bed . . ."

In fact the kitchen staff did bring them ice cream in bed, along with carbonated water that came all the way from Italy and towels that by some wild contrivance were warm when they arrived. Cordelia had been a great many places since she had last bathed, and so she spent some time marveling at the full, hot stream of water produced by the Calla Lily Suite's shower, not to mention all the dozens of polished fixtures it required and the many marble surfaces that surrounded it, and also the sheer size of the room, which in many parts of the world would certainly have been sufficient for a parlor. When she emerged, clean and wrapped in a thick terry cloth robe, Astrid was already asleep on the far side of the bed. Cordelia crawled under the blankets, laid her head against a pile of down pillows, and was dreaming before she could even begin to catalogue the great many notable things in her new bedroom.

She slept a good long time, and when she woke, rested, the light of an advanced day was streaming in through the tall windows. She experienced a brief moment of disorientation while her eyes adjusted to the brightness. Astrid was still snoring softly on the other side of the bed, and a silver tray with a silver coffee pitcher and a platter of crescent-shaped pastries had been placed on the nightstand. The room seemed even more opulent in the noon light than it had the night before, and Cordelia exhaled a sigh of pure satisfaction. Then she snatched up the note that lay folded on the tray and experienced her first disappointment as the acknowledged daughter of Darius Grey.

My dear,

I'm sorry, but business has called me away to Canada. I will return in a few days, and we will celebrate our reunion more properly then. I have told Charlie to look after you until my return—you will find that it is no light thing to be a member of my family, but I trust Charlie with my life and yours. Until I return . . .

Love,
Your father

8

"WHAT'S THE NEW GIRL DOING?"

Unlike Paulette, the cigarette girl from Seventh Heaven, her roommates, Fay and Kate, had not yet embraced Letty's name. But even if *new girl* was a little bit of an insult, still it meant that Letty was new to someplace, that even if she was only here until she figured out where else to go, there was the chance she was on her way to belonging. The place in question was a basement apartment, dark even in the daytime and with a warped floor. It was filled with old velvet furniture, tasseled and threadbare, that had the air of having come from what Mother might have called "a house of ill repute."

After the fight with Cordelia and their expulsion from the

Washborne, Letty had returned to the nightclub because it was the only place she could think of, and the nice girl who'd helped her earlier in the evening had helped her again by taking her back here. She'd slept a long time, and when she'd woken up, she had three new friends to replace the one she'd lost.

Fay's hair was peroxided to a shade almost white, and Kate's was frizzy and dark, and they both wore mid-thigh-length kimonos around the apartment even though it was well past noon. Their hair and makeup, however, had been impeccably done already that morning, just after they'd risen, as it had been the morning before, when Letty met them for the first time. Letty, who was lying facedown on a worn Persian rug with a magazine she'd found in the bathroom, couldn't immediately think of a reply and was relieved when Paulette answered for her.

"She's reading notices for auditions she's too shy to go try out for, and circling them for reasons she doesn't fully comprehend." Paulette's voice was flat, and she spoke from the kitchenette without looking up from the coffee she was making. Her dark hair was already marcelled, and the crests of its wide waves gleamed in the afternoon light. Her lips were wine-dark and shiny, anchoring a slightly plump face, and she was as tall as Cordelia. The ceiling in the kitchenette was low like all the ceilings in the house, except a little more so, and her head almost seemed to graze its tin tiles.

"Aw, why won't you go?" Fay took a seat next to Kate on the plum-colored velvet couch, with its faded and ripped upholstery leaking white fluff from the cushions, so that she could peer over Letty's shoulder. "Won't kill you, you know."

Letty glanced up at her and gave a diminutive shrug. "I will soon, just not yet," she said. Paulette was right—she knew that she wasn't really going to go to any of those auditions—though she wouldn't have been able to say why exactly.

"Oh, honey, look at all these fancy jobs you're thinking about!" Fay's kimono was white with blue flowers, almost as pale as her hair and complexion, and her sleeve brushed Letty's shoulder as she peered over it at the last page of the *Weekly Stage*. "You've got to start with something a little less ambitious." They all hoped to make it on the stage one way or another, but Fay was currently the only roommate who earned money at it, as a chorus girl in one of the big variety shows. Glimpsing her long, coltish legs crossed and dangling from the edge of the couch, Letty found herself wondering if she would ever have the height for a job like that.

"Oh, hush, we all have to find out for ourselves," Paulette said, coming toward them with a steaming cup of coffee in her hands.

"Sad," Kate interjected from the couch, upon which she reclined as she repaired a wide, beaded belt that she had damaged the previous evening, "but true."

"Oh, *no*—not the new Gordon Grange play. How tiresome," Fay went on, continuing to spy over Letty's shoulder at the wanted listing. He was a playwright Mother used to speak admiringly of, and the part called for a waiflike brunette, which was exactly Letty's type. Though she couldn't admit it to these girls, who all spoke as though they'd never been surprised by anything, she had already decided that the part was perfect for her and that if only she could get up the courage, fate would make it her first real job. "They call him a genius, but geniuses are just like other men, you know."

"Except they expect more and do less," Kate put in.

"You just have to start trying out," Fay said, patting her white-blond bob. "You'll be scared for a while, and then you won't be scared anymore, and eventually something will stick. I can't tell you how many times I heard *no* before I—"

"Before she said *yes*!" Kate interjected bawdily, and then threw back her frizzy head and howled in laughter.

Bewildered, Letty sat up and crossed her pale legs under her navy skirt. She wasn't quite sure what Kate meant, and if she meant what Letty thought she meant, whether it would hurt Fay's feelings. But then she realized that Fay thought it was just as funny—she was laughing even harder than Kate was. Letty, who had started to blush, refocused her eyes on the paper.

"Oh, sweetheart, don't mind them," Paulette said

quickly. She handed the cup of coffee to Fay, bent down on Letty's other side, and began rearranging her hair. "You'll get there your own way. Anyway, Fay, you know you really aren't so bad. You'd never do anything as bad as what Clara Hay does."

"That is very true," Fay said, leaning back on the couch and crossing her legs the other way.

"Who is Clara Hay?" Letty asked.

"Oh, just a girl who works with me at the club. Hasn't got an ounce of real talent, but she gets by—doing things other girls won't." Perhaps Paulette saw the new girl squirm a little, because she waved her hand in the air and said, "Never mind. Don't think of it. What we need to think about is your hair—it's really *too* old-fashioned. Can I fix it? Please?"

Without looking up, Kate passed her the scissors that had been resting on a side table. Letty's large eyes rolled up toward Paulette, who was smiling so kindly that it was impossible to do anything but nod in agreement.

"Come over here." Paulette pulled a wooden chair out from the small table in the kitchenette and gestured toward it.

Tentatively, Letty took a seat. She closed her eyes. Holding her breath, she tried to banish the thought of what Mother would have said. The room grew quiet as Paulette placed the blades an inch below her ear and began to cut. In the few days that she'd spent in New York, she hadn't yet heard a noise quite as loud as that, and she could not help but gasp out loud as the dark locks began to fall into her lap.

"Better already," Kate said dryly.

Letty squeezed her eyes tighter. Cold metal slid against her neck, and then she felt more hair fall down her back. Her face went numb and there was a buzzing in her ears, and she lost the sense of time passing. When it was over, she only knew because Paulette said, "There!" and set the scissors down.

The room seemed brighter when Letty lifted her lids. Fay passed a hand mirror to Paulette, who handed it to Letty. More than two-thirds the length of her dark hair was gone now, and it framed her neat, pale heart of a face. A row of bangs drew a straight line across her forehead, bringing out the iridescence of her complexion. She appeared more grown-up and more fragile at once; her neck had never appeared so slender. In the reflection, she could see Paulette, eyes bright and expectant, watching to see if Letty liked the new cut, and Letty did attempt a brave smile. But then her bottom lip trembled, and she knew that she was going to cry. She stood and hurried to the front door.

Outside the sky was a lazy arch of tranquil blue, and neighbors went about their business. All Letty could hear were her own rough breaths as her little legs carried her down the block. By the time Paulette caught up with her near the corner, her cheeks were streaked and damp.

"Oh, honey, I wouldn't have touched your hair if I'd

known you cared so much!" her new friend exclaimed, frowning with exaggerated sympathy as she reached forward and began to blot the tears away.

"I don't!" Letty had to bring her arm up to cover her face. "I don't care that much."

"No, 'course not. You'll like it tomorrow, I promise."

A final sob worked its way up through Letty, and when her shoulders had relaxed again, she felt Paulette take hold of them and spin her around.

"Look!"

Letty did as she was told. They were standing in front of a barbershop, and in the reflective window glass she saw a girl she barely recognized. All the elements of her appearance had been altered by the bobbing of her hair, and what might before have come across as slight and girlish now seemed petite and rakish—sophisticated, even. The sorrow ebbed, and for a moment there was only a quiet empty inside. Her long silken hair was gone, and her best friend was gone. All the old familiar places and people, whether comfortable or hurtful or dull, were very far away, and she didn't have the money to return to them even if she wanted to. A sensation of weightlessness came over her, and her lips parted.

"I wasn't crying about my hair," she said, and the shadow of a smile crossed her face. Until that moment, she realized, she hadn't really stepped out of her old name, and for the first time she glimpsed Letty Larkspur in that shopwindow. She had lost many things, but she could see herself more clearly all of a sudden. There was a glistening in her eyes when she turned around to face Paulette. "I feel so light!"

"Well, you look gorgeous." Paulette smiled and reached forward to adjust the new girl's bangs.

"I'm sorry for being such a ninny. It's just that all of a sudden Ohio, and everything, seemed so far away."

"Well, that's 'cause it *is* far away," Paulette deadpanned. "Though pretty soon you'll forget there's anything or anybody west of Twelfth Avenue."

Letty, who wouldn't even have known how to get to Twelfth Avenue, could only nod.

"You know, I'm not from here either. Kansas. I can't even remember which train I'd take to there anymore, or how I used to talk. I took up with a waiter from the Plaza when I first arrived—he'd spent a long time listening to how fancy people talk, and he taught me to pronounce consonants, thank heavens. Before that . . ." She trailed off and crossed her eyes clownishly, which brought both girls to giggles.

"And, oh! I made you run out in your nightclothes, didn't I?" Letty said, through her laughter, once she'd realized that under Paulette's belted black coat was probably nothing more than the slip she'd been wearing during the haircut, and how mortifying that must be for her.

But Paulette shrugged and opened up her palms toward the sky. "Who cares?" she said. Then, lacing her arm with Letty's, she added, "Aren't you starving?"

"Yes!"

"Come on, let's eat some breakfast."

So they strolled to a lunchroom on Sixth Avenue, where diners sat packed in at rows and rows of long tables, their mixed origins even more salient against the spare, white-tiled room. Policemen took their break with corned beef hash, side by side with the local swindlers who were their sometime antagonists, while men with long hair put aside their ukuleles to eat pastrami sandwiches beside socialites, still in their evening finery of the night before, bent forward over steaming coffee and plates of fried eggs.

"Pancakes—I want pancakes. Don't you want pancakes?" Paulette asked, facing Letty across the long gray marble table.

Eating a sweet breakfast dish so late in the afternoon seemed at first terribly frivolous to Letty, especially since the dinner hour in Union was often about this time of day. But once the idea had settled in, she found that pancakes were precisely what she wanted. She was, in fact, starving. She could have eaten a stack of ten. They ordered pancakes and coffees and looked around at the multitude of characters, chewing and gossiping, just in from being terribly busy or on their way to do something awfully grand. While they waited for their food,

Letty told Paulette about the dairy farm and the daily dance lessons Mother used to give, and Paulette told her stories about the nightclub and what it was like working there.

"And when her beau nodded off at the table, on account of the too many Bacardi cocktails he had drunk, she merely moved over to the next table and took up with the fellow there!" ended one such anecdote, as the syrupy remnants of their meal were being cleared away. The girl who used to be called Letitia might have found herself discomfited by this story, but Letty was now sufficiently citified to find the humor in it and laugh out loud.

By the time they returned to the sidewalks, the brightest part of the day had already passed and Letty felt she knew Paulette almost twice as well as she had only a few hours before. They were heading across Barrow Street when Paulette took the lollipop out of her mouth and said, "You really want to be on the stage, do you?"

"Yes," Letty managed after a minute.

"You'll never be the queen of high kicks, I'm afraid."

"No." Letty sighed. "But I can sing."

"Even better. Show me."

"Show you . . . now?" They came to a busy avenue, where people were walking by on both sides. The first floor of every window was a storefront, inside which shopgirls leaned against counters and stared out at the passing pageant. "Here?"

"Why not?"

"But—but there are all these people."

"Oh, what does it matter? Everyone is always just paying attention to themselves anyhow."

They were still walking, but Letty let her eyes drift closed and stopped thinking about her forward motion. She remembered the reflection of the girl with the smart bob, and she lifted her hands and began to sing a song she knew from the radio, about the joys of dancing barefoot until two o'clock. Her voice was timid at first, but then it rose to full capacity, and when it did she forgot the people around her and began to move a little with the melody.

When she was finished, she did a twirl and bowed toward Paulette. Then she peeked, with a mixture of pride and fearfulness, to see what she thought. Paulette's eyebrows were raised, and her eyes were round with sincere admiration. "You got it, kiddo," Paulette said.

But before Letty could thank her or even absorb the full pleasure of that subtle, stylish endorsement, she got another.

"Bravo!" a man called out, and she turned toward the sound of clapping.

There were people all around, some of them watching her with sudden attentiveness, but most of them going about their business, just as Paulette had predicted, and it took another few moments for her eyes to settle on the gentleman in question. He was fair, wearing a straw boater, and he was hanging from an idling electric streetcar. Though his nose had decided character, his face was soft and gentle like a college boy's. There was something teddy bear–like in the way his gray herringbone suit fit. His eyes were observant but not piercing, and set back so that his brow cast a shadow over them, and when he noticed that Letty had spotted him, he began clapping again.

"Bravo!" he repeated.

To hide her blush, Letty gave an even deeper curtsy, bowing her head so that the tips of her dark hair cut across her cheekbones. Then she stood up quickly and grabbed for Paulette's hand, so they could hurry away before anyone noticed the embarrassment coloring the skin from her face down to her clavicles.

"Where can I see you again?" the young man called after her. The car had lurched into motion and was now passing the girls as they ran hand in hand up the avenue.

"You know where Seventh Heaven is?" Paulette called out.

The man nodded.

"She works there! Come by and see her sometime."

The man lifted his hat and tipped it in their direction as the car continued uptown, and the girls' run slowed to a brisk walk.

"He was nice!" Paulette said, laughing and catching her

breath. "You see the kind of attention a little talent and a good haircut will get you?"

Letty nodded in agreement. "But I don't work at Seventh Heaven," she said when her giggles had subsided.

"Well, rent doesn't pay itself, sister. We've gotta get you something to do."

"Rent?" They turned off the avenue onto a side street, and Letty let the word echo in her mind. She found it had never held so much appeal. "You mean, I can be your roommate?"

"Yes. You're one of us now, which—I'm sorry to inform you—is pricier than life back in Indiana."

"Ohio," Letty corrected her, but she smiled anyway.

"Ohio. But the manager, Mr. Cole, he likes me—he'll hire you if I ask nice."

"Thank you," Letty whispered, though no matter how she tried, she wouldn't have been able to convey the gratitude she felt toward this girl who, in less than a day, had turned her fortune around so completely.

9

ON CORDELIA'S SECOND MORNING WAKING UP TO THE Calla Lily Suite, at Dogwood, she experienced not even a hint of disorientation. It was as though she'd opened her eyes to exactly this room every day of her life. By then she knew that the flaky, crescent-shaped pastries they brought in the morning were called *croissants*, and she had gathered—although she still hadn't heard anything to confirm it—that the bizarre flowers filling the tall, rectangular silver vases all over the room were calla lilies, even though they were more austere and futuristic than any lily she had ever seen, like flowers that grew on the moon.

She pushed herself up against the white leather upholstered headboard. The sun must have been high in the sky already; it flooded the room. The dress she had worn the night before was thrown over the white stuffed chair nearest the bed, and she had slept in her black slip, which itself had cost considerably more than any dress she had ever owned. On the other side of the room, across a carpet that spread out like a soft acre of new-fallen snow, sat a dozen or so packages from Bergdorf Goodman. Bergdorf, she now knew, was a place on Fifth Avenue that sold ladies' clothing for outrageous amounts of money where she and Astrid had spent much of the previous day. Later, they had eaten dinner at a fancy hotel, and Charlie and his gang had met them, and then the girls had been sent back rather late to White Cove in the Daimler. She smiled, thinking of her new clothes and all the evenings on which she would wear them, but before she could help it her mind had turned to Letty and how much she would have loved all this, and her joy dimmed.

She poured a cup of coffee and crossed the room toward the terrace. Outside the air was warmer, and it was full of pollen and the smell of leaves. The white tent that she'd danced under two nights before—it seemed a lifetime ago—was still intact, although all the evidence of broken champagne glasses and discarded shoes had been carried away. Two men wearing undershirts and trousers held up by suspenders were walking on the lawn in the direction of the entrance, one of them with a rifle resting over his shoulder.

"Miss Grey . . . ?"

She turned at the sound of her name and went back inside. "Yes?"

Elias Jones, standing in the doorway, averted his eyes when he saw she was only wearing a slip. "I'm . . . sorry. We aren't used to ladies—young ladies, ladies like you—here. Mr. Grey has instructed me to hire a maid for you. Then we won't have any more of these awkward intrusions."

"That's awfully nice." Cordelia smiled at the idea that someone was bowing to propriety on her account, and though she tried to look unfazed by the mention of the maid, a little private corner of her heart squealed at the notion that another girl's whole job might be to wait on her. "But I'm not angry."

"I'll find someone by tomorrow," Jones continued, clearing his throat and ignoring her smile. "In the meantime, please let me know if there is anything you need."

"Thank you."

"And there's a telephone call for you."

Cordelia nodded and followed him into the adjacent study, which housed a polished desk, a marmalade-colored rug with a geometric pattern on it, and a black telephone.

"Hello?" she said as Jones disappeared.

"Darling, it's me. I hope I didn't wake you . . ."

"No, not at all." The sadness she'd felt over Letty faded at the sound of Astrid's voice, which reminded her that she did in fact have a friend with whom to delight in this new, rich world. Anyway, had Letty believed Cordelia when she'd finally told her about Darius, she might have been waking up here now, too. "Though I'm still in my slip, which it seems I've slept in."

"Oh, dear, did I just make Elias walk in on you like that?"

"Yes!" Cordelia couldn't help but giggle as she pictured how Jones had blanched at the sight of her. "Do you think he'll ever forgive me?"

"Forgive *you*! Darling, I'd put money on that being the most exalted moment of his day." She snickered.

"It's going to be a beautiful day, isn't it?"

"They're all going to be beautiful days from now on. Which is why I'm calling, as it happens. Have you eaten?"

"No."

"Then come have lunch with me at the club, won't you?"

"Isn't it a little early for a nightclub?"

"The country club, silly."

"Oh." Cordelia fidgeted with her hem. Of course, the White Cove Country Club—she'd read once that the Greys were not members, because someone else supplied the club's liquor, but naturally all the other wealthy families in the area were. "Yes, of course. Should I tell Charlie?"

"No!"

The swiftness of Astrid's reply startled Cordelia, and she

wondered if she had done something wrong. "But I thought you loved him?"

"Oh, yes, I love Charlie and Charlie loves me and everyone knows it," she replied in a breezy, childlike voice. "Only—I'm not in the mood for him just now."

"All right."

"So avoid Charlie on your way out, and try to get Danny, you know the young one, the guard you fooled the night of the party, to drive you . . ."

Cordelia cracked a smile and then remembered that Astrid couldn't see it. Few of the small houses in Union had telephones, and Aunt Ida's certainly didn't. It was new for her and a little peculiar, having a casual conversation like this with someone's disembodied voice. "I'll see you there in an hour?"

"Perfect, darling. *Bisous, bisous!*"

"*Bisous*," Cordelia replied, though she didn't know what the word meant.

An hour later, when the long-lost daughter of Darius Grey, whom everyone was dying to catch a glimpse of, walked onto the terrace luncheon room of the White Cove Country Club, Astrid Donal was already ensconced in a corner table with a particularly good view of the green. Like everyone else under the blue-and-white-striped awning, which shielded the round tables, Astrid was wearing white—a crewneck sweater and an

A-line skirt—and a wide straw hat drooped over her pretty face.

Beside her was Billie Marsh, her stepsister, who was a student at Barnard College in Manhattan, and who usually favored darker shades but had that afternoon complied with the unspoken dress code of the place by donning white slacks and blouse. She had not, however, bowed to the tradition stating that women who smoked should do so discreetly; her pack of Chesterfields sat on the table in front of her. Her dark, mannishly cut hair was slicked behind both ears, and her eyes were covered with small, perfectly round black sunglasses. These two girls did not, at a glance, appear to be members of the same family, and it was possible, given the lives their parents had led, that they viewed every domestic arrangement as more or less temporary.

"That can't be her," said Billie, exhaling a cloud of smoke, in a voice devoid of shock that implied of course it must be.

There was a chorus of porcelain teacups being placed back onto porcelain saucers. The din of conversation fell to silence and then rose back to a low hum. Astrid's big eyes sailed to a tall girl approaching the Marsh table in a red boatneck dress that was loose in the middle but clung lightly to her hips. Astrid had seen that dress on Cordelia yesterday at Bergdorf and had told her new friend she really ought to have it. The thing just fit her too well. But the cut was a rather audacious choice for an institution as old and formal as the White Cove Country Club, and the color put her completely afoul of many decades of tradition.

"How brave," Billie commented.

"Yes," Astrid replied, just before Cordelia came into earshot. "That was one of the first things I noticed about her."

A moment of awkwardness ensued, in which Cordelia appeared perplexed about the right way to greet them, but then Astrid lifted up her arms to bring her new friend in for a kiss on either cheek.

"Cordelia Grey, this is my stepsister, Billie Marsh." The girls shook hands. "She insisted on meeting you."

"Charmed," said Billie.

"Yes, exactly," Cordelia replied and sat down.

"I'm starving," Astrid said. "Can we order, please?"

For a moment they turned to their menus, but then Astrid noticed that Cordelia was looking over her shoulder at all the people uttering low murmurs and covering their mouths were their hands.

"They're staring at me," she whispered.

"Yes." Astrid slammed her menu closed. "Ignore them, darling. They are quite shocked that you wore red. We dress in white for the club."

"You've performed a public service, really," Billie elaborated in her usual dry tone.

"True." Astrid signaled the waiter. "Everyone will have something to talk about at dinner."

"They all want to meet you, you know." Billie put out her cigarette and smiled. "I'm not the only one."

"I had no idea I was supposed to wear white." A cloud of confusion lingered briefly over Cordelia's brow, and then she shrugged, and the light came back into her eyes. "But I am always happy to be of service, and anyway, didn't you say you were starving?"

"Yes!"

They ordered bacon, lettuce, and tomato sandwiches and iced tea, and enjoyed being watched by the staid old members of the club, who were so obviously pleased to be scandalized. Their food arrived, and as Astrid began to eat with her hands, she felt her contentedness soaring upward to its high point of the day. Each bite was salty and crunchy and fresh, and she had a new friend who was really such an interesting person—and she'd had no one interesting to talk to in a long time—and she was glad for having successfully avoided Charlie. Plus, she'd lured his sister to the club where it was a point of pride for him not to go.

He had lied to her—it was subtle, but she was sure of it, because Cordelia and he had crossed paths at a nightclub on an evening she distinctly remembered him saying he was doing nothing, just a little business. Last night, when she and Cordelia were out with Charlie's gang, it had been confirmed for her—Danny, the youngest of Grey's men, kept apologizing for some scene he'd made at Seventh Heaven, and saying that really, it was all Charlie's fault. Which Astrid was sure it was. Though she was not particularly put out about the lie, she felt that a girl should always return even the smallest transgression with a day or two of cold shouldering, to make her fellow wonder what is wrong and to remind him that he should try extra hard to please her. Yet none of that seemed particularly bothersome to Astrid now. The day was fine and clear, and when Billie finished her food and lit another cigarette, it seemed to punctuate the slow-moving pleasure of the day.

But in another moment, Astrid's contentedness shriveled away to almost nothing.

"Hello, dears."

On the other side of the low stone wall that demarcated the edge of the luncheon room stood the third Mrs. Marsh, wearing jodhpurs and a black velvet riding hat. Her mouth was smirking, and the expression she wore seemed to suggest she was terribly pleased with herself. A few feet behind her stood Luke. Astrid's throat constricted. There was that same incongruity to his appearance as the other day—the hard, ropey body and the sweet, sad lashes—and she found she liked looking at him now just as much as she had then. The sun was very bright, and she was glad that she had to squint, which somewhat obscured the flirtatious face she might otherwise have made.

"Whom do we have here?" Astrid's mother asked.

"This is my new friend, Cordelia Grey." There was a kind of pride in Astrid's voice when she said it, but she could not bring herself to smile. "This is my mother, Virginia."

"Ah, *the* Cordelia Grey!" Mrs. Marsh said grandly, and then she stepped forward and extended her hand to grip Cordelia's. The older woman's eyes burned with fascination, a kind of voyeuristic interest that might have irked Astrid at another time, except that Astrid was having a hard time not gazing past her at the handsome boy in denim, and he was having a hard time not reciprocating. The skin under his eyes was delicate, and his black hair kept flopping in his face when he tried to avert his gaze from the young Miss Donal.

"We have all heard about you, you know," Virginia Marsh continued. "What a wonder that you have been returned to your father. You'll have to come over and visit. We—my husband and I—love to entertain."

"Thank you," Cordelia replied.

"This is Luke, my riding instructor."

Billie lit another cigarette. "I wouldn't think you'd need lessons, Mrs. Marsh."

"One can always be more perfect." Astrid's mother moved her body so that she eclipsed her daughter's view of Luke, an act that flooded Astrid with irrational sorrow. She didn't want anything particular from the boy who had once walked her pony for her, except that she found his eyes so nice to look into, and she wanted to go on doing it and not think of anything else. He was just like summer, and she loved summer. If she had any wish, it would be to live a lifetime of summers. "And Luke is such an excellent instructor."

"Yes, he must be." Astrid inclined herself so that part of the riding instructor's face was again visible, and she let her fluffy blond hair fall girlishly across one cheek. "You'll have to give me a lesson one of these days," she added, and for extra measure gave Luke a slow, flirtatious wink.

Virginia Donal de Gruyter Marsh stiffened and reached for the young man's hand. "He's quite busy, dear. We'll ask for the club to assign you someone else. You *do* need the discipline."

Then the elder lady turned on her heel and went striding forward across the green, pulling the handsome young man after her, as though he were an accessory. Astrid simmered—she couldn't *stand* her mother. Her desire for the young man to turn back and look at her one more time was almost equal to her desire for her mother to twist her ankle right then, in the bright sunlight, with all of the White Cove Country Club watching. But Virginia Marsh didn't falter, and when Astrid forced herself to stop gaping at their receding figures, she noticed that her new friend was pushing back from the table.

"Where's Miss Grey going?" Billie asked as Cordelia

strode purposefully away.

"I haven't the faintest."

Cordelia, too, was heading out into the sunshine, on light feet, toward the realization that New York, for all its millions of souls, was just a small town like any other. Because there, standing on the grass by himself, a cigarette between his fingers, gazing out toward the golf course, was the boy with coppery hair who had said such pretty things to her the night she'd fought with Letty.

"I'm sorry I left so quickly the other night, before I even got your name," she said when she was a few feet from him.

He turned to face her. His lips parted in surprise, and then he smiled. "I kept hoping you'd show up somewhere."

"Did you?"

The air was warm out in the sunshine, and any remaining self-consciousness over wearing the wrong color to a country club evaporated with the appreciative way his eyes lingered on her. He inspired that whir of agitation in her stomach just as he had at the nightclub, although now she knew that it had nothing to do with her first taste of alcohol and was entirely to do with him.

"Yes, I've thought of nothing else. In fact—"

"Thomas!"

They both turned at the sound. A slender woman whose face was obscured by the brim of her white hat waved from some distance away on the green.

"Now you know," he said as he lifted his arm to wave back at the woman in the white hat. "Though everyone calls me Thom. I hope you aren't disappointed—it has always seemed rather common to me."

"Thom." She nodded, pondering the sound of the name. "I don't like you any less, now that I know."

He smiled at that.

"Thomas!" the woman called again.

"My mother," he explained with a look of patient irritation. "I don't care for golf particularly, but I told her I'd accompany her today. I suppose I ought to go do as I promised . . ."

"Oh." Cordelia smiled bravely and hoped that there was nothing on her face to betray how dismayed she would be to see him walk away, maybe forever, with no guarantee of another meeting. "I hope you enjoy the day. Good-bye."

"Wait," he said, although neither had budged from their position. "Can't I see you again?"

She could not help the smile spreading across her face. "Yes."

"Tomorrow?"

She nodded and bit her lip.

"I'll pick you up at six. Where do you live?"

"Do you know where Dogwood is?"

The shade of his eyes darkened almost imperceptibly.

When she first met him, she'd thought his eyes were green, but now she saw that they looked almost brown when he was under a different light, or in a different mood. She supposed he probably knew who the proprietor of Dogwood was, and perhaps he was intimidated by the notion of taking a bootlegger's daughter out. But if this was the case, still he did not waver. "At six then?"

"Yes, only—" She broke off, wondering if Charlie would have to accompany her as a chaperone. "Only, pick me up on the road in front?"

"Thomas!" his mother yelled a third time.

Thom grinned and bowed forward to kiss Cordelia's hand. "Until tomorrow then," he said before stepping backward.

Even after she turned, she knew that his eyes remained on her. She could almost feel the delicate pressure of his gaze on her shoulders. As she crossed the emerald grass—drawing a streak of red against a background of blue sky and white clouds—she realized that he was not the only one watching her. All those white faces floating above white-clad bodies, under the awning or out on the green, moved so as to get a better view of her. By the time she had returned to the luncheon room, the Marsh table had already become the most talked-about table of the afternoon—and she began to sense that they weren't just interested in the color of her dress.

"Do you know who that boy is?" Astrid asked as Cordelia took her seat. There was an excitable, incredulous quality in her voice that warned Cordelia of a weightiness on the other end of that question.

"His name is Thom." Cordelia took a sip of her iced tea and winked at her friend. "But I don't think I want to know anything more about him just yet."

Astrid's eyes glittered and one of her eyebrows went upward, but in the end she only smiled and obliged her friend. She knew something about troubled love, after all, and she was not about to get in the way of Cordelia making her own mistakes, much less having her own fun.

10

"LET ME DO THE TALKING, AND IF HE ASKS YOU ANY questions, just look pretty and try not to seem too bright, okay?" Paulette whispered as she hustled across the floor of Seventh Heaven.

"All right." Letty was just a step behind her, but she was distracted by how different the nightclub felt before it was open, when there was still light left in the day filtering in through those high cathedral windows. There was something drab about the scuffed plank floors and the little round tabletops with no candles on them, but the scene contained an air of promise, too, of the glamour and gaiety to come after sunset.

"Oh, Mr. Cole!" Paulette singsonged, putting on a sweeter voice than she used around the apartment.

Letty recognized the small man in the tuxedo right away, from when she'd come here with Cordelia and the Washborne girls.

"Yes?" he replied crisply, glancing up from a pile of papers that were spread out at the corner of the bar.

"Mr. Cole, this is the girl I was telling you about. Letty Larkspur. Isn't she divine?"

Mr. Cole's eyes shifted indifferently from Paulette to the petite girl in her wake. "She's short."

"We'll get her some high heels," Paulette replied brightly.

"But I don't need any more cigarette girls."

"Oh, Mr. Cole, I know." Paulette batted her long lashes, and her voice got even sweeter. "But don't you remember how you were just complaining that us girls disappear on you soon as we get a callback? Don't you think it would be a good idea to take a new girl on now, so you'll be ready next time someone defects? I'll show her how to do everything myself, and she'll work hard, I promise."

Mr. Cole sighed. He shifted his gaze once or twice more between the two girls, and then he turned round in his barstool, back to his papers. Letty's heart sank, and she glanced up at Paulette, who was holding her breath. It had probably been silly of them to think that Letty was sophisticated enough to walk among all those beautiful city people night after night.

But then, with his back to the girls, Mr. Cole said, "One week. I'll try you out for one week. If I still don't like you at the end of it, you'll have to go—and no complaining."

It didn't sound like a job offer, but after a few seconds Letty realized that it was. She beamed. "Oh, thank you, Mr. Cole!" she gushed. "I'll work hard and be no trouble, I promise!"

Paulette gave her a wink and reached for her hand. "Come on, doll, let me show you how it's done."

As they headed toward the far end of the club, Letty couldn't help tilting back her head and taking in the expanse of the room with a certain reverence. Later, music and shrieking laughter would fill that space up to the arched ceiling, and by then Letty would belong there, instead of being a shy outsider just peeking in on the scene the way she had been before. Someday she'd be even grander than that—she hoped so, anyway—but for now, a gate had opened into a new, shimmering world.

Her attention was brought back to the main floor by a few strutting notes from a cornet.

When she turned toward the sound, she realized that all the boys in the band had been watching her for some time already, and her cheeks colored. The cornet player was standing near the edge of the stage, in shirtsleeves, and he bent toward Letty and met her eyes as he played a few more bars. For a moment, she thought she might be swallowed up by her embarrassment, but when she realized that the melody was familiar to her, she felt not quite so shy of him.

"Where do I know that song from?" she asked, stepping toward the stage.

He lowered the instrument from his lips. "Just a tune we used to play in the college marching band, a lifetime ago, back in Cleveland. I doubt you've ever heard it, little lady."

"No, no, I'm sure I have. I'm from Ohio—and if I hear a song even once, I never forget it. I'm a singer, you see."

"What part of Ohio?"

"Union, Ohio, but Mother was a dancer in the Cleveland ballet, and when we were young, she used to take us to the big city whenever there was a parade." Letty blushed again. "That seemed like the big city, then, but of course none of us had ever dreamed of going to New York yet."

"I was born in Defiance," he replied, grinning. "Though you must have still been a girl when I left that dusty town behind."

They both laughed at this evidence that the world was not so vast after all. Then the man lifted his cornet and played a little more of the song. Letty closed her eyes and hummed along, her heart lifting with the music and the memory of how much her mother had loved a parade.

"Come on, Letty," Paulette said, reaching for her hand and pulling her gently along.

"Stay late some night and sing with us, Letty," the cornet player called as she moved along behind Paulette.

"They seemed like nice boys," Letty whispered, still smiling at the invitation, as she and Paulette passed off the main floor and into a dressing room on the side. Racks of clothes and mirrors lined the walls, as though chorus girls and not cigarette girls dressed there. The far corner was occupied by an old daybed, where Letty supposed the girls rested on their breaks.

"Oh, sure!" Paulette laughed. "The boys in the band are always concerned about the welfare of the newest cigarette girls. But listen, honey, I have a few simple rules of comportment for while I'm at work or out on the town—and you'd be wise to follow them, too. Number one is: No going out with musicians."

"Oh, I don't want to go out with him! He must be at least ten years older than I am, anyway. It was only that he seemed nice . . . and it *would* be fun to practice with them."

Paulette gave her a smile out of the corner of her mouth. "Okay," she said. "But be careful."

Mindful of how much she owed to Paulette, Letty softly asked, "What are the other rules?"

"Number two: Never accept a drink during your shift. That's how you end up having to pay back all your wages to the house, on account of all the money you've lost. Number three: If you do accept a drink from a gentleman, after your shift or on your night off, always keep him one drink ahead of you. This one is to prevent you from waking up in strange apartments." Paulette winked and stepped toward a rack of cream-colored outfits. "Our uniforms," she interrupted herself. "Mr. Cole insists on white. Something about us looking like heavenly virgins—ha! Number four: If a customer gives you a big tip, don't gush and act like it's some giant favor. Act like you deserve it, because, honey, *you do*. They like that sort of thing, anyway."

Letty nodded and peered over Paulette's shoulder as she pushed one outfit and then the next aside.

"Number five: Say as little as possible. Men find that mysterious, and then they want to learn more about you, and they'll keep tipping you excessively trying to do exactly that. Or buy you more drinks, or bring you more presents. Whatever it is you happen to be fishing for. Here! Isn't this perfect?"

With a wide smile on her face, Paulette pulled a tiny jumper off the rack and held it up in the air. In the end, Letty chose a more girlish, conservative style, with flounces at the neckline and hem, cinched at the natural waist. Except for the fact that it showed a good deal of her legs, which were covered in mahogany fishnets, even Father might have approved. As they dressed and made up their faces, other girls trickled in, shouting out the latest gossip and waving half-lit cigarettes as they took the curlers out of their hair.

Paulette shared a few more tips with Letty, though if her new friend had been more honest, she might have included this lesson in her list of survival tips: That it is often advantageous to forget. Forget your wincing humiliations, forget life's blows, and get on. For blocks in every direction, down every street in the city, people not yet old enough to have lines on their foreheads were laughing away memory, warmly ensconced in shrines of forgetfulness. Those who followed the word of God and those who preferred what the priests called "hoodoo" alike. People everywhere forgetting with drink or forgetting with religion or forgetting with the numbing quality of their many heaps of things. They looked forward and imagined rosy tomorrows, and gave up whatever horrors heckled their dreams, and listened to the pretty stories of whomever ruled their pulpit.

In the dressing room of Seventh Heaven, just as Letty was beginning to grow comfortable with the banter, Paulette announced, "It's time."

Letty gulped.

"Go get 'em," said Colleen, the girl she'd just been discussing the club's female singer with. Apparently her name was Alice Grenadine, and she was Mr. Cole's special lady friend, and couldn't carry a tune to save her life.

"Don't worry, you'll be great," Paulette said, as she

strapped a tray neatly packed with cigarettes and candies and other treats to Letty's middle. With a reassuring smile, Paulette turned toward the noise and the light. Letty took a deep breath and followed her friend as she strode onto the main floor of the club. In the time it had taken them to dress and go over the particulars of the job, Seventh Heaven had been transformed. The light was low and warm, and the tables were filling up. The buzzing of excitable voices hung in the air.

"Oh!" Letty suddenly shouted, pain shooting out from the spot on her elbow where she had collided with a barstool. But the pain was not as bad as the embarrassment over her klutziness. She squeezed her eyes shut and hoped she wouldn't cry. She'd been concentrating on all the potential customers out there, and had collided with the tall wooden chair hard. "I'm so sorry. I—"

"Don't worry." It was a man's voice, sincere and kind. "In fact, I came here hoping I might run into you, but now I find that it's you who has run into me."

Letty opened her eyes. It took her another moment before she recognized the man who had yesterday applauded her singing from a streetcar. Letty was so relieved to see a kind face that she smiled back. This seemed to please him and cause the color of his skin to change, too. He was sweet on her, she realized, or at least he found her pretty, and the nature of her embarrassment changed. Then it occurred to her that he had made a joke.

"That's a good one, Mr.—"

"Mr. Lodge. But my first name is Grady."

The edges of her mouth flickered upward, and her eyes became bright. He had a nice name and a nice face, and he was wearing the same herringbone knickerbocker suit as the day before, although his boater had been removed from his head to reveal fair hair parted down the center.

"What's yours?" he asked.

"Letty Larkspur."

"Letty Larkspur," he repeated, and for a moment she thought he might enjoy the sound of that name almost as much as she did. "What a pretty name. You must be from New York, with a name like that."

"I'm from Ohio," she said, noticing Paulette watching her from among the tables out on the nightclub's floor. "But this is home now."

"Well, welcome, Miss Larkspur. You look like a city girl to me."

She glanced down nervously at her outfit, which she certainly would never have dared wear in Union.

"Thank you, Mr. Lodge. And where are you from?"

"I'm a rare native-born New Yorker, so I should know. I'm a writer, also, thus I spend a great deal of time observing people, and I see it when a person has something about them particularly worth watching—and you have that, Miss Larkspur."

Before she could wonder what he meant, Mr. Cole approached from around the bar.

"Larkspur, you're not here to flirt. Move along."

Shame washed over her, when she remembered that she was only trying out, and that she didn't have time to act shy. She could not bear to look at either man as she stepped back onto the floor—although, once she had, she discovered a strange new confidence. Anyway, Paulette had warned her to say little, and perhaps it was for the best that she'd moved on right when she did. She tried to appear busy—which she very quickly was—and tell herself that her exit had seemed smooth and purposeful.

Despite her embarrassment, she couldn't help but feel excited by the attention. No one had ever seemed interested in her that way in Union, except a few bucktoothed farm boys with unclean hands. Cordelia had always said it was just that, in their backward part of the world, men were only interested in a thick girl who could stand up to years of hard living and childbearing, and that someone delicate and sparkling like Letty confused them. And though everything Cordelia had ever said was now shadowed with doubt, Letty wanted to believe that maybe, in that one instance, she might have been speaking the truth.

After she managed a few sales—somewhat blushingly and bumblingly, but nonetheless—she got up the courage to glance back in Grady's direction. He was still there, watching her from the same barstool as she ferried her tray of wares between tables crowded with patrons. It was almost as though he was clapping for her like he'd done the other day, although privately.

A lithe woman wearing what looked like a beaded bathing cap bought a pack of Lucky Strikes, and once Letty had counted out her change, she heard Paulette at her ear.

"One night on the job," she whispered, with a wise grin, "and Letty Larkspur already has a fan!"

Letty smiled and said nothing. But after that she began to believe that she would last through the week and have a job for herself as long as she needed one. Then she would know for sure that she could make it here on her own, and that she hadn't needed Cordelia to survive at all.

11

DESPITE THE AGONIZING BEAUTY OF CORDELIA'S waking life and the unusual luxury of the sheets she now rested upon, dreams more vivid and darker than she'd ever known had invaded her sleep. But when she pulled off her eye mask after a restless night, she encountered nothing terrifying in her room. Instead she saw a girl with uneven blue eyes and a dirty-blond bob, wearing a black-and-white uniform, standing at her bedside and holding the tray of coffee things.

"Good morning, miss," she said in a singsong English accent. "I'm Milly, your maid."

"Good morning." Cordelia sank back into her pillows and let her eyelids drift shut. Heaps of sun-streaked hair fanned out around her head. The elements of her dream were fading, although she believed they involved John, and that John was dead, and that she was somehow or other being chased. Her dream self had been wearing the same peach satin slip that she was wearing now, except it had been ripped and torn.

"Coffee?" the girl persisted.

"Thank you." Cracking her right eye, Cordelia regarded the girl, and an unpleasant possibility occurred to her. "Where do you sleep?"

"On the second floor . . . over the kitchen."

Cordelia nodded, relieved, for that was far enough away that she might not notice, later in the evening, when her mistress tried to leave the house without her brother accompanying her. That was the source of the anxiety that fueled her dream, she supposed—every inch of her was determined to meet Thomas, or Thom, or whatever his name was, but she feared that if Charlie found out, then he would insist on coming along, and that wouldn't be nearly as much fun.

"Good. I was only curious. You can put the coffee over there."

As the maid crossed the floor and put the tray down on a little table, Cordelia draped an arm over her face and thought she might drift off again . . . but a swift, explosive sound from somewhere on the property brought a harsh end to her languor.

The sense of dread that had pervaded her dream now returned.

"What was that?" she demanded.

Milly's shoulders rose upward toward her neck as though she were frightened.

Cordelia threw back the covers and fastened an oat-colored linen robe around her body. She descended the main stairs two at a time. As she rounded the final landing and came onto the final flight, she heard another explosion, louder this time and much closer. She knew that sound. It was the sound of a shotgun. She had heard it often when Uncle Jeb was trying to scare coyotes.

She passed through the pocket doors, beneath a strange mounted animal head, and into the ballroom. The filmy curtains that covered the south wall billowed with the breeze blowing through the open French doors, over the waxed dance floor. Cordelia stepped onto the stone verandah, which was composed of several levels connected with switchback flights of stone steps, each one decorated with carved stone balustrades and statuary.

Outside the light was bright and white. Her eyes adjusted, and then she saw her father wearing a thick terry cloth robe, from which black pajama pants emerged over loafer-style suede slippers. He stood near the edge of the terrace, his back turned to her, and his figure framed by the rolling blues and greens of Dogwood's acres, a shotgun cradled under his arm. A little farther behind him, under the protective shade of the stone arch, Elias Jones sat on a canvas folding chair, his face pointed toward the distance, his eyes obscured by the shadow his hat brim cast. Jones was holding on to the end of a wire, which snaked along the ground toward a contraption just in front of her father's right slipper.

"Pull!" yelled Darius, and Jones's hand flinched, and then a circular object was launched from the contraption and went soaring past the lower levels of the terrace and over the south lawn. Cordelia watched as her father lifted the gun, swung its long shaft to follow the trajectory of the pale object, and fired. The object exploded, and its parts fell on the grass below.

The air filled with mingling odors of citrus and sulfur. Relieved that the shooting was benign, Cordelia sighed—apparently loudly enough to get the two men's attention.

"Cord!" her father exclaimed once he had turned and seen her standing on the threshold from the ballroom. She smiled and walked toward his outstretched arms. It was strange to see him like this, in the daylight—those bursts of white in his sandy hair looked more aged than elegant, and though his broad, tan face was still handsome, there was something puffy and middle-aged about the wear around his eye sockets. He rested his hand on the back of her head and gave her a squeeze.

"Jones, what can we do?" he called out jokingly. "I go

away for a few days, and now she's sleeping till noon, just like Charlie. Soon she'll be as bad as her brother, and then I'll have no one to leave my kingdom to."

Cordelia's eyes flickered toward Jones, briefly fearful that he would inform her father that she had in fact been out every night with her brother's entourage—although Darius had *wanted* her to be under Charlie's watchful eye, and so she had not technically done anything wrong. Then she remembered something else—how she had flirted yesterday on the green—and experienced something curious and for the first time. She'd never before had a father to be protective of her and to frown on young men's intentions toward her, and suddenly she felt secretive about her interest in Thom and hoped that Darius hadn't heard of it.

"Here," Jones said, standing. "Take my seat, Miss Grey. I have things to see to, anyway."

"Yes, sit, my dear," Darius said, and as Cordelia moved to the chair, he called after Jones: "Have them send us some fresh coffee, would you?"

Jones did not acknowledge the request but simply closed the ballroom doors loudly as he left. Whether it was an accident or an expression of anger, Cordelia couldn't tell. Her eyes returned slowly toward her father, but his face showed no sign of perturbation, and when he spoke again, it was with such gentle affection that she decided he could not possibly know that she had told a young man—a stranger—to pick her up on the main road in only a few hours.

"Toss me a few grapefruit, dear." She followed the direction of his pointing finger, to the right side of her chair, and saw a crate full of pale yellow orbs. So that was the source of the citrus smell. She leaned over, took hold of a few, and threw them toward her father one by one.

"Have you ever eaten grapefruit?" he asked as he caught the last of three.

In movies she had sometimes seen svelte women eating half a grapefruit for breakfast, but she herself had never tasted one.

"Lousy fruit. These come all the way from Florida." Her father bent, placing the fruit in the contraption. "Ten dollars a crate."

"Ten dollars a . . . ?" She couldn't believe he would use something that expensive for target practice, but she tried not to appear shocked.

"Oh, don't worry, I won't bankrupt myself. I have a great excess of these because a special lady friend of mine was on the grapefruit diet. Never heard of that? It's when a woman eats grapefruit and melba toast for breakfast, grapefruit and olives for lunch, grapefruit and grapefruit for dinner." He made a disgusted noise and spat. Then, as though he had just remembered the company, his brow rippled and he shot his daughter a sorrowful look. "You mustn't think that . . . this friend—that she could ever replace your mother. Dear Fanny." He sighed. "How she would have loved this house. I only wish I'd already made it, then, when I first knew her . . ." A storm passed through his features. "Then none of the bad things would have happened."

"You still love her?" Cordelia did not want to sound like it mattered to her, although of course it did. She had wondered that probably every day of her eighteen years.

Darius closed his eyes, and some exquisite pain of long ago seemed to twist up the corners of his mouth. "Your mother had a very pure kind of beauty. She would have done anything I asked her. I was always pawning her things, borrowing from tomorrow to scrape by today. I thought I'd live forever . . . I certainly thought *she* would." When he opened his eyes, they looked particularly dark. "Yes, I still love her. But now I have you back, and it makes me feel I haven't lost her so completely."

Despite herself, Cordelia beamed. There was no way to reply to a statement as momentous as that, so she leaned forward and picked up the end of the wire that Jones had been holding on to. "Would you like me to . . . ?"

Her father grinned. "Thank you, dear. When I say 'pull,' you push that button."

"Okay," she said, leaning against the canvas back of the chair and crossing her long legs. Sleepiness was still blurring her at the edges somewhat, but it felt good to sit like this, with her father, before the day had shown her very much. The sun came out from behind a hazy cloud, making the steps below them and the lawns stretching out toward the orchards almost sparkle.

"Anyway," Darius went on, settling into a wide stance and propping the shotgun against his shoulder. "Florida is entirely crooked. You agree to a weekly shipment, and they won't let you out of it no matter how you scream and yell. So I have another four months of grapefruit, and no skinny broad around to eat them by the crate." He shrugged indifferently. *"Pull!"*

The sudden loudness of his voice startled her, but then she regained herself and pushed the button. The machine launched the grapefruit into the sky, and her father followed its trajectory with the body of the shotgun. He pulled the trigger. A shot rang out, echoing against the stone arcade, and far off over the lawn, the fruit exploded in the air. That smell—as though a whole book of matches had been set aflame and then put out with orange juice—rose up again. His nostrils growing wide, Darius inhaled.

"Smells like America," he said grandly. "As I was saying: Never invest in Florida. Can you remember that? It's a snake-infested swampland."

The only investment Cordelia had ever considered was a one-way ticket to New York City, but she nodded anyway. "Never invest in Florida," she repeated.

"It's like the Australia of the Union. Entirely inhabited by crooks." He cleared his throat and reloaded the gun. Before the thought could even take form in her mind, he went on: "And I know I seem like a crook to you, but believe me, I'm not like most of them. I do things honorably, and I'm not a violent man. I provide wealthy people with harmless spirits, good ones, imported from Europe through our neighbors to the north and south, and I am paid handsomely for the risk I take doing so. But I am not a criminal, and sooner or later I will have amassed enough wealth that I'll be able to go entirely into legitimate business. So don't let anyone tell you your daddy is a criminal, all right?"

Besides churchgoing busybodies, no one minded much how Darius Grey made his money, at least Cordelia didn't think so, and many others regarded him with a kind of awe. But she did not want him to know how fervently she'd always read newspaper articles about him, so she only said, "All right."

"All right. Now, would you like to learn how to use this handsome piece of equipment?"

"Me?" she asked, already rising and trying not to appear frightened.

The shotgun was heavier in her hands than she had expected, and when she tried to lift it, she became clumsy. He had been right about it being handsome, though—burled wood sidings and gold inlay detail—and she almost wished that Thom could see her now, looking like an outlaw in the picturesque sunshine.

"Like this," Darius said, gesturing how she should hold it. "Put the end there, against your right shoulder. Now, when you're ready, call 'pull.' Watch where the target is going, but don't waste time, got it?"

"Yes." Cordelia mimicked his posture of a few seconds before: her stance wide, her shoulders braced, her gaze focused down the length of the gun. She listened to her father shuffle back across the stone, and took a deep breath as he yelled, "Pull!"

She had to pull hard on the trigger, and barely noticed which way the yellow fruit went. The gun kicked back, and she couldn't help but gasp at the force with which it met her shoulder. Meanwhile, there was a great cawing of pigeons as they emerged from a large bush somewhat off to the left of the fallen grapefruits on the south lawn.

Big brown eyes wide, she turned to her father. "That wasn't very good, was it?" she said.

Darius laughed, and smiled his toothy, charming smile at her. "You like the truth straight without no chaser, don't you?"

"Yes," she answered.

"It wasn't very good." He winked and patted her shoulder. "But you'll learn. It takes practice. And I don't have anywhere to be—do you have anywhere to be?"

The awful thought darted through her mind that he might be hinting at a certain road, where a certain young man was planning to meet her in not so many hours. Darius's smile was in place, however, and after a few seconds passed, she wondered if she wasn't being a little paranoid.

And so she offered a simple "no."

"Well, then, let's see if we can teach you."

She didn't improve immediately, but by the time they got to the bottom of the crate, Cordelia had managed to blow a few grapefruits out of the sky. Jones had never sent their coffee, but her father was being so attentive, so diligent in his instructions, that she didn't want to risk the growing sense of camaraderie between them by bringing up an unpleasant observation. After a while, he set the rifle down and said, "I think you're ready to learn how to shoot a pistol."

So they took the remaining grapefruits and lined them up on a low, whitewashed wall by the turquoise pool, and he showed her how to load the six-shooter. It felt heavier in her hand than she had anticipated, and before she could reconsider, she heard herself say, "Have you ever . . . used one?"

"Used?" he laughed. "I think I take your meaning. No, no, of course not—I told you, my business is not a violent one. And anyway, I am far too important to carry my own gun."

"Oh . . . of course."

By then she had become rather obsessed with shooting targets, and she wanted badly to show him what a quick learner she was. She assumed a solid stance, raised both arms, narrowed her eyes, and pulled the trigger. The first shot hit its target, exploding pink citrus all over the wall. But the next few were misses, and in the end she only managed to hit two. She turned toward her father, to see what he would say, but he wasn't even watching. A far-off look had come into his eyes, and he was gazing north.

"That's enough, don't you think?" His tone had become low, almost weary. Her heart sank, and she wished that she could go back to a few minutes ago, when they had been joking and talking easily.

She tried her best to smile, even though she was disappointed their first afternoon together was going to be cut short. "Yes—thank you for teaching me."

He put an arm around her shoulder and patted it. "You've got a good eye. You'll make a fine shot soon." Then he took the gun out of her hand, opened the chamber, and dropped the casings onto the pool deck. "You look sleepy, though. No more firearms practice when you're yawning like that."

"I wasn't yawning," protested Cordelia, who had not thought she'd shown any signs of fatigue—but he ignored her.

"Aren't you sleeping all right? Isn't the bed comfortable?" he demanded as they began to walk back up the steps toward the house. "Whatever you need, just ask. I'll see that you get it."

"Oh. Thank you." Cordelia's cheeks flushed. "But I'm sleeping very well, thank you."

"Good! Good." They had passed back through the white curtains and onto the vast dance floor, which, Cordelia realized for the first time, couldn't get much use in a house where most parties required guests to stay outdoors. "I hope I didn't bore you with talk of my business." He paused, as if considering his words. The pocket doors were still open, and on the other side of the gleaming teak floor was the gloomy paneled space that had been her first glimpse of the house. "It's my hope you'll take an interest someday."

Cordelia's eyebrows shot upward with surprise. "I—I certainly would" was all she could think to say.

"Good. In my business, you have to read people, and sometimes, you have to know when to let them go. An old associate, Duluth Hale, has been much on my mind these days. He was one of those I had to let go. He was a friend, and I let him get very close to my business, but he'll never be more than the personal bootlegger of middle-class college boys and the odd roadhouse." Cordelia's brow furrowed, but she remained silent, listening. "He seduced a socialite, and she married him to make her parents angry, and eventually they let him supply the White Cove Country Club, which they own, just so they wouldn't have to worry about her anymore."

"I read in a newspaper that you never go there—is that why?"

Darius nodded.

"Astrid and I went there for lunch yesterday. I'm sorry—I wouldn't have gone if I'd known."

"That's all right. Miss Donal is a very high-class young lady, and you should go wherever she takes you. The point is, you must be unsentimental and let go of deadweight, or else not kid yourself when one of your intimates cannot be trusted. You have that, I can tell—you know when to let go."

She swallowed and tried to look sincere and worthy of his compliments. It felt as though he'd seen into her whole history—that he knew she had watched John Field flash by as she left Ohio, that she had stalked away from her oldest friend after a silly argument, the particulars of which she could not even quite remember. Her intention had never been to let go of deadweight, exactly—she had only done what she had to do—but then once she had, she'd risen effortlessly. There was a sadness to this realization, but there was also the comfort of being so completely, so mysteriously understood.

"Thank you." Her voice was quiet, and this time she was voicing her gratitude for all he had given her, the many things great and small.

"Now go put your head down, my dear," he said. "You look like you might collapse from exhaustion. We are having dinner together as a family tonight. Six o'clock. I've had enough of you young people carousing without me."

"Oh, but . . ." Blood rushed to her face, and though she

so wanted to tell her father that she would love to have family dinner, she felt that she must let nothing stop her from meeting Thom. "But I promised Astrid I would go to her mother's dinner party tonight."

"Ah." Darius shrugged, and he smiled magnanimously. For her the lie soured the afternoon a little, but he seemed unaware that anything was amiss. "Don't worry, my dear. You enjoy yourself tonight, and we will have our dinner tomorrow . . ."

Then he kissed her forehead and sent her up the stairs. She had nearly made it to the third story when she heard him call out, "My girl is back." When she glanced over the railing, he was nowhere to be seen, but she heard him calling, "I always knew she'd come back to me!"

12

DOGWOOD, AS IT HAPPENS, IS EASIER TO SNEAK OUT of than into, a fact that applies to many places in this world but very few of life's situations. Among Cordelia's new possessions was a watch with a rectangular face and roman numerals, attached to her wrist with a delicate gold bracelet, and so she knew it was at precisely 5:49 that she discovered this to be true about her new home. She had taken a roundabout walk across the grounds, in a boatneck dress of midnight blue chiffon with a dropped waist and a low, open back, and snakeskin T-strap heels that kept sinking into the soft earth. Tonight she'd wanted to be pretty but not too attention-grabbing, and by the time she tiptoed past the turned back of her father's guard, she was confident that she had succeeded in that mission at least. He was leaning against the guardhouse, his gaze directed up the road, and it took only a little courage for her to dart past him in the opposite direction.

The traffic was sparse at that hour, and everything around was quiet, so she listened as her heart's thudding became less loud, and she let her pace slow to an amble. Even her feet scarcely made a sound, for every step was cushioned by clumps of fallen pine needles. A breeze picked up around 5:52, and the sun cast a long shadow. She worried that Charlie or someone would come after her now, and also that it would be difficult to regain access to the Grey estate later. But by 5:56, when she went around the next bend, every tiny shard of negative thinking left her mind completely.

Thom was there already, wearing a white suit and tie, leaning against a gleaming black automobile. The dust around him had settled, and he had the air of having been there for some time already, though the waiting did not appear to have caused him any agitation. His arms and ankles were both crossed comfortably, and his chin was pointed up the road, in the direction from which she had come. When he saw her approaching, he grinned.

They both regarded each other for a moment, considering the right greeting. Then, before she could become nervous, she thrust forward her hand.

"So you're Darius Grey's daughter?" he said, still grinning, the skin of his palm pressing against hers.

"Yes, I guess I am."

He whistled and let go of her hand. "Everyone at the club was talking about you. I must know: What *do* long-lost daughters do with their time while awaiting the moment of their joyous and unexpected returns, anyway?"

Cordelia laughed, showing her broad white teeth. She wondered briefly what it was that Astrid had nearly told her about Thom, and then replied, "Maybe I'll tell you when I know you better."

"That's fair enough, I suppose," he said, and then walked round the vehicle. Several seconds later, she realized that he was opening the passenger-side door for her, the way gentlemen were supposed to, and that she should come around the side, too.

Lowering herself onto the seat, she felt the sweet weight of his attention upon her. His stare was concentrated but nonetheless subtle and untroubled, and even after she had settled in he did not immediately close the door. Her breath rose slowly inside her, and she turned her face up toward him and blinked. He was almost too handsome to look at straight on, but she didn't have to for very long, because he grinned again and pushed the door shut. With the sound of metal against metal, she felt that she'd once again crossed over into another world—Thom's world, whatever that meant. Whoever he was, he certainly owned a fine automobile, and she took advantage of her brief solitude while he walked back around to the driver's side to run her hand over the soft leather upholstery.

"To the city?" he said, as he put the car in reverse. She was relieved she didn't have to tell him she'd rather not risk driving past her father's guards again.

"I'll go wherever you're driving." She had wanted to say something cute, but once she heard the words aloud, she realized how much she really meant them.

So they did—down the White Cove main road, catching glimpses of the blue water through the trees, small colorful vessels moving calmly across the sound, and then into the low suburbs, with their dense, careless structures. They exchanged easy words—about the warmth of the day and the taste of old-fashioned cocktails—as twilight came on. By the time Cordelia experienced the elation of rising swiftly upward onto the Queensboro Bridge, a sliver of moon was hanging against a lavender background and the setting sun was already half obscured by the striving and clambering of New York's big buildings at a distance.

"What's that?" Cordelia asked, pointing at a long stretch of land in the middle of the East River, which they were then passing over.

"Blackwell's Island," Thom explained. "That's where they keep criminals, didn't you know that? Mae West spent ten days there, bragging that she brought silk panties to prison with her. Not to mention Dutch Schultz—"

"Who's Dutch Schultz?" Cordelia asked before she had time to wonder whether she ought to already know.

"Dutch Schultz? He controls the Bronx," Thom replied slowly. He paused and glanced over at his passenger, and the brief meeting of their eyes caused her to forget what they had just been talking about and made her heart soar. "You really are new to this town, aren't you?"

Cordelia laughed. "You didn't believe me till now?"

"I suppose you haven't got any reason to lie to me, since you don't know me at all." To her chagrin, his tone had become serious, as though he was turning something over in his mind.

The car passed under the shadow of one of the bridge's spans, and Thom stopped squinting, and his words became weightless again. "Anyway, if you really are a stranger to New York, all the better for me—it'll be much easier to impress you."

"Don't count on it," she shot back playfully.

The roadway was descending now, and in the thickening dusk the playful brilliance of his eyes and smile were even more prominent, and she found that every inch of her wanted to sing, *I can't believe I'm out with a boy like him! I can't believe I'm out with* him*!*

"Well, baby," Thom began, turning the wheel sharply and picking up speed as they cruised down the off-ramp, toward the streets. She was surprised by the way his voice could change all of a sudden, from careful and florid like a college boy's to clipped and a little rough. It was like the color of his eyes, she supposed—not quite one shade or another, and utterly unlike anyone else's. She loved the idea of driving in a car with a boy like that. "You stick with me. I'm gonna show you what's really hiding behind all them straight-faced facades."

As they sped down a broad avenue, past slower cars and grand entrances guarded by green awnings and uniformed doormen, it occurred to her that she didn't know Thom at all, that she'd never known a man of Thom's type—or even if he was a type—and this added to the shivery pleasure of his playing tour guide with her. In a matter of days, everything about her life had changed, and she couldn't really be blamed for regarding every future moment as though it contained a surprise, some treasure better than any she'd yet seen.

Such was her experience when she stepped into a small oak-and-mirror-paneled room in the lobby of an elegant hotel and felt the floor begin to rise beneath her feet.

"Oh," she gasped and grabbed Thom's arm. Then she realized this was what was meant by a lift, that they were going to the top of the building, and they both laughed.

On the roof there was a little bar and a number of lithe people swaying gently in the cool darkness. Thom ordered old-fashioneds and ushered her over to the building's edge, and Cordelia felt a pleasant rush of fear when she saw how high up they were. She peered down those many stories, where miniature-sized people got in and out of cabs. Beyond them lay Central Park, the tops of its trees forming a forest far more vast than she could possibly have imagined while on the ground, but which was nonetheless neatly framed by the uninterrupted progression of buildings and streets that seemed to cover every other inch up and down the island.

After a while, Thom turned and propped his elbows against the carved stone barrier that protected them from what surely would have been a fatal fall. For a moment she thought he might kiss her; her face began to tingle.

But then he didn't.

"You're bored here, aren't you?" he asked, furrowing his brow.

There was nothing to do but smile at his concern, for though she was afraid to say so, she felt she would never be bored, no matter where she was, so long as she was in his company. But perhaps he heard her silent thoughts, because he smiled back and held her gaze. Then he took her hand, and they hurried to the elevator and out of the hotel.

"Good night, Mr. Hale," the doorman said as they brushed past.

The name sounded familiar, but before she had time to really think about it, they were driving downtown, the wind and the whole evening giving her pleasant chills. They stopped into a place in the West Fifties with no ceiling fans, where another doorman knew Thom by name. An all black five-piece band played in the basement, sweating through their button-down shirts, and Cordelia watched glittery-eyed at the sound they could make with their instruments. But the little tables were too crammed together for dancing, and they both agreed they wouldn't go home satisfied unless they found a place to do just that. Next they went to a pool hall—a long, vast room with lights dangling over green tables—and Thom taught her to play. She didn't try to hide how competitive she was when it came to a game, and he was undeterred by this characteristic; she beat him, but barely, and they walked down the single flight of stairs to the sidewalk hand in hand.

Now when they drove, she began to recognize her surroundings—the great monolith of Penn Station, the night clouds above the Hudson, which were made visible against an indigo sky by the reflected glow of an electric city, the stream of traffic, substantial even as late as it was, past buildings a girl had to crane her neck to see. There was so much of everything—the headlights coming at them and the thousands of windows above, which held little flickering scenes from lives she would never know anything about. Her chest grew warm thinking of all that plenty, and also with the idea of expressing what she was feeling to Thom. Later, when this evening had crystallized into a perfect memory, the driving would be the part that characterized everything else—the two of them, sitting side by side in that great, polished piece of machinery, traveling fast to new places . . .

"Thom Hale," she said when his name surfaced in her thoughts again. "I hope you're not related to Duluth Hale."

His eyes darted toward her and back to the road. "He's my father," Thom answered after a minute.

"But your father and my father—"

"—do not get along." Thom grimaced.

"You knew I was Darius Grey's daughter . . . and you still wanted to take me out?"

She wondered if this meant the end of the evening, now that they couldn't avoid each other's identities, and began to experience a sinking disappointment.

But then Thom shrugged. "At first I didn't know who you were. And then, after I did—how could I stay away from you?" he asked.

They had come to a stop at a traffic light. The motor was shaking, and the smell of gas was sweet and sickening in the air. She opened her mouth to reply, but before she could think of an answer to a statement as beautiful as that, she felt his hand on her waist, and when she turned her face toward him, she saw that he was going to kiss her. His mouth was a pressure simultaneously soft and intense, and for a while she forgot that there was anything more to her than the spot where their lips touched. She felt as though they might go on kissing forever, but then horns blared behind them and they realized the traffic signal had changed and the hold-up they'd caused.

After that, their banter was different. A closeness filled up the vacant air between them on the bench seat, and the joking ebbed. The car proceeded another block, and then a slow smile crept across Thom's face.

"I know where there'll be dancing," he said.

"It shouldn't surprise you by now," Cordelia whispered, curling against the seat and watching Thom with starry eyes. "I wanna go wherever you're going."

13

IN WHITE COVE THE SKY HAD TURNED FROM BLUE TO mulberry, which in that part of the world is synonymous with cocktail time. So it had been since the first American merchant decided to build himself a country castle there, and probably even before, for the local fishermen had an almost hereditary tradition of ending their days in the shacks that faced the sound. Astrid Donal had never set foot in anyplace like that, but she had attended plenty of gatherings that began in the late afternoon and stretched into the giddy hours following midnight. Many of these, like the party at which she was currently playing a somewhat unwilling guest of honor, had been hosted by her mother.

"Oh, yes!" the third Mrs. Harrison Marsh II was saying, as the skin of her eyelids squeezed ever tighter in a show of mawkish joy, to her neighbor and most closely held rival, Mrs. Edgemont Phipps, née Narcissa Beaumont. Mrs. Phipps and Mrs. Marsh had been debutantes together, but they both had decidedly more gaunt faces now. "We are *so* happy to have her back."

Astrid, ten or so feet away, smiled faintly and gazed out the window. From the parlor on the first floor, one could see all the way down the drive to the inlet and the road that ran along the shell-strewn shore. Like her mother, she wore white; the dress was composed of a loose-fitting bodice with slender silver straps and a skirt that skimmed the hips and then flowed outward to the feather-lined hem at midcalf. Her mother's gown was decidedly more décolleté, though it had been created with a touch of the same whimsy.

"She's more like a lady every time I see her," replied Mrs. Phipps, who was decked in severe red, which brought out all the other severe aspects of her appearance. Then she turned her back on Astrid, perhaps because her own daughter, Cora, was nothing to brag about in the looks department, and changed the subject. "What a summer we're going to have! I can just imagine all the parties, I have so many ideas, and . . ."

Mrs. Phipps went on like this, but Astrid had moved away from the window until her voice became part of the symphony of ice cubes clinking against crystal and sotto voce gossip and smug laughter. The crowd was composed mostly of people who could afford to have begun their day long after noon. Astrid's stepfather had opened up his booze larder, and their guests were all sipping from goblets of real French champagne or else tumblers of the latest intoxicating concoctions. Her mother had redone the parlor along with all the other rooms when she became the mistress of the Marsh mansion. There was a high gleam on the gold-inlaid palmwood furniture, and the neutral South American rugs underfoot suggested the classy minimalism of the house's occupants. The white and black cloisonné floor vases were stuffed with pink flowering branches; the prevailing mood, as usual, was one of unhurried luxury.

"Miss Donal?" said a waiter, approaching her with a vast copper tray. She was not in a festive mood and had thought her mother might realize how unwelcome this party was if she noticed that her daughter was uninterested in drinking. But now Astrid saw that the rims of the drinks were frosted with powdered sugar and she couldn't help but take a glass, before moving on across the floor.

She bent her head, which was encircled in a yellow haze of hair, and sipped. The sweet, exhilarating drink made her current circumstances instantly more palatable. Not that her situation was so *very* bad . . . but she was feeling distinctly left out. Her new best friend Cordelia had promised to be there early, but then had rung up a few hours before the party to say she wasn't feeling well. The afternoon had brought many deliveries—from the florist and the grocer and the iceman—but the ringing phone was never Charlie calling for her.

"You don't seem particularly thrilled."

Over the sugared rim of her glass, Astrid glimpsed Billie, who was wearing black trousers with a high waist and a bejeweled little matador's jacket, which she'd bought in Spain from a bullfighter she knew, for a cask of red wine, or so the story went. The house was large and so the stepsisters crossed paths less than one might think, and it was almost a surprise to see her now. No one would ever have called Billie pretty, but she certainly was handsome. Her dark hair was parted straight at the middle and smoothed down behind her ears, so slick with pomade that it appeared wet, and her tone was as dry as ever.

"No, I'm having a swell time," Astrid replied.

Billie raised a high, thin semicircle of an eyebrow and surveyed the crowd. "And why shouldn't you? Same faces as always, same topics of conversation."

"I suppose it should have been a party for you, too," Astrid continued, after a pause. "You've returned from school as well."

Billie batted the suggestion away with a breezy: "But I haven't returned, really. I'll be leaving for Europe in a few days, and anyway, I don't like being the center of attention."

"How dull!" Astrid returned, without particular animosity

or even any certainty about which part of Billie's statement she was responding to. She had spent a good deal of time in Europe as a little girl, in between her mother's marriages, mostly waiting for ships to depart and trains to arrive, and her recollection of that continent was not overly rosy. She also believed it was a girl's duty—if she was bright and good-looking—to try to be the center of attention at least half the time.

"I prefer to watch from the sidelines," Billie went on, a touch wistfully.

Before Astrid could wonder what she meant, a loud guffawing drew their attention. They both turned toward the arched entryway to the ballroom. It was Harrison Marsh II, who shared with his daughter a fierce intelligence and a protuberant nose, but was a good deal thicker all over. He had an old sportsman's physical breadth, and his considerable middle was currently stuffed into a paisley waistcoat. His face had gone red in blotches. Astrid's stepfather liked to believe that he always knew more about everything than the person he was speaking to, and at this particular moment it would have been difficult for that not to be true, for Narcissa Phipps had glided into his orbit. From the way they were laughing, however, it was clear that the topic was not the cultural changes wreaked by the Great War, or Greek philosophy, or even Greta Garbo.

"Stop!" Mrs. Phipps was shrieking, in a manner that

seemed conversely to insist that he go on saying or doing whatever it was he had just been saying or doing. "You're too much, really! Oh, ha-ha-ha-ha-ha!"

Twenty or so well-dressed bodies separated Mr. and Mrs. Marsh, although they all became noticeably quiet and subdued in the moments that followed this outburst. Surely these guests had registered the rather flirtatious pose that Mrs. Phipps had assumed, and the sharp quality coming into the eyes of the woman whose husband's every word Mrs. Phipps was currently hanging on. In the next moment, Astrid's mother gripped the young stranger who had just entered the parlor—he was handsome and overdressed, and he carried himself with a guilty slouch. The pair crossed the floor—the hostess with her eyes roving a little wildly, making sure everyone saw what she was doing, and her companion without looking up from his brand-new shoes.

"Have you met Luke?" Mrs. Marsh said, teeth bared, as she approached her husband and Mrs. Phipps.

Then the piano music from the next room picked up again, and the guests resumed their polite conversation.

"I wonder what they're finding to talk about . . . ," Billie mused, watching her father and stepmother from the middle of the room. Astrid, still by her stepsister's side, wondered no such thing. The tightness with which her mother's bony arm had encircled her young companion's, the way she was pressed against his side, the slightly unhinged manner in which she was glancing at everyone near her, made it perfectly obvious that she'd had more to drink than to eat that day, and that she now had a point to prove. All of which was more than Astrid had wanted to know in the first place.

She turned from the bristling scene—and what she saw outside the window made her preoccupations of the previous hours melt away. There was Charlie, wearing a suit, holding a bouquet of plain daisies.

"Should I come in?" he mouthed, putting a hand on the glass pane.

Astrid gave a slow, subtle shake of her head and then stepped away from Billie and the confrontation masked as light social discourse in which her mother and stepfather were currently engaged. Through the crowd she went, like a white bolt, turning her face right or left to offer a wink here and there. When she passed through the foyer, she couldn't help but skip a little across the stone floor, and she bit her full lower lip to keep a giddy smile from fully forming.

The great front door was open to accommodate latecomers, and by the time she stepped through it, she'd made her smile vanish. Charlie was standing there, wearing a pale blue suit, his hands and the daisies hidden behind his back, waiting. Behind him the grounds rolled tranquilly toward the water, the foliage only slightly ruffled by the wind, the lower lawn populated by various species of automobile. Astrid leaned against the door frame and crossed her arms over her chest.

"Do I know you?" she asked.

"I hope so," he replied in a tone less joking than hers had been.

She cocked her head. "Hard to say for sure—if I *do* know you, it's been just ages, hasn't it?"

He stepped forward, dropped the daisies, and bent his knees, wrapping his arms around her thighs and lifting her off the ground, as though she were light as a rag doll. "I'm sorry, baby. There's been trouble," he said, resting his chin against her belly, staring up into her face. "Otherwise I would've called sooner."

"Put me down." She set her hands against his shoulders and pushed away from him, struggling showily.

Once he had, she averted her eyes and fussed with her skirt to make sure he hadn't wrinkled it. He leaned toward her face, aiming his lips for hers, but she twisted so that instead the kiss landed on her cheek.

"Don't be like that! I'm here now, ain't I?"

"But here is exactly where I don't want to be," she answered, her haughty, humorous veneer breaking midsentence.

Charlie grinned and grabbed for her hand. She was so charmed by that grin that she could not help but lay down what remained of her defenses. "Come on, then," he said. "Let's get out of here!"

They ran across the lawn, through the small city of parked cars to Charlie's own. By the time he had reversed out onto the road that ran along the shore, she had forgotten that she had ever been angry with him, and she was only vaguely reminded when he asked, "What was the party for?"

"Why, for me, of course!"

"Was it? Think they'll miss you?"

"Naturally." Then she laughed and threw her arms around his neck and planted kisses up and down his neck. They were going fast along the bumpy one-lane road now, and she found she didn't mind that he hadn't realized the party was in her honor, and that she was simply grateful to have been rescued. "But I don't miss *them* at all. I have never been so glad to leave a party in my life."

"Yeah?" Charlie held the wheel with one hand and lit a cigarette with the other. "Well, where'd you rather be now?"

"Oh, I don't care." She sighed and leaned her head against his shoulder, curling against him.

So they did what young couples everywhere—in the city and the country, couples whose daddies went to the same prep schools and couples who grew up on opposite sides of the tracks—do when they wish to be alone and unsupervised. They just drove. Drove up and down hills, away from the water and toward it again. They delighted in the chill on their ears and the jostling that the car afforded them and the cool fizzing of the sodas they bought when they stopped at the filling station. Neither said very much. They passed great chestnut trees that were older than they were and dunes that grew smaller by invisible increments every year. Just as the sun slipped away beyond the horizon, Charlie parked by a dock and they settled into the backseat of the car.

"Aren't you starving?" she asked, some minutes later, after he'd pulled down her silver strap several times in a row and she'd grown tired of putting it back in place.

"Yes," he growled, and put his mouth back on her neck.

"Don't be a boor!" she cried, and pushed him away. To underscore her point, she scooted to the opposite side of the backseat.

"Well, what would you like to eat, then?" Charlie asked after clearing his throat.

"Oh, I don't care . . ." Astrid sighed and pursed her lips as she examined her face in the compact. The water beyond the worn wooden platform was still and black and reflective, and she felt little urgency to be anywhere in particular. "Let's go to your house."

"Now you're talking," Charlie said, climbing into the front seat of the car and starting the engine so quickly that she was thrown back against the seat when it lurched into motion.

"Careful!" she squealed in delight as she clambered back into the front. The wind whipped her hair horizontally. She almost lost her footing, and the idea of the awful consequences of falling out of a moving car gave her a queasy sensation of being very keenly alive.

She did not discover the truth of her hunger until she was all the way in Charlie's oak-paneled bedroom, situated cross-legged on one of the great, worn-leather club chairs that occupied the corner nearest the windows, and eating a hamburger that the Greys' cook had prepared for them off a folding tray. She was very happy to be fed. Charlie, who always ate in great gulps, had already finished his, and he had put a phonograph on, and was in the chair next to hers listening now to the sorrowful swaggering of a trumpet. His napkin was still stuffed into his collar, his big arms were folded up behind his head, and his toes were wagging. The windows were open onto the verandah, and a leafy breeze reached them in the lamp-lit room.

"Done yet?" he asked, without opening his eyes.

"No." She took another nibble, chewed thoughtfully, swallowed, and then put her thumb in her mouth to suck the ketchup off.

"Do you like the record?"

She nodded. To her, it sounded like every other record he owned, but music was something she trusted Charlie to know about and understand, and that she only half paid attention to. When she grew weary of working her way slowly through the meal, she put down the remainders of her hamburger and sighed.

Charlie opened his eyes and turned to her. "Done now?"

"Yes," she replied.

He stood and moved the tray out of the way, and then, hovering over her, waited until she pushed up to kiss him. Her arms hung round his neck as their mouths met. For a few minutes she teased him, pulling away and then sweetly bringing her lips back to his, until he lowered himself down against her. His fingertips circumnavigated her long naked arms, sending little pleasant tremors across her skin. The music, meanwhile, grew faster and more heady; there was a *rat-tat-tat* from the phonograph that was closely echoed by the accelerated beating of her heart. Charlie's kisses became more intense, too, and his hands moved down along her ribs to her waist. She was having trouble getting air, and as he pressed closer against her, she felt the nudging of something forceful and unyielding on her thigh, the grown-upness of which made her go sad all of a sudden.

"Charlie!" There was a loud knocking at the door, and she felt a surge of relief when she knew the intensity of the moment was passed.

"What is it?" he called inhospitably, as he drew back and turned his attention to the door.

She averted her eyes and pulled her skirt down over her bare legs. The skin of her cheeks was hot.

One of Grey's men stood in the hallway, and he said a few

hushed words that Astrid couldn't hear. Charlie glanced back at her, and though she widened her eyes irritably, she was glad when he followed the man out of the room.

Once he was gone, Astrid tiptoed to the white-tiled bathroom and washed her hands and splashed water on her face. This helped a little, but when she stared at her reflection, she still found a disheveled girl staring back. Her hair was a mess, her lipstick was smeared around her already ample lips, and her pupils were big and black. She pressed her lips together in a way that hollowed her cheeks, and wondered at what hour her mother had noticed her absence, if at all, and also if the party was still going. She jerked open one of the drawers of the cabinet, looking for a brush to smooth her appearance.

Instead she saw a single dangly earring of black jet beads. She froze, staring at this feminine object, unfamiliar to her and odious in equal measure. Immediately a picture of the kind of woman who would wear that sort of bauble began to form in her mind.

Holding the earring in a tight and furious fist, she stormed back through Charlie's bedroom and into the hall. As always at Dogwood, the distant sounds of low male voices emanated from somewhere in the house. The great hanging light in the front entryway created silvery pathways along the polished floor of the otherwise dark third-story hall. Astrid had taken several angry steps without any particular intention when she noticed that the door to the Calla Lily Suite was ajar and began running in that direction.

Earlier, she had been disappointed when her new friend had said she wasn't feeling very well and couldn't come to the party, but now she was glad there would be someone to talk to about the hateful earring and the hateful girl who had left it there.

"Cordelia!" she cried, as she crossed onto the carpeted floor inside the suite. "Cordelia?"

But there was no answer. As she stepped out onto the suite's verandah, she saw a car start up and drive toward the gates of Dogwood, and she knew that it was Charlie and that he was leaving. A few minutes ago, she had felt frightened of him and wanted him gone, but now she needed him to be back, whether to shriek at him or be held by him, she wasn't sure.

After a minute, there was nothing to look at but darkness and trees. She stood there with her white arms wrapped around herself, wondering why, on a night that a party was thrown in her honor, she felt so stupidly alone.

14

"WHAT IS IT?" LETTY ASKED AS SHE STEPPED AWAY FROM the mirror in the cigarette girls' dressing room and toward the doorway. Several girls were huddled by the threshhold, whispering excitedly.

Paulette hung back from the others, her long frame leaning against a wall, a cigarette resting between her fingertips. "It's that playwright you were so interested in—Gordon Grange."

Letty stepped over toward the huddle and peered out at the nightclub floor, where there stood an older man in a well-worn tweed blazer. He had a dapper quality, like an Englishman whose greatest pleasure derives from smoking a pipe in a musty library, and hanging on his arm, her body pressing close against him, was the cigarette girl named Clara Hay. *Shouldn't she be out hustling cigarettes like the rest of us?* Letty wondered, before the graver implications began to dawn on her.

"Clara Hay was cast for my part?" she gasped before she could think better of it. "But she's blond!"

"Well, you can't call it your part if you didn't even try for it," Paulette laughed. But when she saw Letty had nothing to say to that, she went on more seriously. "Men are disgusting. They'll do anything for a girl who'll let them give her the business, which is why God gave us bigger brains, so we can outwit them. Right now, Miss Hay's wits have gotten her further along than yours, but don't worry, sweetie—you'll catch on." Paulette dropped her cigarette and stubbed it out with her toe. "Currently you're paying your own bills, though, and me too. So come on, before Mr. Cole thinks better of it and kicks us both out."

This was reminiscent of something Cordelia might have said, and before she could help it Letty's mind had turned to her old friend, who was out in the world somewhere and enjoying herself without any thoughts for the people she used to know. Letty sighed heavily and knit her brow.

"Don't take it too hard," Paulette said as she stepped toward the racket of the busy nightclub floor. "No matter how many old playwrights Clara Hay lets seduce her, she'll never sing half so pretty as you."

Despite her sunken mood, Letty couldn't help but smile at that. She pushed into the main room of the speakeasy, where there were cigarettes to sell and a crowd spinning ever faster. The tray of goodies led, with her red smile following shortly behind. She hummed a little now as she went from table to table, leaning in here and there in a gesture of offering. A middle-aged man, with a girl who could not have been much older than twenty, purchased a paper carnation for his date and a few chocolates wrapped in silver; two women in dramatic dresses, who barely spoke to each other while their eyes searched out something more interesting, bought a pack of cigarettes each. She was moving steadily to the far side of the room when she heard a snapping near her ear.

"You, new girl!"

Letty turned, bewildered, and saw Mr. Cole, the manager. His small eyes flickered nervously, and he straightened his tuxedo jacket.

"Yes?" she said, keeping pace with him as he darted between tables.

"A very important customer has just arrived." He pointed in the direction of a couple approaching a table just to the left of the stage. "See if they want anything, but don't linger, know what I mean?"

"Yes," Letty answered, although Mr. Cole did not bother to listen for her reply.

The couple was tall and slender—the back of the woman's dress, which faced Letty, was low and deep, exposing the lovely bones below her shoulders—and they moved effortlessly together, as though they had been in love a long time. His hair was a light brown, almost metallic, and it was neatly arranged over a high, smooth forehead. There was an unmistakable aura of privilege about him—he seemed to have just stepped down off a yacht—and Letty found herself longing to be part of a club as exclusive and well-dressed as their crew of two. She placed her hands firmly on her tray and stepped forward. The man had moved to pull back the seat for his girl, who gracefully lowered herself, rotating her neck as she did to take in the room. When the line of her jaw came into the light, Letty stopped suddenly.

She would have known Cordelia anywhere—but oh, how transformed she was! In the brisk, dark dress she wore, she was as much a lady as anyone in that room, and the gold band that circled her head suggested the imperious ease of a Grecian goddess.

For a moment, Letty was flooded with relief and excitement to see her friend looking so enviably well, but then she remembered how it was when they had last seen each other—she had been staring at Cordelia's back then too, before she had stalked off into the night without so much as glancing behind her in apology.

The thick emotion within Letty began to turn, and she became self-conscious of the tray of goods strapped to her middle, the girlish dress she was wearing, and the way she'd thought cutting her hair might make her appear cosmopolitan, simple as that. Her heart went low. Mr. Cole's brusque instructions were still in her ears, but her feet were stubborn. In a few seconds she realized that the rest of her didn't want to have to face Cordelia, either, and an idea seized her.

Across the room, Cordelia's eyes were so full of Thom that she hardly saw anyone else. She didn't even notice which establishment he'd had in mind until they were inside, and the riot of color and noise brought her back to the last evening she'd spent with Letty. There were the same stained glass windows and the same hysteria from the band on stage, but she regarded the room as she might have some fairgrounds she'd visited as a young girl. Everything looked different now, when she was so much more traveled in New York's after-hours.

"I guess they like you here." Cordelia put her elbow against the table, draping her body forward.

"You'll find they like me everywhere," Thom replied, letting his fingers linger on her bare back and turning toward the band.

The music was wild and fast, blurting and bouncing in every direction; the beat echoed across the room in the ecstatic shaking of shoulders, the furious tapping of toes, the jittery clicking of fingertips. When the song ended, the room erupted in applause. The waiters continued to wind their way between the tables, and the poor souls hanging back in the entry inclined forward to see what was so exciting.

Cordelia's red lips bent upward in a natural smile as Thom's fingers grazed her spine, sending shivers from her neck every which way along her skin. Then her eyes returned to the stage, where a girl was stepping, a little shyly, toward the microphone. She was petite, with cropped dark hair, and she was turned away, saying something to the cornet player. All the members of the band were straining to hear her, and some of them wore expressions of surprise. She was wearing a flouncy cream-colored dress and brown fishnet stockings, and when she turned around, Cordelia couldn't help a whispered exclamation of shock.

"Oh!"

But if Thom heard her, he didn't respond. Cordelia sat frozen, her lips parted, as the frightened pallor disappeared from Letty's face, replaced by a broad smile, and she fixed her hands to her hips. A low rumble was beaten out on the bass drum, and Letty's big, blue irises went theatrically left and right. Then the rest of the band joined in, and her brows moved flirtatiously up and down. After the first few bars her hands rose up, fingers splayed, and she opened her mouth. The crowd gasped, and even Cordelia, who had heard Letty sing many times, felt a shudder of surprise at what a deep voice that slip of a girl could produce. But mostly she felt a surging pride: Letty sang with such beauty and confidence that it carried to the rafters. And it was obvious that all these strangers heard the same thing, too. She recognized the song, but only vaguely—Anabelle Baker had performed it on a radio show they'd listened to back in March, something about dancing barefoot—and wondered if Letty had practiced it in private, or if she simply knew it from memory.

When the song ended, Cordelia couldn't help herself. She stood and began to clap, almost forgetting in the moment the man she'd walked in with.

Letty's chest rose and fell. She turned in the direction of the tall girl who'd shot up, so quickly, from the crowd. Their eyes met, but by then everyone else was standing and clapping, too. Letty's attention turned to the audience that had risen like a wave, and she regained the flashy smile of her performance. Someone yelled, "Encore!"

With all the excitement, Cordelia hardly noticed the bodies crowding in behind her, and the noise was loud enough to drown out her yelp.

By then it was too late. She was being hustled back

through the tables, and the two men behind her were so large that she wasn't even able to glimpse Thom when she turned. Danny was ahead of her, pulling her by the arm, a fact that only stoked her anger. None of the other patrons, who had gawked so freely before, so much as glanced in her direction now.

"What is this?" she demanded, as they came stumbling onto the sidewalk. The single bulb above the entrance cast a pool of light around her and the three men. After the mania inside the club, the blue night seemed especially calm, though inside Cordelia was heaving with fury. "Who do you think you are?"

Danny wouldn't look her in the eye, and she saw that he was sheepish, that he hadn't wanted to pull her away any more than she'd wanted to be pulled. The two men with him were older, and they were large—standing side by side, they constituted a rather formidable blockade. On the other side of them, the door to the club opened, and for a moment all the music and voices within became audible again. Dress shoes sounded on the single stone step. Cordelia craned her neck and saw Thom coming toward her. What was in his face—anger, concern, humiliation? Before she could read it, Danny opened a car door and one of the other men pushed her inside. The car was in motion before she even managed to speak.

"What—?" she began. But when she saw Charlie's big furious face, his simian brow tense and his lips taut, she lost her breath.

A long way, but only a few blocks west, in a church still used for its original purpose, a reverend railed against bad behavior for a handful of midnight faithful. "This lewd new music," he lectured, "this unspeakable jazz!" But down alleys and up rickety stairways hundreds of feet moved along, as dancing bodies for the first time contemplated a very modern cadence. This was the tempo of the time, and for a brief moment Letty, on stage with her innocent face and experienced voice, was its perfect expression.

She beamed and sparkled and caught her breath. She was just trying to think what song she should sing next, when she noticed a gaping hole in the audience where a few seconds before had been one truly familiar face. Letty had felt so full of glory, but now she experienced the sting of rejection. *Why would Cordelia have left so quickly?* she asked herself. Was she still angry at Letty, or simply embarrassed by her former friend? There was no way of knowing, so Letty smiled sadly at the boys in the band, and stepped off the stage toward her waiting box of wares. As she was strapping it to her waist, she heard someone call her name.

When she turned, she saw Grady.

"I'm so glad I got to hear you sing again," he said from the same barstool he had occupied the night before.

She gave an appreciative bow, and the great blues of her eyes gleamed. With her hair short and her lungs exercised, she was even lighter than usual. And so Letty kept on through the crowd. She looked right and left until someone met her eye or whistled or summoned her with a gesture of the hands. Suddenly she was the most sought-after girl in the room. They were interested in her for being precisely what she was: a cigarette girl who had done the unexpected, something exciting and gay that stoked their imaginations and their curiosity, and now they all wanted to buy their Lucky Strikes and gumballs from her.

She went forward until she felt a tightening around her waist. Someone, she realized with a pinch of fear, had taken hold of her. Bewildered, she turned, but she was already being pulled backward.

"Would you like something?" she said, a little hotly, to the man in the tuxedo who was holding onto her apron strings as if she were a marionette. He had manicured eyebrows, long and horizontal, and a trim, dark mustache hovering above a grin. His features were handsome, though his face reminded her of an overly polished apple.

"No, no, nothing for me just now." He glanced at the other men at his table, all of whom were dressed similarly, with the same high shine, and all grinning like rakes. "Boys?"

The boys shrugged.

"Nothing, pretty baby."

A long pause followed, during which Letty began to feel especially self-conscious about the way he was restraining her, as though she were a small child or a pony. A few people at the surrounding tables looked, or pretended not to look, and over by the bar she saw Paulette next to Grady Lodge, both of them watching the spectacle she'd stumbled into.

To Letty's relief, the man let go of the strings and patted her gently on the elbow. "I only wanted to tell you that you should be on that stage every night." He leaned forward, resting his arm on his knee and staring intensely into her eyes. "And I ought to know."

There was something haughty about his *I ought to know*, but Letty smiled complaisantly and remembered Paulette's instructions. Saying as little as possible, she went back to work. She worked until her legs were tired and her bones felt heavy, and then she worked another hour, until they felt numb. Later, after they had counted out their tips in the backroom and put their coats on over their girlish uniforms, Paulette and Letty finally stepped out into the refreshing night air.

The darkest hour had already passed, and the first signs of dawn to the east were becoming visible. Revelers were still stumbling home from long evenings of debauchery, and there was a street vendor selling hot popped corn with melted butter in wax paper bags for five cents. She and Paulette each bought one, paying with a quarter and telling him to keep the change. They ate as they walked toward home, not in any particular hurry.

"You know the fancy pants who grabbed you by the apron strings?" Paulette asked as she brought a handful of popcorn to her mouth.

"Yes," Letty replied distractedly. She hadn't known how hungry she was until she'd taken her first bite, and tasted how rich the butter was on her tongue, and heard her belly growl for more.

"Well, he's Amory Glenn." Letty didn't respond immediately, and then Paulette went on. "Of the theatrical Glenns. His family owns some of the biggest houses on Broadway!"

"Really?" Letty pictured him sitting there at that prominent table, with his crisp white collar and neat bow tie, with the slick hair and dark eyes, and she realized that he *had* had a moneyed, important way about him, and what he had said to her—"I ought to know"—didn't seem so haughty after all. She thought then of Cordelia and the handsome man with her, and marveled at how, in the span of so few days, both girls could catch the attention of such important-seeming fellows. They really had been too big for Ohio, she supposed, and perhaps they *both* had what Mother used to call "magic."

Letty let out a long, contented breath. There was a touch

of moisture in the air, and it was refreshing on the tip of her nose. She looked at Paulette, with her long legs and her head full of information about the secret workings of the world—what a lucky stroke it had been to find a new best friend like that!

A few stars were still visible in the brightening sky, and Letty sensed that at least one of them was for her. She was charmed—she just knew it, and she felt the tingle of the many possibilities laying in wait for her tomorrow and all the days after that.

15

"THERE'S NO NEED FOR—" CORDELIA BEGAN, AS HER kidnappers pushed her into the library of Dogwood, but she fell silent when she saw the ashen face of her father waiting for her. The lie she'd told earlier had been exposed, she realized, and any calmness she'd derived from her cool anger with Charlie, in the car en route to White Cove, left her now. Her heart was beating awfully fast, but she pulled her shoulders back and smoothed her skirt over her legs and blinked.

Charlie had been furiously silent all the way home, but her father, when he saw his children coming through the door, appeared only tired and concerned.

"I hope they weren't rough with you, my dear. Men like that

don't have much experience with nice girls." Darius spoke softly, tentatively, as though he were afraid of causing her more harm.

"They weren't that rough" was all Cordelia could manage in reply.

"Why shouldn't they have been rough?" Charlie broke in angrily. "It's like I told you the first night she came here, Dad: She's nobody. She came out of nowhere. Who knows what she's up to, or who she's working for, especially now that we've seen her out with Thom Hale—"

"Charlie, shut up." Darius closed his eyes, pinching his forehead as though he had a headache. "You were supposed to keep an eye on her. You were supposed to be always at her side. How could she know to stay away from Thom Hale if you didn't tell her?"

Charlie said nothing, but his eyes burned with invective.

After a moment Darius stood up and crossed to the doorway, where he put an arm around Cordelia's shoulder and escorted her back to the circle of stuffed leather chairs where he had been waiting. For a moment they sat there in silence, an awkward family of three. "I can understand how you might think I don't care what you do, since I went off so soon after your arrival. Because of all the years I let go by, without trying to get you back . . . But believe me, I do care. I want you to enjoy yourself, but also to be safe. And I'm afraid neither of those things are possible with—that young man."

"But Thom's nice," Cordelia whispered, remembering how easy she'd felt in his company. But the grave mood in the room made it difficult to hang on to that lightness.

Charlie snorted.

"I'm afraid not." Darius let go of her hand and leaned back against his chair. He rested his mouth against his hand contemplatively, and let his eyes drift out the window for a moment. The mysterious noises of the country at night—crickets and rustling leaves—filtered inside. Eventually, Darius sighed heavily. "Thom is Duluth Hale's son. You remember this morning when I told you about Duluth Hale?"

"They want a chunk of everything we got," Charlie interrupted. "Furthermore, they'd kill us if they thought they'd get away with it."

"Charlie!" Darius turned, slapping his son's shoulder. Both men were large, but in that moment, Cordelia glimpsed the formidable force of which the elder Grey was capable. "Say another word and I swear you won't leave this house the whole summer." He leaned his elbows against his knees and pushed himself toward Cordelia. "He's no good, all right? That's all you need to know. Stay away from him. Can you promise me that?"

A cold front was advancing within her.

"Yes," Cordelia answered, but she could not bring herself to look as though she meant it. The way the city had rushed by the windows of Thom's car—bright and fast and full of music—was becoming less tangible to her with every passing second. It seemed excruciating that the kiss they'd shared in his car was going to be their only kiss. Thom's touch, and the giddy, perfect way it made her feel, was fading, and she couldn't help but be stricken by that. She was crushed, and she knew that it was visible all over her face.

"Both of you will be staying here at Dogwood for a while." Darius stood again, more heavily this time, and walked toward the entryway on tired legs. "I am telling the boys. You are both punished. Good night, children."

When he was gone, Charlie faced Cordelia. There was even more fire in his eyes now. "Look what you've done," he said. "You *fool*."

But the hatefulness of his tone was no match for the memory of the brilliant sensation Thom Hale had created within her when he'd turned that sideways grin in her direction, and it was with all the joyous confidence that the hours in his company had imbued her with that she stood, nose in the air, and declared, "You're a beast, and you don't have even a third as much class as Thom Hale."

If she glanced back, she feared there might be tears. So she kept her eyes focused forward as she climbed the stairs and walked across the third-floor hallway to the Calla Lily Suite.

"Cordelia!" Astrid wailed when Cordelia came into the bedroom.

For some hours, Astrid had been making use of the Calla Lily Suite. She had showered and redone her hair and gone through Cordelia's closet, examining the new frocks hanging there and imagining all the trading of clothes they would do over the summer. Then Milly, the maid Darius had hired for his daughter, had come with milk and cookies and also to turn down the bed, and for a while Astrid had engaged her in gossip about the strange inhabitants of Dogwood. But since Milly was new, she had little to add, and eventually Astrid grew bored and dismissed her. She was becoming truly, profoundly bored when she heard the sound at the door. The fact that Cordelia had claimed to be feeling too bad to go out earlier, and was now wearing a very expensive dress, was lost in the relief of having her friend back.

"What's the matter?" Cordelia said as she kicked off her heels.

The two girls moved to sit side by side on the bed.

"Oh, *look*." Astrid opened her fist and showed her friend the earring.

"What is it?" Cordelia leaned forward to better examine the offensive object.

"I don't know!" Astrid groaned and set her head against Cordelia's shoulder. "All I know is, it's not mine, but it *was* in Charlie's things . . . I suppose I was half hoping it was yours?"

"No . . ." Cordelia's brown eyes flickered from Astrid's hand to her face. "It's not mine."

"I mean, how did it get there, and under what circumstances?" Astrid went on, although the questioning tone was disingenuous, because already the picture in her mind of the woman whose ear it had dangled from had become a lurid scene that involved Charlie and another girl, or possibly two. The image made her feel foolish and powerless, and before she could help it, the corners of her eyes had become damp.

Astrid slumped and sunk her hands into her lap. She felt diminished; she didn't know how she would confront Charlie, or even to put into words what she feared he'd done.

"I know you love Charlie," Cordelia began cautiously, "but he can be such a bully—"

Before Astrid could respond that that wasn't the way she saw him at all, she was distracted by a noise down the hall on the stairway and raised her finger to silence Cordelia. As soon as Charlie saw she was gone from his room, he would be coming this way. She felt on the brink of some crisis, and the only thing she was sure of was that she didn't want to see him yet. She brought her finger to her lips, telling Cordelia to hush. "I'm not here," she mouthed, and then she tiptoed to the bathroom, soundlessly closing the door and putting her cheek against it to listen.

From the bathroom, with its expanses of gray-streaked marble and shining gold fixtures, she heard Charlie barge into Cordelia's suite. This was the way everyone redid their bathrooms nowadays, though she supposed Cordelia had never encountered anything like it in Ohio.

"Have you seen Astrid?"

The sound of Charlie's voice jarred her, even with the wall separating them. His tone was tense and breathless, and he didn't sound pleased to be asking the question.

"No," Cordelia, on the other side of the door, replied in that laconic way of hers. "Have you?"

"Yes, but now she's gone." The floorboards groaned beneath Charlie's feet as he walked across the floor. "She was in my room, but she isn't anymore—she's not here?"

"No." Another pause. "What a shame, I would have liked her company tonight."

There was no reply, and after another moment, Astrid knew he was gone. She could just picture Charlie leaping up the steps, searching for her with that brash, important way he had. When the door slammed, she hurried back to Cordelia, who was still sitting in the same position, her hair hanging down around her shoulders.

"He's looking for you, you know," Cordelia said slowly.

"I know." Astrid bit her lip. "Only, let me stay here a little while? Can I sleep here with you?"

"Of course you can . . . but why not just confront him tonight?"

"It will do him good to think I've gone off . . . and I can't decide what to do until tomorrow." Astrid sighed and threw herself back against the bedspread. What she couldn't bring herself to say was that if Charlie had betrayed her, she didn't want to know. "Anyway, I always sleep in this bed when I'm here too late to drive back home. I did before you came, that is. Which I'm *awfully* glad you did!"

"You sleep—here?"

Astrid let out a loud, flat laugh. "Where did you think I'd sleep? Not with Charlie."

But she could tell from Cordelia's face that this was exactly what she had thought. Cordelia's lips parted, and she went on watching Astrid, as though for a sign that she was telling a joke. "Oh," she said quietly, and nodded.

Astrid slapped the bed and laughed again at the notion. Cordelia took to everything so quickly, it had momentarily slipped Astrid's mind how far away Ohio was. It was different there, she supposed, now that she thought about it. Perhaps boys and girls on farms acted like married people long before they actually were. "Of course not! Oh, he'd *like* me to, but there are some things a girl doesn't do before, well—anyway, I wouldn't want to end up like my mother."

Astrid groaned, remembering the party she had left behind and all the horrid antics. "Anyway, it's all so dull. Let's talk about you, can't we?"

She scooted up the bed and pulled the cover over her

evening gown. A breeze picked up, pushing against the white curtains and moving them about in a ghostly manner. Cordelia ran her long fingers over the bedspread and seemed to be silently considering her words. The corners of her mouth twitched for a moment, as though she were trying to keep a smile at bay, but she could not stop it from coming into full bloom.

Cordelia tossed a heap of sun-streaked hair over her shoulder, and stars shone in her eyes. But that hair *was* a bit country—Astrid saw that now. They were going to have to fix it. The rest of Cordelia was so elegant, after all; it was a shame to let this one detail remain off-key.

"I met a boy," Cordelia finally whispered.

"Aha!" Astrid exclaimed. "I *knew* something very thrilling had happened. Why else would you have suddenly become so elusive? Tell me! Tell me *now*. Tell me everything."

"Well, his name's Thom, and—"

Astrid gasped. Her mouth fell open, and her tone became serious. "Thom Hale? Oh, when I saw you speaking at the club . . . Well, you can't fall in love with Thom Hale," she said quickly, giving a stuttered shaking of the head.

But Cordelia did not match her seriousness yet. She laughed and lightly replied, "Not you, too?"

"The Hales and the Greys—how can I explain?"

"Oh, I know. I know everything. Charlie and Father told me I'm *not* to see him, and they've locked me away in the castle just to make sure." She bit her lip, glancing from Astrid to her hands, as though she were frightened by what she'd done, or maybe frightened by what she felt. Cordelia lay her head on the pillow so that she was just next to her friend, and she lowered her voice as though she were about to tell a very dark secret. "Only, I've never felt that way before. The way I felt when I was with him. I'd never known life could be so grand . . ."

Astrid's eyes had become very large. "Oh, but you mustn't. Charlie and Darius take family very seriously . . ."

There was a long silence after this, and for a moment it seemed that Cordelia had regretted her confession. But then a little mischief began to play at the corners of her mouth. "But do you know how handsome he is?"

Now Astrid could not help but smile, too. "Yes—he is handsome, I suppose."

"So you know him?"

"Of course, everyone knows Thom!"

Cordelia let out a dreamy sigh and buried her face in the pillow. She was in trouble, and yet she seemed almost happy. Watching her friend, Astrid wondered if the rivalry between the Hales and the Greys really mattered so much after all. Sometimes people questioned Charlie and Astrid's affections—and perhaps they were right—but in Astrid's heart, she knew she couldn't help loving Charlie, despite his flaws. Even now, when her head was cluttered with anger, she loved him.

Who was she to doubt anyone else's love affair?

They began to drift off, briefly, but were awakened by the sound of shouting down below. Creeping toward the window, they giggled a little as they realized that it was Charlie and Elias calling Astrid's name into the night.

"Maybe we should tell them?" Cordelia whispered as they peered outside.

"No! That can wait until morning, just like everything else." Astrid took her friend's hand and they padded back across the floor and tucked themselves under the covers.

"Anyway, none of it can be all that bad." Cordelia gave Astrid a reassuring wink. "How could it be, when we get to fall asleep in a room as soft and bright as this one?"

This was a new concept for Astrid—but once she closed her eyes and considered Cordelia's logic, it seemed irrefutable.

Even as the night sky became tinged with the pink of sunrise, it was likely that down in the back corners of White Cove, and in its finer social rooms, gaudy laughter was still ringing to the ceilings, or else vast sorrow was being drowned. But in the Calla Lily Suite on the third floor of Dogwood, layers of expensive bedding held Astrid, and the rhythm of Cordelia's breathing on the next pillow gave her the sense that, at last, she had a true friend.

16

"YOU'LL NEVER GUESS WHAT THE NEW GIRL DID LAST night!"

Letty had just stepped out of her bedroom, wearing a charcoal-colored dress she had borrowed and was thus a little long for her. She looked even more petite than usual and was feeling rather delicate for reasons she could not yet quite pinpoint.

"What did the new girl do last night?" Fay asked as she walked out of the kitchenette and over to the plum couch, where she sunk down next to Paulette. A black silk eye mask was pushed up on her forehead, beneath the curve of her pale blond hair, and she was still wearing the usual knee-length kimono.

"She jumped onstage and sang an impromptu song with the band!" Paulette announced, as though she still couldn't believe it. "The crowd loved it. Amory Glenn was there, and later she found a way to flirt with him."

Fay's lower lip fell and her eyes glistened. "Good girl!" she exclaimed. "It's those big innocent blues."

"Amory Glenn?" Kate exclaimed, emerging from her bedroom. Her frizzy dark hair was tucked under the folds of a white turban, and her long, slender features were already made up. "You brilliant little dog!"

But her roommates' glee at her conquest only made Letty feel embarrassed. Last night, it *had* seemed very grand, but she'd woken up this morning in a different mood. In her dreams, Cordelia had been a kind of princess, and she had mocked Letty from a passing carriage, and when Letty had opened her eyes and heard Paulette's noisy breathing beside her in the bed they shared, her life hadn't seemed quite so bright as it had before. If she retold the story of jumping on the stage at Seventh Heaven, then she would soon arrive at the part where the song ended and she realized that Cordelia was gone again. The memory made her throat tight.

"I'll tell you all about it later." She mustered a small, brave smile. "It's just that it's such a beautiful day, I can't bear to be inside . . . ," Letty offered, a bit lamely, as an excuse.

"Oh!"

"But—"

"*Tell* us," chorused her roommates, as they pushed themselves up and inclined themselves toward her. But she was already hurriedly crossing the alcove by the entry. She pulled a cocoa-colored felt cloche over her bob and pulled open the door.

"I'll be back later!" she called with a frantic wave of the hand, and then she went out of the dim basement and into the day.

As she came up onto the sidewalk, her embarrassment and sorrow began to ebb, and with it her desperate need to flee. She paused there on that narrow, curving street, in the kindly shadow of the two- and three-story brick townhouses and the tall trees in full leaf overhead.

That was when she saw Grady Lodge across the street, leaning against his black roadster, with his hands in his pockets.

A floppy cap created a wedge of shadow on his face, but it could not hide the patient yearning in his deep-set gray eyes. He was wearing the tweed trousers of a knickerbocker suit, his rust-colored socks visible to his knees, although the jacket was nowhere in sight. That was what they called "natty," Letty supposed, except that everything about him was just slightly askew.

"Hello there!" he called.

Feeling bashful again, she glanced behind her, but the curtains to her apartment remained drawn. Seeing him in the daylight was peculiar, but she was happy now to have been given a direction. With a little feint of surprise, she let out an "Oh . . . hello!" and then crossed to him.

He reached out for her hand and kissed her knuckles.

"How did you know where I live?" she asked when he brought his eyes up to look at her again.

"Your friend Paulette told me last night," he explained. "Maybe she felt sorry for me, when she realized how many hours I'd sat at the bar waiting to talk to you . . ."

For a moment he appeared to lose himself in looking at her, so Letty simply smiled in a girlish way and waited for him to say something more.

". . . and when I woke up this morning, I thought perhaps, you being from Ohio and all, you would like a tour of the city."

Reasons why not brimmed in her throat. But the day *was* lovely, just as she had told her roommates, and she had after all not ventured very far beyond Greenwich Village. Cordelia seemed to be going everywhere, and why shouldn't she? "Well, all right, but I haven't got the whole day," she said, trying not to sound too eager.

A grin filled his boyish face. "I'll take you for as long as you can spare."

Hurrying around the side of the car, he opened the door for her, posing in a courtly way until she was settled in. Once he'd secured the door behind her, he came around and started up the car. For a brief while she felt nervous and a little shy, sitting in a car with a stranger, but eventually the sights drew her in. They drove down blocks where every storefront was filled with flowers by the bucket, and streets where the signs were in red Chinese lettering.

Perhaps sensing how foreign these sights were to her, he said, "You're awfully brave to come all this way by yourself."

"Oh . . . I didn't," Letty replied. "I came with a girl named Cordelia, but we don't know each other anymore."

Grady glanced at her. "I'm sorry," he said quietly. "Perhaps I could help you find her?"

"That's very kind, but—but—I don't think she cares about me anymore. You see, she came in the club last night, but left as soon as she caught sight of me."

"I can't imagine anyone not wanting to know you."

"Oh, that's very kind," Letty told him, pushing aside the melancholy that had crept into her dreams. The day was so pretty and the city so full, and she didn't want to be sorry over anything—and anyway, it felt good to tell someone about Cordelia and her unkind departure. "I've made better friends since then," she said brightly.

When she announced she was hungry, they pulled alongside a street vendor's cart and Grady bought hot dogs, and they ate them as they drove up and down the shady roads and grand tunnels that ran through the big park at the center of the city.

"This is what they call the Central Park . . ." Grady's attentive gray eyes traveled from the road and back to her.

"It looks like it goes on forever!" Letty said between bites of soft bread and juicy meat. "How many blocks is it?"

Grady paused and then admitted, "I don't know . . ." He reddened and gave her one of his easy smiles. "But I promise I'll find out. Many, I suppose. It's its own little kingdom; you can get lost in there, you know."

The canopy of green over her head rustled in such a peaceful, quiet way that for a moment she forgot that she was in a city at all. Elegant women with mincing walks followed poodles on leashes, and children clutching balloons begged for treats from their fathers, and all the while the sky above remained an impervious blue. She had taken long drives before, but never ones that were so aimless and leisurely, and never ones with such grand scenery.

They changed directions, going downhill somewhat and driving through the low-lying areas by the water, past loading docks and factories puffing smoke and little forgotten structures crammed onto the island at its edges. Ferries made their way across the river, and men smeared with grease idled in front of garages.

"I apologize for having taken this route," Grady said, chagrined, as they motored through a particularly industrial patch.

"But why would you be sorry?" Letty exclaimed. Whatever

filth lay heavy in the air, she could not help but feel thrilled by the very multitude of smokestacks and brightly colored tugboats, the distant yelling of working men, the far-off blaring of maritime horns. "I think it's beautiful here. In fact, it's such a nice day, I wouldn't mind putting my toes in . . ."

"Not here!" A shade of worry crossed Grady's face at the very suggestion. "No, no, no—the water and the shoreline here are dirty in ten different ways. I would *not* let you go down there, even with an army of bodyguards, even with a fleet of Sherpas to hold you up above the muck."

Letty put her elbow against the back of her seat and gazed behind them at the receding view of the water. The area that they were heading into now was one of higher buildings, and the river, though still pungent, was no longer so visible. Disappointment bore down for a minute on the corners of her mouth, but it passed quickly, and the sentiment of what he had said began to sink in and create a decided glow along her cheekbones. For Grady—though he was only a writer, and though his humble face did not create such wild disturbances in her breast—thought that she was worthy of being carried like a queen.

"I know a pretty spot where we can go down close to the water—I still don't believe you should put your toes in, but maybe for a look-see."

So Letty smiled, and they sailed on. He took them on a

looping route, through streets whose sidewalks were crowded out with produce stands, streets where the smell of onion was heavy in the air, streets paved with cobblestone.

Eventually they puttered to a stop under the shadow of an enormous bridge.

"Where are we?" she said, as he helped her out of the car.

"Just a place where I like to come and gaze at the borough of Brooklyn, from time to time, when I'm thinking of Walt Whitman . . ." Grady closed his eyes and inhaled a deep, contented breath.

Letty's legs felt a little wobbly after so long in the shaking, rumbling automobile, but Grady offered her his arm. As they headed toward the water, she saw the spans of two other enormous bridges, stretching all the way across the river to where she could just make out the houses and factories and piers on the other side.

As they walked, she listened to the lapping of the water and the scattering of debris underfoot—but the tranquility was broken by the sound of two thunderlike claps. A shudder passed from the sides of her skull down to her toes. The howling of two or three dogs followed, as if in furious confirmation that some very violent deed had been done.

"Oh!" she gasped, and she put her hands up against Grady's chest.

They hurried forward and saw a car parked under the wall of the bridge. A man's wide back faced them—he was bent, examining something, so that his large rear was pointed toward the span above. Then he stood, lifting the sleek, limp body of a creature and hurling it onto a pile of similar, lifeless forms. When Letty gasped again, the man glanced briefly in their direction.

"Get out of here," he said in a tone that was equal parts gruff and weary, before looking away. He opened the door to the car, and the howling started up again. For a minute or so he struggled, and then slammed the door, holding tight to a dog's leash. At its end was a very skittish greyhound, long legs quavering and eyes rolling in terror. The man pulled, jerking the frightened animal away from the car and cocking his gun.

"He's going to kill that poor animal," she whispered desperately to Grady, who had already put his arm around her, gently trying to goad her back. But her chin had begun to quiver, and her feet were quite stubbornly planted. "Look!" She couldn't find words for what they were about to witness. "*Do* something."

"I don't think—" he began, as the greyhound shook and whimpered.

"Stop him!" she persisted. "Listen—the dog's *crying*."

The man, whose white collared shirt had grown see-through

in places with sweat, and whose jowls were shaded by stubble, raised his gun and fired twice. The dog's elegant legs collapsed, and then the whimpering was over.

"Oh!" This time Letty's cry had become low and guttural—true wailing. The succinct cruelty of the big man's movements was so terrible that for a moment she felt it was her skin that had been ripped apart, her own blood that would now begin to spill.

Inside the car, a lone dog yelped, its paws clawing desperately at the window.

The man straightened and shook the casings out of his gun. He stuffed his hand in his pocket and produced another handful of shining bullets, which he slipped one at a time into the chamber, before clicking it closed. "I told you to get out of here."

Grady glanced down at Letty, his eyes glazed with fear. "I think we should go."

She gave a furious shake of her head.

"Why are you killing those dogs?" she demanded, walking several lengths toward the big man.

"Because they're old, and they don't run fast anymore, and they're no use to me now," he replied, with a kind of resigned menace, as though it were obvious and he were irritated at having to explain himself. Then he opened the car and grabbed the leash of the final dog, who jumped to the ground and began dashing in circles around the man until the leash had ensnared both of them.

Untying himself required several clumsy attempts, and perhaps after that Grady was not quite so frightened of him. "She looks pretty fast to me," he told the big man.

"Yeah, well, everyone runs fast when they're scared for their life," the man muttered back.

"Do you operate a racetrack concern, sir?" Grady continued, returning to his usual buoyant, educated way of speaking, and putting on a smile.

"Something like that," the man replied, yanking at the leash and pulling the dog closer to her fallen brethren.

"Mister, please don't kill that dog," Letty implored.

"Don't give me that act, princess." The man cocked his gun. Letty brought her hands to her face, bracing for tears.

"Stop!" She heard Grady's steps as he hurried forward. "Please stop. What do you want for her? A dollar? Five? Please don't kill that dog."

Cracking one eye, and peeking through her pinkie and ring finger, Letty caught a glimpse of Grady as he begged the man. The greyhound whimpered, her head swaying back and forth, her paws scraping the ground in agitation.

"You'll take her off my hands?" the man said eventually.

"Yes," Grady replied.

Letty's hands fell from her face, and she clasped them in front of her heart.

"I'll never hear from either of you again?"

"No." Grady shook his head perhaps a few more times than were necessary.

Letty rushed forward and bent on her knees, taking the dog's face in her hands; her lovely brown eyes were wary for a few seconds, but then once the man had handed Letty the end of the leash, she began gently pawing the front of Letty's dress and licking her face.

"Five dollars," the man said irritably.

"Yes, of course, right." Grady went fishing in his wallet. "Here you are."

Letty came to her feet and narrowed her eyes at the man. "Come on, gorgeous," she said to the dog, and then began to walk at a rapid clip away from the horrid scene.

"Thank you!" Grady called out as he hurried along behind her.

"Don't thank him!" she admonished, and then immediately felt bad for speaking harshly. "I—I'm sorry. Thank you, Mr. Lodge. I'm very—" She paused, looking down at the animal's sleek snout. "*We're* very grateful. I will pay you back every penny."

Grady must have been truly frightened, for there was a little quaver in his voice when he spoke again. "Don't mention it. Only—I won't be taking you to any more secret places anytime soon."

The light was going out of the day by then, and they both agreed he should be getting her home. All the way she cradled her new pet, who alternated between trembling and licking her face.

"Thank you so much again, Mr. Lodge," Letty said when they slowed to a stop on Barrow Street. "It's been quite an afternoon."

"It has." He had been quieter than usual on the drive home, but seemed to be regaining his composure now. With his fingers on the brim of his cap, he made a few nervous adjustments. "I hope you'll let me take you out again sometime."

"Yes." She bit her lower lip and gave him a sincere smile. "I'd like that."

"There's one other thing I wanted to tell you . . ."

"Yes?" she said sweetly, though she didn't like what his expression augured.

"I saw you talking to Amory Glenn, and I just wanted to say . . ." Grady averted his eyes awkwardly. "I've known people who know him well, and—he's not a good egg."

Letty blinked for a moment, and another car swerved onto the street and passed them before she thought to laugh. "Oh, don't worry about me, Mr. Lodge! I know a thing or two, and I can spot a good egg when I see one." She crouched, nuzzling the dog's face. "And this is a good egg. That's what we'll call you: Good Egg Larkspur!"

When she stood again, her eyes were misted, and she shrugged at the wonder of it all. "See you at your usual end of the bar, Mr. Lodge!" She blew him a kiss as though she were a big star, and ran across the street with Good Egg loping ahead of her, feeling altogether ready for the next chapter of her day.

17

CORDELIA'S FIRST WEEK AS THE DAUGHTER OF A famous bootlegger was nearing its close, and she was beginning to see that parental love comes with its own irritations. Her father had been true to his word; she was not allowed off the property. Two days in one place is a long time for any young person, especially one with a formidable curiosity, especially if that person happens to be a girl who is learning for the first time that *lovesick* is not a figure of speech or an old wives' tale. The idea of Thom Hale made her feverish and ruined her appetite, and she'd had to excuse herself from dinner early the night before because she couldn't think of any words besides *Thom* and *Hale,* and was afraid she would make her obsessions obvious if she opened her mouth again. All night she turned in bed, her temperature going from hot to cold. She couldn't love him, she knew, not after just one night with him—but if it wasn't love, she didn't know what to call the jittery longing that was making it impossible to sleep or sit in one place very long.

Plus, there was the sad fact that now she knew where Letty was, and she couldn't even visit her. How she would have loved to see her old friend's entire act, and congratulate her on her great success, and tell her how ridiculous their fight had been!

Her movements were curtailed even further by the knowledge that her brother was always at Dogwood now, too. She couldn't be angry at her father, really—he'd been kind to her, despite her dishonesty. But Charlie had been odious, and she had come to think of him as the single reason that Thom was now probably petrified of phoning her. She supposed Charlie had had it in for her since that first night at Seventh Heaven, before either of them had known they were family. But on the second day of her imprisonment, when she came back from a long walk on the grounds, she found that she wasn't going to be able to avoid him after all, because he was clearly seeking her out.

"Have you talked to Astrid?" he barked as she came up the rise toward the front of the house.

Cordelia paused, looking rather like a lady golfer in her sporty white dress with the sleeveless, crew-neck bodice and the accordion pleats on the skirt. The directness of his address surprised her, as did his misguided notion that she might share information with him, after the things he'd said. "Maybe, but it's really none of your business."

Charlie had been coming from the garage and was now striding toward where she stood on the gravel. When he arrived at her side, they began walking in the direction of the house. The sun was high in the sky, and it almost seemed as though golden dust was floating on the air.

"Come on, she's driving me crazy," Charlie went on, and though his voice was still a touch bullying, there was a pleading to it, too. "She won't take my calls."

Cordelia sighed. Against her better judgment, she couldn't help but feel a little sorry for him—after all, she felt crazy, too. "I've talked to her. She's angry with you." When she saw Charlie hanging his head and nodding, she added a touch more gently, "I haven't known Astrid as long as you have, but it seems to me that she's not one to budge when she's been wronged."

"You're right about that. But she *hasn't* been wronged," he replied quickly. "I don't even know what she's angry about."

"Perhaps." Cordelia glanced at Charlie dubiously and considered telling him about the discovery of the other night, and how Astrid knew that a mysterious girl had been in his bedroom. Although she did have to admit, to herself at least, that the Greys threw a lot of parties, and she supposed the earring really could have come from anywhere. "But I don't think that matters very much now."

"No, I guess not. She can be awfully stubborn. But don't think Astrid's sullen or selfish," Charlie went on as they moved into the shadow of the house. "She values you."

Though his statement made Cordelia happy, she responded with a cool "Why do you suppose that is?"

Charlie shrugged. "Maybe because you're my sister? Who cares, just be nice to her."

"I'll be nice to her because she's my friend," Cordelia replied sharply. "Not because of your say-so."

"Don't you get difficult, too. You're a Grey, after all, and Greys have to stick together."

"But the other night you accused me of—"

"I'm sorry I said that." When Charlie exhaled, he did so with the whole force of his big body. There was something about that sigh—so heavy with responsibility—that made it difficult for her to go on regarding him as a mere obstacle. "I was wrong to say that, especially to the only sister I've got."

They climbed the grand marble steps toward the house, and in a moment she glimpsed what Astrid had said about him the other night—that he cared above all about the family. Having spent her entire life as a kind of changeling, she couldn't help but like him a little for this characteristic and want to be taken in under his protective wing.

"All right, but just today," she said, her tone turning light. "I can't make any promises for tomorrow."

Giving her a sidelong glance, Charlie opened the door so that she could pass. Inside was dim—there was only the natural light coming in through the windows, plus the walls were paneled with dark wood. Cordelia stepped forward, into the hall; the house seemed rather cold to her for a moment, and she realized that she hadn't even spoken to Darius since last night at dinner, when she had been so silent and awkward. Of course, she felt her father's presence constantly—in the attention of his staff and in the continual arrival of clothes and shoes and hats, and especially since her punishment. But the absence of his face all morning struck her at that moment and made her feel a little sad.

"Charlie—"

Both Grey siblings looked up at the sound, although Elias Jones, wearing a trim, unflashy black suit, barely appeared to register Cordelia's presence as he emerged from the shadows. Charlie stepped toward him, and the older man began to whisper in his ear. Her brother's face grew serious again, and he nodded, listening until Jones finished what he had to say.

"Thanks," Charlie said. Then he turned his back on both Jones and his sister and bounded up the stairs.

After clearing his throat, Jones informed her, "A few more

packages arrived from the city—your father asked that I put them in your suite."

By the time Cordelia managed to say "thank you," Jones had turned and headed outside. She could hear his footfalls scattering gravel, and also the creaking of boards under heavy footsteps above. Craning her neck, she looked up the three stories, to the carved ceiling and the great chandelier, which remained off during the daytime.

"Charlie!" she cried.

A few seconds passed, and then his head appeared over the banister. "You need something?" he said eventually.

"No . . ." She shifted on her feet. "I just wanted to tell you—I didn't know who Thom was when I agreed to go out with him. I wouldn't have, if I'd known."

There was another pause, but then Charlie smiled, wide enough that she could see it, even way below him on the ground floor. His head disappeared, and then she heard his steps as he began to descend the stairs. By the time he had rounded the final flight and stood facing her on the second-to-last step, his smile had gone away, but there was a new genial quality as he paused to appraise her.

"Thank you for that."

"It's not a favor." She held his gaze, her face neutral, her back straight. "That's just who I am."

"Even better," Charlie chuckled. "I never trust favors,

anyway, until they've been given."

"Me neither."

An awkward lingering ensued, during which Charlie appeared unsure whether to return upstairs or not. Cordelia, who had nothing much to do, remained steadily in place.

"No good being cooped up, is it?" Charlie said eventually.

Cordelia gave a silent shake of her head.

"If I got you out of here, do you think you could persuade Astrid to meet you?"

Her eyes shone, and her blood quickened. That sounded like the most fun she'd had in days. She looked around, but there was no one watching them, and then she gave a swift nod.

"Come on," Charlie replied with a grin.

They began to walk in the same direction that Cordelia had gone during her first moments in Dogwood—down the hall, toward the kitchen, which she now saw was a large space, crowded with ranges under iron hoods, high, worn tables, and hanging copper pots. A heavy man wearing an apron, his multiple chins rising out of a collared shirt, stood at the stovetop.

"Charlie!" the man exclaimed, shaking a sauté pan from which rose the rich smell of mushrooms cooking in butter. It was obvious, the way he said the name, that he had known Charlie as a child.

"Cordelia, this is Len—he's been with Dad since the beginning."

"So you're the young lady," the big man said, nodding as he assessed her.

Cordelia answered with a slight nod. "You've been cooking all my meals, haven't you?"

"Yes, ma'am."

She smiled, but before she could thank him, Charlie asked Len if he could pack them a picnic lunch for an afternoon on the grounds.

"You still eating like three grown men, kid?" Len asked, and Charlie nodded almost bashfully.

They waited while he packed it for them. Nobody said very much, and Cordelia couldn't help but glimpse something horrible and strange near his feet: He wore one normal black polished shoe, but his other pant leg appeared to hang around a wooden post.

"Charlie," Cordelia whispered, once their lunch had been finished and they were crossing through the formal dining room. "What was wrong with that man's leg?"

To her surprise, Charlie chuckled. "His leg? He lost it."

A wave of dread passed over her as she tried to comprehend a thing like that. She had to reach down and press her palms against the fronts of her thighs, just to experience the relief that she was all there. "But *how*?" Cordelia pursued.

"Why else do you think a man his size would be in the kitchen? He's big; Dad says he used to be good muscle." Charlie shrugged. "Anyway, it was a long time ago now, back in the early days, when they were just starting to enforce Prohibition. Territories hadn't been worked out yet. And Dad, Len, some others, they had a gang—they delivered liquor—and one night a rival gang challenged Dad, tried to edge in on his customers. Dad took a bullet, and Len got run over. Pulverized his leg. They both ended up in St. Vincent's—the doc said he was just lucky he lived."

"Oh," Cordelia said in a very small voice.

"Like I said, long time ago," Charlie went on matter-of-factly as they entered the ballroom. "We don't eat much in that dining room," he commented. "Only since you been here—it's funny, I guess Dad wants to impress you."

"Why funny?" Cordelia demanded.

"Don't take it personal—it's only that you've spent all your life in Ohio, and it seems like he worries a lot more about impressing you than some of the ladies he brings back here—I mean, real ladies, grew up on Fifth Avenue and have been to Paris and own poodles and all that. Ladies like Astrid. But it makes sense he'd want you to have the best . . . you're his blood."

Cordelia smiled at the thought that her father cared so much about treating her well. "Dad has a lot of girlfriends, huh?" she asked.

"Yeah, well." They had nearly crossed the gleaming dance floor, and Charlie opened the door on the far end, and paused to allow Cordelia to pass into the library before him. "That's why he redid the Calla Lily Suite. There was this chorus girl, Mona Alexander—they were engaged for a while. But she was a bad drinker, and eventually Dad decided she was the wrong element. I think that's the only room in the house that has really new furniture, actually. Furniture he bought himself, I mean."

Cordelia nodded and glanced up at the plasterwork angels on the ceiling and the fine chandelier that dangled in the center, wondering where Mona Alexander was now, and whether or not Darius had thought of Fanny Larson when he proposed to the chorus girl.

"Never mind all that," Charlie said as the siblings continued into the shady library. It had an even more solemn air in the daytime, and the ferns seemed overgrown, almost as though they had been there a hundred years. Charlie stepped over the Persian carpets toward the floor-to-ceiling bookshelves that lined the south wall. He studied the spines for a minute, searching for something.

More words had been exchanged between them that afternoon than over the entire week, and for the first time she was really curious about her brother. "It must have been pretty nice, growing up like this," she mused.

"Like this?" Charlie gave a short snort. "Wish I had. Dad bought this place in '24. Year before that, he rented a beach place in Whitewood—that's east along the sound—not as high-class, if you know what I mean. Before that, it was one apartment to another in the city."

"Oh?" It was difficult for Cordelia to picture Charlie like that, without the chauffeur and entourage and fine clothes.

"It seems like another life. It was. Prohibition *made* Dad—he was pretty small-time before that, though don't tell anybody I said so."

"Have you always been part of his . . . whatever it is he does?" Cordelia asked.

"Ever since I could talk—first racket I ran was as the distraction for Dad's pick-pocketing schemes. I'd act lost in a crowded place, and some broad would make a big fuss about me, and meanwhile Dad would be slipping billfolds out of pockets . . ."

This sounded like a good adventure to Cordelia, but she couldn't be certain if Charlie thought so, too, because he turned his face away from her and changed the subject.

"What I'm about to show you?" he said. "You can't tell anybody about it."

"One thing to know about me, Charlie Grey: I can keep a secret."

His eyes went to her, and he put on a half smile. "I'll bet you can," he replied, and he placed his hand against a red book and pushed.

There was a groaning mechanical noise, and then with a whoosh the wall began to rotate in a slow circle. Cordelia's mouth opened in surprise as the wall of books disappeared and another tableau came into view. With a click the movement ceased, and the shelves had become a bar of polished wood, with a semicircle mirror behind a collection of bottles holding seemingly every kind of spirit, and a large case stocked with glasses of various shapes.

"Very impressive! But I thought you were going to get me out of here?"

A little light caught in one of Charlie's eyes, but they were otherwise dark and inscrutable as he watched her. "You really can keep a secret? Only Dad's inner circle knows about this. He'd go crazy on me if he knew I was showing it . . ."

"I already told you I could!" she exclaimed.

"Right. Well, truth is, this is really just a false front for a kind of passageway."

Taking a breath, Cordelia assessed her brother. "A passageway to where?"

His eyes glinted again, and he reached behind the bottles on the bar to press another button. The contraption groaned, but this time the bar rotated only halfway, so that a space was left open between the real wall and the false one. Cordelia stepped forward and saw a stairwell leading down into the darkness.

"Follow me," he urged her. They walked down a curving flight of stairs dimly illuminated by the natural light coming through the slits in the ceiling. The air was cool in the darkness, especially as they traveled farther down under the ground. By the time they reached the bottom, it was almost completely black. Charlie searched for something, and in a moment he had found a switch, and the light of a single dangling bulb made their surroundings visible.

They were standing on a dirt floor in a cavernous space, just beside a door secured with a great padlock, and beyond that a passageway branched right and left. The space underneath Dogwood was nothing much to look at, but Cordelia felt that vague excitement that comes from being someplace so secret.

"That's the storeroom." Charlie waved his hand toward the padlocked door. "There are others, of course, but that's the one on the property."

"Where do those lead?" Cordelia pointed down the two passageways.

"One goes to the garage, so that deliveries can be brought in underground. Doesn't happen very often—like I said, only a few of Dad's men know about this place, and we want to keep it that way. The other goes to the bay."

"To the bay?" The smell of earth surrounded her, and she folded her arms around her torso and shivered. "What for?"

"Oh, lots of reasons. In case the roads are blocked or being watched, and we need to get the goods in or out another way . . . Sometimes Dad says the feds are watching or waiting around the bend, and he doesn't want them to know he's leaving . . . or if there's a raid someday, this'll be the escape route, I guess."

"Where does it end?" Cordelia asked, taking a step in the direction of the bay passageway.

"Little rundown pier by a fisherman's shack—it's a good half mile of tunnel to get there."

For a moment, Cordelia thought she caught a faint whiff of sea air, and her pulse quickened with the idea of escape.

"You ready?" Charlie said, a touch of urgency heightening his voice.

Their eyes met, both sets glinting with mischief, and then they struck out, walking in easy silence. For the first time, Cordelia began to feel what it was to have a sibling—even if he was a half sibling—and having been placed in Charlie's charge began to seem a little less of a nuisance. If he was an irritation, then he was the kind of irritation one is comforted by and rather likes having around.

"How do you know the fisherman won't tell?" she asked as the darkened tunnel came to an end at a flight of old wooden stairs that led to a trapdoor.

"Old man Ostrander? He'd never—Dad did him a big favor once. He's more loyal to the Greys than he is to his own people. Plus, he drinks for free, and that's the most important thing to him."

He pushed open the heavy door and they came out on a rundown pier. Blinking in the bright light and breathing in the salty bay air, they couldn't help but shoot each other conspiratorial grins. The day was gorgeous, and they paused for a moment to share in the exhilaration of finally being free.

18

THE SOUND OF PEBBLES AGAINST GLASS AWAKENED Astrid from an anxious slumber. At first she hoped whoever it was would just go away, but when the barrage of pebbles continued, she cracked an eye and saw that she had fallen asleep on a daybed on the far side of her bedroom and that she was still wearing her pale peach silk evening frock from the night before. It was sleeveless, in a boyish cut, with a scalloped pattern of beads on the gauzy overdress, and when she'd put it on last night, she'd thought how much Charlie would have admired her in it. One high-heeled shoe was half on her right foot, and the other lay across the room, near the undisturbed coverlet she ordinarily slept under. She pushed herself up enough to shove open the leaded windowpane.

"What?" she called irritably.

"Astrid, it's me!"

At the sound of Cordelia's voice, she scrambled to her feet and popped her head out the window. The air outside was unbearably fresh. "Oh, thank God! I've *missed* you," she caroled. Down below, on the drive, stood her new best friend in a blindingly white dress. Astrid pushed her piles of blond hair out of her face and beamed.

Cordelia waved and smiled and stepped out of the shadow of an oak tree. "I've missed you, too!"

"How did you ever escape Dogwood?" As soon as she said it, her happiness flagged. There was no way Cordelia had escaped alone. Plus, the place where she was standing was too far for a girl's arm—Charlie was with her, hiding behind the tree trunk, probably. Cordelia cleared her throat and stepped forward, but before she could answer, Astrid pulled back and slammed the window shut. She threw herself down on the daybed, put a silky pillow over her face, and told herself to go back to sleep as quickly as possible. But her heart kept ticking, almost audibly, and pretty soon she realized that she wasn't going to have any peace. For a whole day she had been very good and not returned any of Charlie's calls and not even thought about him any more than was necessary. She still hated him for what he might have done—for all the ugly jealousy he'd made her feel—and yet she knew she wouldn't be able to stand it if he left before she caught at least a glimpse of him.

With as much cool hauteur as she could manage, she removed the pillow from her face, retrieved her wayward shoe, and made her way down to the main foyer. By the time she cracked the heavy front door, Charlie was visible. He wore a white T-shirt tucked in to brown trousers and carried a paper sack in one arm. His hair had less grease in it than usual and so appeared fairer and thicker; it was parted down the middle and rose up in two hills on either side. Astrid crossed her arms over her chest and leaned against the door frame until they noticed her. For a moment, it seemed as though Charlie was going to rush at Astrid, but his sister put a hand up to his chest to stop him. Then Cordelia approached the house alone.

"I'm glad to see *you*—but what is *he* doing here?" Astrid demanded.

Cordelia smiled apologetically. "I know that earring looks bad—but if you could only see how he misses you. All morning he begged me to see if I couldn't get you to take his call. He said he doesn't know what he's done to deserve your anger—"

"And you believe him?"

Cordelia turned and glanced over her shoulder. Charlie was watching, hands stuffed in pockets, his big frame inclined toward the girls as though it was all he could do to keep himself put. "I don't know. What I do know is, it's a beautiful day, and we're finally free, and it won't be any fun without you, and we have three egg sandwiches, and only two of us to eat them."

Astrid knew the thing to do was to put her nose in the air and say she'd love to if her afternoon weren't so packed. But seeing Charlie walk away now would be agony, and before she could stop herself, she'd stepped forward onto the drive. Her heart was still tight as a fist—but at least now he would get to see her in the peach dress.

"All right, Charlie Grey!" she called defiantly. "You can have me for the afternoon if you dare."

Though the day was utterly cloudless, Astrid's face was occasionally made cold by the currents created by various flying contraptions zooming up and landing on Everly Field, in Queens. She reclined like a princess on the checkered picnic cloth, with her head rested against Charlie's hip. A few feet away Cordelia sat with her long legs folded under, her hair tied back in a loose bun, watching the pilots pop the balloons that occasionally rose from the crowd and high into the vast blue arc above the enormous green field. The whole day had such charm, Astrid thought; she was happy to be here, watching the crowds at the airfield, instead of lonely at home and wondering what her boyfriend was doing without her.

"Charlie, why haven't you ever taken me up in an airplane?" Astrid demanded, turning her remaining half sandwich in her hands, contemplating the best place to bite into the white bread. After an absence of some days, he looked particularly handsome to her, and she was struggling to keep part of her heart angry at him. But being difficult was a talent she'd mastered at a young age, and she was managing to be difficult with Charlie now, even if he was so broad and strong. "It's only five dollars a person, and they take you all around."

"No, thank you."

Astrid and Cordelia exchanged glances over the odd swiftness of his reply.

Then Astrid frowned theatrically, which caused Charlie to return to the sweet tone he'd been trying to win her over with all afternoon. "Maybe a boat ride instead? I could take you out on one of those ferries that tour all the inlets and serve champagne. Wouldn't you like that?"

"Boats bore me," Astrid replied acidly. "And if I find out you've taken your other girl up in an airplane, that will be the end of us."

It was not her first comment of the kind that day, and she could see that this latest really chafed Charlie. "There's no other girl, so stop laying into me," he shot back.

"I don't see any *other* reason why you wouldn't take me up," Astrid went on airily.

"Not after you disappeared the other night. If I let you go up in a plane, what's to guarantee me you'll ever come down?"

Astrid's lips assumed a pout. "Aw, I said I was sorry, didn't I?"

Cordelia, supporting herself on a long, sun-darkened

arm and shielding her eyes with the flattened fingers of her other hand, leaned back to look at the show high above them. "I've never been in an airplane," she said to no one in particular.

"Take us, Charlie!" Astrid demanded girlishly.

But all her prodding must have irritated him too much—she was trying to be kittenish now, but it appeared to be too late. "No," he said and turned away.

There was something very stern about the vertical slabs of his face, which must have amused Cordelia, because she laughed and asked, "Oh, why not?"

Charlie cleared his throat, and when he addressed Cordelia, he softened his voice. "I'm afraid of—I don't like heights."

"*Charlie,*" Astrid said, smiling. "You've never told me that!"

"Yeah, well, now you know."

Cordelia changed the subject. "Well, I could go and make sure she behaves," she offered. "I'm blood, after all."

Charlie, who was resting on a thickly muscled forearm, squinted at his sister, seeming almost to consider her proposal. "Yes, you're blood, and I'm just starting to feel grateful for it, but it's still too soon after your little indiscretion for me to let you go off by yourself in a flying contraption."

"Oh, Charlie," Astrid exclaimed flirtatiously, spreading her fingers against his stomach. "Don't be mean to dear Cordelia!

She didn't even know who the Hales were . . . and who knows, maybe it's true love, and they'll be like Romeo and Juliet, and bring peace to rival houses."

"Juliet dies at the end of the book," Charlie snapped.

Perhaps he was just fearful of the idea of going up high, or maybe she had teased and pushed too much, but either way his tone stung. The sound of his voice had ruined her afternoon. "It's not a book—it's a play, you big fool," she huffed.

Cordelia, seeing that she had not been successful in bringing harmony back to Astrid and Charlie, watched a little red-and-black biplane making figure eights high in the air. All across the field, arms reached heavenward, pointing to show young children or old folks what daring feats were possible in the modern world. For a while it had seemed that the novelty of escaping Dogwood, and the company of good friends, would be enough to distract her, but now that Astrid and Charlie had retreated into their lover's quarrels, Cordelia's thoughts returned to Thom. Soon after that came the longing. She would have taken any tiny scrap of him—a glimpse of his sideways twist of a grin, or the grazing touch of his arm if by lucky chance they passed in a crowd.

"That's Max Darby's plane," Charlie said after the girls were quiet awhile.

"Max Darby?" Cordelia's eyes met her brother's. "How strange—I saw him flying my first day in New York."

Astrid, who was glaring off into the distance, stood up

suddenly. "I'd like to be taken home now," she announced to no one in particular.

"That boy's going to get himself killed." Charlie shot Cordelia an exasperated expression, ignoring Astrid. "He's only eighteen, and he's always trying to do some ridiculous stunt just for the attention—he's planning to fly to the Florida Keys now, and they say he wants to be the youngest man ever to make a solo transatlantic crossing."

"Transatlantic?" Cordelia listened to the word echoing in her thoughts, trying to imagine the vastness it implied. "You mean—"

"New York to Paris," Charlie interrupted.

New York to Paris—Cordelia wasn't sure she'd ever heard such a wondrous phrase. The delight of it faded, however, when she realized that Astrid was stamping her foot, her fists placed angrily at her hips.

"What?" Charlie shook his head, but did not wait for her to answer before standing. "All right, all right, we'll take you home."

Then Cordelia rose, too, and the three of them walked into the wind, toward the car they had borrowed from the Marshes' garage. Astrid charged ahead. As her hips swished, the peach overlay of her evening gown was pulled tight against her skin. Charlie walked along beside her, and Cordelia, who was uninterested in whatever game it was they were now playing, turned and walked backward for several strides, taking in the great expanse of green and brown, the crowds of spectators off to the side, and the big glass-and-metal hangars beyond them.

Before she could turn again, she heard a collective gasp rise up from the crowd: The black-and-red biplane was heading straight for the ground in a nosedive. Cordelia's hand jumped involuntarily to cover her mouth. But just when the plane seemed perilously close to crashing to Earth, the pilot pulled back and his trajectory reversed—for a moment, he seemed to skim the ground, and then he climbed upward in the direction of infinite blue.

"Hey!" Charlie called. "You coming?"

Cordelia shivered and turned toward her brother's voice. He had reached the car, and Astrid was already situated in the front seat, her eyes gazing directly in front of her. Smiling privately, Cordelia hurried after them. That morning she had felt bound, but she didn't feel that way anymore. It was as though she'd drawn some inspiration from the aviator's fearlessness, the way he charged toward heaven or hell just as he pleased, as though there were no such thing as gravity. She wanted to be fearless, too, and follow the yearning within her heart to see Thom Hale again.

19

CORDELIA HAD ONLY THE SOUND OF HER OWN breathing to keep her company as she stepped through the cool darkness. Occasionally she put out a hand to touch the wall, which was lined with unfinished planks, and she quickly learned to do so gingerly for fear of picking up splinters. Taking the secret tunnel that began in Dogwood's library was more frightening by herself, but more thrilling, too.

Still she was relieved to come upon the flight of stairs that ended in a trapdoor. She pushed up through it and found herself, for the second time that day, in the tall reeds of a sandy stretch of land near a pebble beach. The sky was a deep blue by then, and the pier where she and Charlie had hailed a passing fisherman that morning jutted out in front of her, over the smooth, lustrous water. She went to the edge of the dock and stood there in her red dress. She had been specific about the red dress. The air was warm enough that she didn't even need to cover her shoulders; all that was required was a few yards of silk, secured with inch-wide straps above a U-shaped neckline, falling loosely away from the skin.

Then she went through the series of actions, just as she had described them on the telephone. She took a cigarette from the small eel-skin purse she carried and lit a match. The flame flared up, a flash in the warm night air. A few seconds passed, and then she heard the lazy splashing of oars moving through still water. She didn't make him out until he was almost at the pier, and by then her face tingled with anticipation.

Thom was sitting in a rowboat, wearing white slacks and a navy collared shirt with tiny gold stripes under a beige cardigan. His hair was burnished with oil, and his face was lit with a subdued smile that grew when they were close enough to see each other in detail. It was strange to see him now, when she knew what kind of life he came from, for he wasn't at all like Charlie—he had none of her brother's bluntness, and his features were so much more whittled and fine, and he seemed to take everything in stride instead of going so extravagantly hot and cold.

Placing her cigarette between her teeth, she lowered

herself so that she was sitting on the edge of the pier. He stood, balanced himself in the well-worn boat, and then extended his hand. She bent, took it, and falling a little against him, came down into the hull. There was unsteadiness beneath her, but Thom had her solidly by the shoulders. A bird cawed overhead, and the sound echoed across the lonely bay waters. He took the cigarette from her lips and threw it over the side, and then paused, studying her with those calm green-brown eyes. She waited for him to kiss her. When he finally did, any trepidation she had had—about seeing him against her father's wishes or using Charlie's secret to her advantage—all but disappeared. She swayed with it, her consciousness rising up to the place where her mouth was open to his.

"I've been thinking about doing that since I last saw you," he said, bringing his head back but still holding on to her by the torso.

"Is that right?" she answered playfully.

His only reply was that heartbreaking smile.

How interesting she felt to be out in the world without a single soul knowing her whereabouts, and at the same time wearing a very fashionable dress. Something he'd said to her on the first night they met, about it being a perfect moment, repeated in her thoughts. Now it seemed to her that every moment with him was its own variety of perfection, and she was happy to be in this one as long as it lasted—the boat rocking just slightly, the mingling smells of salt and musk, his grip on her light and strong at the same time.

What followed was a string of moments, each following the last in a glittering strand: They coasted across the water, coming eventually to an abandoned stretch of road where he'd left his car. She hardly cared if they went anywhere, but then he started the motor and they headed in the direction of the city.

"More speakeasies?" she asked as they drove.

"You'll see," he answered.

Along they went, in no particular hurry, into the darkness and the city beyond. The weather had been fine for some weeks now, but that night was the first that held the heat of the day even long after dark had settled in. All over town, in every kind of joint, people were drunk with summer.

Eventually Thom pulled over on an East Side block at the heart of the metropolis, although it was quiet at that hour. He came around and helped Cordelia out, draping his sweater over her shoulders as she stepped onto the curb.

"But I'm not cold," she protested sweetly.

"You might be, where we're going" was all the explanation he gave.

The darkened building in front of them appeared to have no solid walls—it was difficult to see anything, except where little lights strung on a wire illuminated a structure of massive beams. They stepped forward, into the shadows, over piles of cable and brick and steel. This was not the kind of scene she had imagined Thom escorting her to—but by then she had frequented drinking establishments lurking behind all manner of incongruous facades, and so, for a few brief minutes, she considered herself now too sophisticated to be surprised.

A man in a hard hat and undershirt came forward from the gloom. He met Thom's eyes but did not so much as glance at Cordelia. Their hands clasped for a few seconds, exchanging something. Then the man lit a lantern.

"Watch your step, miss," he said, before leading them deeper into the site. Thom's hand rested on the small of her back as they followed. "Stand there." The man indicated the place with a burly arm, and Thom eased her toward it.

There was the sound of a lever being pulled, a creaking of hinges, a slipping of ropes. She reached for Thom's arm, and he pulled her closer to him, brushing his lips against her cheekbone.

"I hope no one is drunk up there," she joked as they began to rise faster.

"No," he replied lightly. "I thought I'd show you something more interesting this evening. Just you and me."

As they went higher, they passed through less-completed parts of the structure, and they could just make out the faces of other buildings, patchworks of illumination and darkness, beyond the lattice of beams. By the time the lift came to a stop, they were higher than any of the surrounding buildings. A real city is never dark, even at night; tonight, with the humid air to reflect its limitless activity, Manhattan was a soft purple. Cordelia couldn't be sure if it really was colder up high, or if it was the dizzying height that made her shiver.

"Come on." Thom took her hand, grinning again. "We've only got ten minutes."

"To do what?" she whispered, but he was already stepping carefully along a great steel beam, pulling her behind him. Her breath was short, and she was glad the ground was too far below them to make out. At that perilous height, it occurred to her that despite his charm and beautifully smooth face—or maybe because of it—Thom was a boy she had been warned not to be with. No one in the world knew where she was—a little while ago she had been proud of that fact, but now she began to wonder at herself for allowing him to take her someplace so secret and so dangerous. She shuddered to think what one good push would do and how little all her pretty red silk would do to cushion the fatal fall.

But then she caught sight of the view, and her breath came back to her. "Oh!" was all she could manage.

Below—a long ways below—the island tapered away from them in electric rows that were sometimes neat and that sometimes jerked unexpectedly. Apartment buildings and office towers reached for the sky with varying degrees of success, their broad vertical lines silently striving. There was a good deal of movement through the arteries of the city, everything flowing and bright, around and around, as though according to the directives of a very restless heart. They stood near the edge; one of Thom's arms wrapped around a great thrust of steel, the other holding her secure by the waist.

The height no longer made her feel fragile. Now it created a sense of being above it all, almost invincible, and she couldn't help but think of the tender girl who used to be her best friend and who was now out there, among the lights down there, entertaining a crowd with her voice. Cordelia smiled wistfully and thought that a city is a very wonderful thing, after all.

Letty was indeed out there among millions of New Yorkers, and though her name was not in fact a cause for illumination yet, she was by then at ease in her job. She'd told herself that it was just like acting, and she had put on a persona. After that, she bumped into fewer things, and her movements became more fluid, her smile more winning. Paulette and the other girls agreed: Letty Larkspur was a natural. She'd taken to the job as quickly as any cigarette girl in Seventh Heaven history. Also she was petite, and that helped, because she could move across the crowded floor with such alacrity.

The nights had begun to blend together, and usually she only saw a few hours of daylight in between, because she was returning from work so late and so entirely exhausted. Her feet were always swollen, her head foggy. But it seemed to her a noble kind of fatigue, and in truth, there was no place else Letty would rather have been. Except, of course, onstage—but in the meantime she felt very lucky to have the club to go to. And every day in New York was so obviously a new day—hopeful, chock-full, yawning with possibility.

"Letty!" Grady called out as she passed. He was at the end of the bar, perched on his usual stool, wearing herringbone and nursing a beer.

But she was too busy. She tried to meet his eyes over her shoulder, to let him know she had heard him, but she wasn't certain if he'd noticed. Anyway, she hadn't the time. The room was full, and the patrons were giddy and ready to buy anything that was put under their noses. It was a sea of faces, heads bent together as far as the eye could see: women in turbans, men with a fine glaze over the combed-straight strands of their hair, gesticulating with one hand, balancing glass and cigarette in the other. Girls in cream-colored uniforms that offered varying degrees of coverage rose above their shoulders, inclining forward with stuffed brassieres and glossy smiles. The chatter was rapid-fire, but it was no competition for the band, as usual. She moved between tables with the grace of a swan, bending back and forth, flashing her eyes when necessary. There was a rhythm to the job, which she became more expert at with every passing hour. She listened to her intuition and knew when to be salty with a patron and when to be sweet.

"Letty!" She had done a turn about the room and again passed Grady's barstool in a rush.

"Hello!" she replied this time. No one was waving bills at her now, and two or three other girls were engaged in transactions only a few tables in. Up onstage, Alice Grenadine, the big blonde with the privileged relationship to the house manager, was beginning her first number, pressing her palms into her lap and batting her lashes outrageously.

"If I buy a pack of smokes, will you talk a minute?"

"Why not, mister?" Letty gave Grady a bold wink as she turned away from the stage, bringing her shoulder coquettishly toward her chin. Paulette had given her some pointers on this maneuver, and she'd been practicing in the mirror. "What's your brand?"

"Lucky Strikes." He handed her a coin and waved away the change. Then he began unwrapping the foil and placed a cigarette between his teeth. She struck a match along the side of her box of wares and lit it for him. This, too, was a move she'd practiced in the mirror, although she had not done it for a customer yet.

"Thank you," he said. Then she knew she'd pulled it off,

and she felt almost giddy to have a new trick. As he exhaled, he moved his hand to his head, just above his ear, thoughtfully scratching. "I've been wanting to tell you . . . I think I know where your friend is."

The smile dropped away from her face. "What friend?" she said.

At the front entrance, a man whose face was already pink with drink was yelling about being let in. Every table in the place was already occupied, and the bar was crowded with those who wanted to be inside even if it meant standing, but despite Mr. Cole's calm explanation of this fact, the pink-faced fellow only yelled louder.

"Didn't you say her name was Cordelia? I read about a girl named Cordelia, from Ohio, similar age as you, in one of the papers this morning. She's the bootlegger Darius Grey's long-lost daughter—you must have known? Grey is overjoyed to have her back, sparing no expense, et cetera, et cetera. And I know she was here the other night, when you said you saw her, because apparently she came with Duluth Hale's son, who is of course Grey's sworn enemy, and her father sent some of his goons to pull her out quick." Grady paused to fidget with the stub of his cigarette. His words had been coming in a tumble, as though he was nervous. "So perhaps she wasn't running away from you after all."

Letty's eyes became damp, and she felt that knot of pain

in her throat that means that tears may be imminent, no matter how fiercely one orders them away. The girl she'd called her best friend for half her life had, in less than a week, become unknown to her. Cordelia had climbed several social rungs, and maybe she'd had to be a solo act to do it, but in any event, her clothes and company were now better than any they used to imagine together. Letty no longer thought it was only a secret that had separated them—for Cordelia had seen her, she knew where she was, and still had not bothered to send word, and Grady's kind explanation did not change this fact. Perhaps she was too fine now to be friends with a girl who worked for her keep . . . But there was nothing for Letty to do but hide the wound and try her best not to care.

"I don't know. In fact, I've never heard of any of those people in my whole life." Letty swallowed her tears and then, as if on cue, smiled incandescently.

Before Grady could say anything more, she sashayed forward along the bar without looking back. Grady was nice, and she knew everything he did was well intentioned, but she wanted to be far away from him and whatever he knew. And after she had made a few exchanges and blushed once or twice, half sincerely, she had stopped feeling whatever it was that she hadn't wanted to feel, and forgotten about Cordelia—mostly.

"We just drove down from New Haven today," said a slender man with a smooth chin and blindingly blue eyes as she passed. "Took my last exam this morning and . . . Hey, girlie!"

"Yes?" Letty turned toward him.

"How much are those red roses?" he asked.

She told him, and he scrambled in his pockets. Once she'd handed him the flower, he paused, studied it, and grinned. "Here," he said, extending it toward her face. "Will you marry me?"

All his friends—who were slim and dressed in light-colored suits like him—laughed. Letty colored, unsure whether he was flirting with her or making fun. She plucked the flower from his hand, and broke the stem, which inspired the other four or five boys to hoot and applaud. Drawing herself up, she tucked the flower in her hair, just behind her ear. She paused another few seconds and then stepped away.

"I'll just have to think about it," she said and moved on.

This inspired even more uproarious hooting and catcalling. But she followed Paulette's advice, as usual, and limited herself to a few sentences at maximum, and continued to go about her job.

She was coming around, passing the entrance, when her attention was once again called for. "Hey there, Letty!"

Glancing up, she saw Mr. Cole looking at her with a pleading expression.

"Yes?" She went toward him, wide-eyed. That was when

she noticed the fellow standing next to him. He had a fine jaw line, a trim mustache, brows that were dark and flat, and an intense stare. It was a matter of several more seconds before she recognized him as the man who had pulled her apron strings a few nights ago. Then his name began coming back to her. Amory . . . Amory . . . Amory Glenn.

"This is Mr. Glenn," Mr. Cole informed her in a buttery tone.

Beyond them, she could see the pink-faced man growing irate over what was about to happen.

"He's going to take his usual table to the left of the stage—and he'd like you to escort him."

Letty's eyes darted from one man to the other. Her carefully maintained persona flagged for a moment, and she grew nervous and briefly wondered how she would ever determine the correct thing to say. She wasn't even really sure which table Mr. Cole meant, although she supposed it would be easy enough to find—there weren't many tables open. Summoning courage, she replied, "Of course."

"Excellent," Amory Glenn said, stepping down onto the main floor and then following a few feet behind Letty as they made their way through the crowded club. People were looking at her differently now, she sensed, and she thought it might be a good idea to try and say something. But she was petrified that if she wasn't very careful, she might become clumsy again or lose her footing, so she kept her gaze steady and tried her best to appear natural.

"There you are," she said, when they had reached the small table he'd occupied the other night. She turned her petite frame in his direction. He was handsome, the way a rake in an old-fashioned novel is handsome, but he had another quality, which one could not quite see but which was felt strongly, like a far-off astral body, barely visible yet capable of changing the tides. The candle on the table was already lit, and she was not allowed to take drink orders, so she smiled as best she could and said, "Is there anything else I can get you?" When he didn't answer immediately, she said, "Cigarettes, candy, flowers?"

He smiled from one corner of his mouth, and reached out and plucked the rose from behind her ear. His eyes shone, and twirling the flower between his palms, he let his eyes dart from it to her. "Tell the waiter I'll have my usual," he said.

"Yes, of course." She gave a little curtsy. "He knows . . . ?"

"He knows." With the flower still in his hand, he turned his eyes away from her and lowered himself into his chair. She had moved a few feet back already when she saw him raise his finger in the air and add, almost as an afterthought, "Oh, and there is one other thing."

"Yes?"

His dark eyes rose to meet hers, and he grinned again. "I'd like to take you out."

Now Letty's cheeks turned a truly deep shade of red. She shifted on her feet and glanced at the people around her. If she was being watched, all the nearby patrons were doing a good job of hiding it. Her palms were gripping the side of the tray—they were slick with sweat. Letty blinked. The walk to Mr. Glenn's table had stirred so much discomfort in her that she couldn't really say the idea of an evening with him was desirable, exactly. Of course, she'd never spent the evening alone with any man, and even in the abstract it sounded a little wrong. But as her eyelids fluttered up and down twice more, and she watched Miss Grenadine beam into her spotlight, she felt something old inside of her turn over and something new rise to take its place.

"Tomorrow is my only night off this week," she said breathlessly.

"Perfect." He leaned back in the chair, tossing the flower so that it landed among the foil-wrapped chocolate in her tray. "Write down your address for me when you get the chance. I'll pick you up at eight."

As she walked across the room, she made out no faces, and if anyone signaled for her, she didn't notice. Her pulse slowed to normal, and she stepped more lightly, with a very liberating sense of *why on Earth not?*

That's what Cordelia would say, she thought. Except that Cordelia wasn't around anymore to give advice or tell her what to do, and though the thought had saddened her earlier, she now found something freeing in the great, irreversible distance that had come up between them.

"That's New York," Thom said to Cordelia from their precarious perch, after a few moments of awestruck silence. "I thought you should see the lay of the land, since you're one of us now."

"Thank you," she whispered, finding that she believed it to be true. She was a long way from home, and in the company of a boy she barely knew, and yet she felt curiously more like herself with every passing second. But she couldn't find the words to express that to Thom, and so instead she asked, "What is all this?" as the wind whipped her skirt against her bare legs.

"Right now it's just a lot of metal." He paused to light a cigarette, which was not so easy up there. "But someday it's going to be a skyscraper, the tallest one in the world. It's Mr. Chrysler's project."

"Mr. Chrysler who makes cars?"

"Yup." Thom exhaled. "It's only thirty or so stories now, but they say it's going to be more than seventy by the time it's done."

Cordelia whistled, picturing the tallest building in Union. The dreariness of the place she was from came back to her for a moment, and before she could help it, she heard herself say, "You can't imagine how different my life was a week ago—and Darius . . . my father . . . has been so good to me."

"I suppose he has," Thom replied quietly.

She turned her face away, showing him her profile and focusing her gaze toward the faraway tip of the island. With all the courage of that panorama, she continued: "But I didn't come all this way just to follow another set of rules. That's what I came to get away from."

"We'll find a way." After that he looked into her eyes a long time.

Nothing more needed to be said, and when their time was up, he took her hand to lead her back. They were more careful on their return trip, and though earlier Cordelia had hoped for dancing, it was she who'd suggested they not go anywhere they might be recognized. They spent a few hours sitting in his car by the side of a country road, and she told him all about her childhood and how she'd come to decide to run away to the city. She'd trimmed any mention of John from her stories, of course; perhaps she'd tell him someday, though the image of him from the train had been too private even to share with Letty.

"You'd better get me home," she said, lifting her head off his chest when she saw that the sky was getting lighter.

He nodded sadly.

At the pier, she kissed him good night, but neither of them had had enough, and he insisted on walking her all the way home. This didn't seem like a good idea, and she furrowed her brow, but she couldn't stand the thought of parting yet, either. After a minute of pretending to decide what to do, she showed him the trapdoor, and then he escorted her all the long way through the dark tunnel so that he could really kiss her good-bye, one final time, beneath the library at Dogwood and three floors of sleeping members of the Grey family bootlegging concern.

Their lips parted, and he stepped back.

"I'll figure out a way to see you soon," he said and turned.

She watched as he began walking back down the tunnel. Then she remembered what it was to miss him, how it hurt her like a physical ailment. "Thom!" she gasped.

When he paused, her heart leapt. It was so quiet down there that she could hear both of them breathing.

"I've told you all about my silly childhood, and you've told me nothing of yours . . ."

Then he twisted, and even in the darkness she could see the perfect white teeth that his smile revealed. "I guess I haven't."

"Well, then the night can't be over yet," she whispered.

As they tiptoed up the servants' stairs, her brain began to whir with the implications. But somehow—despite the men all over the house who slept with guns under their pillows—what they were doing didn't feel wrong. They simply had too much more to say to each other.

By the time they had made sure the door was locked, and she had hung her red silk dress up to prevent wrinkles, it was very late indeed. When she lay down in her slip beside Thom, her thoughts grew blurry. Contentment spread through her bones, and just before she fell asleep, his lips brushed gently across hers. Tomorrow he would tell her all the places he'd been and all his secrets and who he really was inside. But for now it was enough that she fit so nicely in his arms.

20

"DON'T TAKE IT HARD ABOUT LUKE, DARLING."

Astrid, who had practically forgotten Luke since she'd last seen him at the White Cove Country Club, lowered the glossy pages of her magazine and peered at her mother, who was unfortunately up earlier than was customary for Mrs. Marsh. A moment ago, Astrid had been happily ensconced under the pale pink bedding of her low, wide bed. Now her mother had joined her, propped against the half moon–shaped, polished oak headboard. The third Mrs. Marsh had washed off the effects of whatever she had done the previous evening, and she was now dressed in an ivory kimono and her hair was drawn back in a simple, flattering bun. She had once been a beauty—so everyone said—and her daughter despised moments when she caught a glimpse of this truth.

"Darling," Astrid replied as she slowly turned a page, "I never take anything hard."

"No . . ." Virginia paused, and her dark eyes roved the room. "I never used to, either."

Astrid had lived in many fine houses, and her quarters in Marsh Hall were neither the best nor the worst that she had occupied. The walls were painted a lovely glacial shade, the ceiling was coved and cream colored, and the furniture was simple and handsome, with either polished marquetry finish or pale pink upholstery. The décor was perhaps a little serious for a girl who so appreciated fun, and was not nearly as fine as the suite sometimes occupied by Billie, who was after all a Marsh by blood. But Astrid had long ago come to view a residence as a very temporary factor in a girl's life, and regarded this particular space with no greater or lesser importance than she would have any other dressing room.

"Never taking anything too hard is a luxury of youth," her mother went on, pushing herself up on one arm.

"Don't be melodramatic!" Astrid tossed her magazine aside and, picking up the oval mirror on the bedside table, began rearranging the hair that crossed her forehead. She found her reflection very pretty just then, and didn't want anything spoiling the joy of that. "I suppose you heard the Greys are having another party tonight, and wanted to see if I could get you an invitation . . ."

"There are so many parties tonight, I couldn't possibly even if they did invite me." Virginia drew her fingers across the bedspread and then began to fuss with its threads aggressively, the way a child might. "Anyway, that isn't what I meant at all . . . it's only—how is it between you and Charlie these days?"

"Oh, very well, I suppose." Astrid put away the mirror and met her mother's eyes.

"Very well?"

"Yes." Astrid watched as her mother's large green irises rolled toward her hands and back to meet her daughter's. She tried to keep her gaze steady and to show no signs of weakness, for she couldn't stand the idea of her mother knowing that she suspected Charlie of cheating.

"It seems to me you haven't seen Charlie lately quite so much as you usually do. And—he couldn't have liked the way you were looking at Luke the other day."

"You may be right." Astrid gave a delicate little shrug. "But he doesn't know about that, does he?"

Now it was the mother's turn to sigh; she pushed herself up and walked across the plush carpet, pausing in such a way that both women could see themselves in the polished oak standing mirror. They had the same eyes, but Astrid shuddered at the comparison.

"All I am saying, my dear, is *do* be sweet with Charlie . . . He's quite a catch for you."

"Well, I should think I am quite a catch for *him*." Astrid threw back the covers, stood up, and wrapped herself in a pink silk robe. "Anyway, I am always sweet with everybody."

"Well, don't be sweet with other boys, or—"

"I wonder that you care," Astrid interrupted aridly. She walked across the sunken main part of the room and rested her hand against the doorknob to the bathroom. "You never *used* to care who was courting me."

Her mother stepped to the window and glanced down. Behind her the grounds stretched out, dense and leafy, and for a brief moment, Astrid appreciated the striking profile that had made her mother famous as a debutante.

"Of course I did," she answered carefully. "Only, it matters more now. You see, things are not very good between Harrison and me at present . . . You know, of course, the difficulties of unmarried women with expensive taste . . . and the Greys *do* do very well."

"Oh!" Astrid rolled her eyes and flipped her short hair. Things were never very good with Mother and any of her husbands, and she scoffed at the notion that she should now be responsible for their keep. "You can't be serious."

The older woman gave a heavy sigh and turned to look

at her daughter. There was something sad, even serious, in her face, and Astrid, who had woken with the conviction that she would allow nothing weighty and melancholy into her day, glanced away before striding into the next room and drawing a very hot, fragrant bath.

But the steaming water only proved to make things worse—as she sank into the vast marble tub, thoughts of her embarrassing mother and the boyfriend whom she could never bend to her will steeped along with the rest of her. And so when she returned to her bedroom, damp and with her blood at a boil, she decided that she couldn't stand the idea of lunching with her mother, and instead dressed for an afternoon at the White Cove Country Club.

"Hey there." Astrid, wearing beige jodhpurs, knee-high black boots, and a starched white shirt, leaned girlishly against the white fence and waited. In a few seconds, Luke turned around to look at her. He tried not to smile, but failed. Then he gave the reins in his hand a gentle tug and came walking toward her in the bright sunlight, with his tall, handsome horse close behind. The club was over her shoulder, and the fine ladies lunching there were too far away to be heard, or to hear.

"What are you doing here?" he asked, his black hair falling forward over his sparkly eyes.

"Don't worry, I don't have any messages from my mother."

Luke averted his gaze.

"I have a present for your friend." Astrid smiled and produced a shiny red apple. The roan horse ambled forward, splashing mud. When Astrid offered her the treat, the animal quickly bent to take it.

"Thank you," Luke said. He had been trying to look at his shoes, but now his gaze returned, fixedly and with some yearning, to Astrid's face. "But you'll spoil her."

"That's exactly the point." Astrid winked and leaned more heavily on the fence. She could smell the sweat on the horse's coat and the grass behind her, but she wanted to be close enough to smell Luke. "*All* girls should be spoiled."

"But you're not," he replied, his voice becoming tentative and intimate.

Astrid shielded her eyes from the sun, which had just emerged from behind a cloud. "Of course I am! And I suspect you rather like me that way."

"Miss Donal—" he began, trying to sound serious.

"Oh, don't worry, darling. I am not here to make things complicated for you. Only . . . I *had* hoped you would give me a riding lesson."

"Yes," he answered, too quickly. The eagerness in his tone could only have been more satisfying to her if her mother was on hand to witness it. A flush overcame his cheeks, and his mouth struggled between a smile and a frown. "Only, I can't today."

"Tomorrow?"

After a minute, he gave a shy, sweet nod. "You wear the riding clothes well, miss," he added.

For a moment they stood silently watching each other. She liked the way his face was transformed by happiness, and it was almost worth coming here for that alone, and not just because flirting with him was excellent vengeance on her mother and Charlie. Then, before she could help it, her thoughts had turned toward Charlie, and the despicable earring—and she decided that she wanted a trophy, too. She stepped forward, and placed her fingers on the back of his neck. Their faces were so close that for a moment there was the suggestion of a kiss. Instead she unknotted the bandana he wore around his neck. It was white and green, the club's colors, and his name was embroidered in the corner. Holding his gaze, she stepped back and tied it jauntily just over her collar.

"Better now, isn't it?" she asked, her mouth twisting into a mercurial grin.

Before he could answer, she twirled and walked back toward the club, slowly enough that he could admire her walk for a good while. At the luncheon room, she found two other of Miss Porter's girls and sat with them for an hour or so, picking at a Waldorf salad, saying little, and feeling tremendously gratified. By the time she walked back into the cool foyer of Marsh Hall, her mood was entirely improved. She had put her mother's shaming gloominess, and her own fears about Charlie, out of her mind, and she undid the bandana as she crossed toward the stairs. When she passed her mother's suite, she dropped her trophy in front of the door, just to let the old lady wonder.

But perhaps that sensation of lightness was something ineffable and wonderful in the air, for at just that moment, in another corner of White Cove, her friend Cordelia was waking up, taking in slow, sweet breaths, and feeling equally invigorated. There was still an imprint in the bed where Thom had slept, and her slip was clinging to her skin with a delicate sweat. Her body felt well rested and warm, and when she put her fingers lightly against the skin of her face, she realized she was already smiling.

"Thom," she whispered aloud, just to experience the shivers the sound of his name always caused, before throwing back the covers, wrapping a robe around her shoulders, and crossing toward the balcony.

The sun was already high in the sky, and down below, the lawn was abuzz with activity. It did not occur to her that she should have been afraid of her nighttime activities being discovered, or worried about whether Thom had been able to sneak out of the house unnoticed, until after she saw her father. But by that time, Darius was walking in her direction—wearing light blue slacks and a matching waistcoat—his arm raised in greeting and his face smiling.

"Cord, my darling dear!" he called from three stories below, in a tone that left no doubt about the fact that she had gotten away with having Thom sleep in her bed, and that all was well at Dogwood.

"Good morning, Daddy!" she called, waving happily.

"You and Charlie have been so good, I thought I'd bring a party to you tonight," he went on, his voice raised so that she could hear him over the hubbub. He gestured to the caterers, bearing crates of lemons and limes and seltzers and other things necessary for a gay time. Lights were being strung along the perimeter of the white tent, and musicians were hauling their instruments across a great stretch of grass. "But in the meantime, get dressed—I want us to have a family lunch on the south verandah."

"All right!" Cordelia turned and tried to forget the exquisite lightness with which Thom had held her. She stuffed her hands into her pockets, as though that would make it easier to act as though nothing in particular had occurred during the night. But as her fingers thrust into the linen robe, she felt a scrap of paper, and by the time she had unfolded it, she knew it was from Thom.

I didn't think it was wise for me to sleep, and slipped out before anyone else was awake. But I can't stand another day without seeing you. Meet me on the dock, whenever you can get away? I will be waiting.

Cordelia bit her lip and wondered how she was going to be able to stand the hours between now and when she next saw him. Her blood had begun to move very rapidly, and it seemed to her that every second when she wasn't looking into Thom's eyes was going to be its own unique form of torture. She crossed to her dressing room and removed a cigarette from the pack that was lying on the top of the vanity table. They were Lucky Strikes—she had acquired them on one of her nights out, when she was still allowed to leave the house, and she was glad of them now, because the measured inhalations of smoke did bring a little calm. Then she held the lit match to the scrap of paper from Thom, dropped it into the silver ashtray, and watched his words disappear in the flames.

When the cigarette was done, she dressed herself in a nude tunic, belting it with a black sash the way Astrid would have done, low on the hips. As she arranged her hair around her face, it occurred to her that a party was the perfect cover—after all, there would be so many people that she would not be easily missed, and the last time there was a fete on the grounds, her father had absented himself rather early. Just when the evening was really getting going, she would tell Milly that she needed a few hours of quiet and privacy, and then she could make her way through the tunnel, to him. She envisioned him waiting for her—crisp suit, dry smile—as she made her way down the main staircase and through the empty ballroom.

"The situation is not good," she heard her father saying as she approached the French doors that led onto the verandah.

"In fact, it's bad," Jones replied. Through the filmy white curtains, she could see the two men sitting at a round table that had been set for lunch. Charlie was standing a little ways in front of them, leaning against a stone column and staring out across the vast property. It was hard to imagine anything bad, surrounded by that quiet and lush summer landscape.

"I never trusted Duluth."

"Well—you did, once."

"I never should have." Her father sighed heavily and cursed, and then she realized that he was truly worried. With a useless little twist in her stomach, she wished there was something she could do to help. "That man has no scruples," he went on.

"None," Jones agreed.

"I'm worried he might—" But Darius broke off when he realized that Cordelia was standing there. He pushed back his chair and smiled, although it was a rather labored expression, and reached out to guide her to her place at the table. "Welcome, my dear. You look lovely."

"Thank you." She smoothed her skirt as she sat.

"Jones," Darius said, "we'll finish this discussion after lunch. But see that we have all the men on duty tonight."

Cordelia tried to smile at Jones as he stood to leave. Charlie turned and gave his sister a private wink. Cordelia pressed her lips together guiltily, thinking how quickly she'd betrayed his trust. But he remained oblivious, and only picked up a silver pitcher, and began to pour iced tea into their glasses.

"Oh, and Jones," Darius said, just before his right-hand man stepped across the threshold and back into the house. "I am particularly worried about my daughter. I want one of my men with her at all times tonight."

"All right," Jones replied, and was gone.

"Don't look sad, Cord," Darius said then, and she realized too late that she'd allowed a frown to tug down at the corners of her mouth. "This is just part of our life here, but I shall see that you are kept safe. After we eat, what do you say you and I have a little target practice?"

Cordelia nodded and tried to smile.

"Good. Now. Let's have lunch together like a civilized family. It's these small rituals, you know, that separate us from the barbarians. What do civilized people do before a meal? They say grace together, don't they?"

He reached out for both their hands, and after a pause, all three bowed their heads and closed their eyes. The oddness of asking for God's blessing beside Grey the infamous bootlegger did occur to Cordelia, but mostly she was glad for the few moments when neither her brother nor her father would be looking at her, because she knew the disappointment of realizing she would not be able to sneak away to Thom that evening was obvious on her face.

21

THAT EVENING, GIRLS IN POSH MODERN BEDROOMS agonized over not being asked out often enough. Young wives on Park Avenue either hoped their husbands would hurry up and get home, or else get home much, much later on, when the smell of other men's cigarette brands had faded with the night breezes. Downtown, Letty Larkspur sat in the company of her new pet, trying to feel comfortable in her borrowed dress, and praying it was good enough for the world she was about to step into.

The dress was one of Paulette's, and they had picked it out together before Paulette went off to Seventh Heaven; it was sleeveless black crepe, with flutters at the midcalf-length hem and gold embroidery on the thick straps. Her dark bob cut across her face like the two wings of a blackbird, and her little mouth was a bright carnelian dot. When she'd arrived in New York, her brows had been rather thick, but by now they were plucked to narrow arcs over her large blue eyes. She had never seen herself so pretty—and still she wondered if her appearance would be good enough to please a man like Amory Glenn.

Good Egg, who had been running in circles, came to a sudden, fatigued stop near the old vanity table and laid her head on her mistress's lap. This made Letty relax some, and she turned her eyes to the ceiling, with its beige pattern of water stains and peeling plaster, and took several breaths. Someday, she knew this place and these petty fears of not being worldly or beautiful enough would seem very funny and faraway to her.

In her head, she imagined lounging on a divan and giving an interview. *It wasn't always easy,* she would say languidly, reclining in the perfumed comfort of her rose-colored sunken living room. *I was a cigarette girl in one of the speakeasies, you know, where I used sometimes to sing with the band.*

Letty looked into her own eyes now and batted her thick, dark lashes. "I lived in a tiny, odious place," she began to say out loud, in a feathery tone that was an exaggeration of her own voice. "With three lovely girls, each talented in her own way, and my beloved Good Egg was with me even then, and she suffered through the indignities of that time right along with me . . ."

Her monologue was interrupted by the sound of a horn—two auspicious blurts—and she pulled a wrap over her shoulders in a rush, kissed Good Egg, and made her way out the door and into the warm evening air.

"Letty!"

She turned to the sound of her name, and hoped that she did not look disappointed when she saw that it was not Amory Glenn but Grady, leaning against his old black roadster in the gathering dusk.

"Hello, Mr. Lodge."

He took in a breath. "You look . . . *beautiful*," he told her seriously.

Her eyes darted up and down the street, afraid that Amory might catch a glimpse of her with another man and think that their date was off. "Thank you," she replied curtly. "But what are you doing here?"

If Grady winced it was slight, and he maintained his smile. "They told me it was your night off at the club . . . and I wondered if perhaps Good Egg needed a walk."

"That's very kind, but—"

Before she could finish her thought, a gleaming black Duesenberg limousine turned onto her street, blaring its horn before rolling to a stop in front of Letty's place. With its long, straight snout in front and the flamboyant curves over the tires, she couldn't help but experience a tiny burst of pity for Grady, who was always trying to win her affection, but who simply couldn't make entrances like that one. A uniformed driver stepped out and approached the awkward pair.

"Mr. Glenn is waiting for you," he announced, without meeting either Letty's or Grady's eyes.

She glanced back toward Grady sadly. His face had fallen.

"I thought you said you were going to stay away from Amory Glenn."

Before she could reply, she had to turn her white oval of a face away from him. "Are you jealous?"

"No—no . . . ," Grady stammered and averted his gaze. "It's only that, as I told you before, he's not a good egg, and—"

"What is this obsession with eggs, Mr. Lodge?" She moved farther away and tried to remind herself that she was about to enter the kind of richly appointed rooms she had only yet dreamed of, and that she should not be swayed by sweet writers who could offer nothing more than afternoon drives in beaten-up old motorcars. "I can take care of myself," she added.

As she lowered herself into the red velvet backseat of the limousine, Amory Glenn met her eyes. Before either could say anything he passed her a long, slender glass filled with pale liquid.

"Excellent choice of dress, Miss Larkspur," he said, and clinked his glass against hers.

At that moment, the name *Larkspur* stopped sounding theoretical to her and began to feel like her own. *Larkspur* connoted bejeweled fingers and feather boas and a constant state of having one's picture taken.

"Thank you," she said, and then lifted her glass to examine the pale bubbly liquid.

"Don't you like champagne?"

Not wanting to admit that she had never tasted champagne, Letty replied, "Of course." Then she took a sip, and felt immediately pleasantly light-headed. "That doesn't taste at all like beer," she exclaimed, before realizing that she had given herself away.

"No!" Amory laughed, and signaled to the driver to start the engine. "I should think not."

A sense of having been blaringly foolish soured her stomach for a moment, but then she saw that Amory was not making fun of her.

"The lady's a comedienne!" he declared to the driver, who nodded a little stiffly and proceeded down the tree-lined street.

By the time they pulled up to the restaurant—the buildings were taller and straighter in this part of town, and the trees were manicured, but otherwise she had no idea where she was—the champagne in her glass was all gone, and with it her nerves, as well as any remorse over leaving Grady standing alone on the street. The doormen stood aside for her as she was ushered down a short flight of stairs and into the dim first floor of a townhouse. Every table was full and illuminated by candlelight, and though this was not how she would have imagined a fancy restaurant—she would have expected something far more vast, with potted palms and electric light and mirrors everywhere—the way they were greeted, with a subtle "Welcome to the Grotto, Mr. Glenn," assured her that it most certainly was.

Amory took one seat at a small table near the wall and allowed the maître d' to pull back Letty's chair for her. Meanwhile, Amory lit a cigarette, propped his elbow on the table, and began surveying the room. "Thank you, Gene," he said as the man arranged the seat beneath Letty. "Has my father been in tonight?"

"No, Mr. Glenn."

"Excellent. We'll have a bottle of Pol Roger and a dozen oysters. For dinner, the lady will have escargots, I will have the steak, rare, with no starch of any kind."

"Very good."

"My father owns theaters," Amory said, as though that explained something about his investigation into the elder Mr. Glenn's presence. "Someday, I will own theaters," he added without elaboration.

"Oh." Letty nodded exuberantly as champagne was poured for them. They clinked glasses again.

"The Grotto is something of a favorite haunt among show-business people. Why, right over there is the actor Valentine O'Dell." Amory pointed, and Letty's eyes went to a corner table, where an immaculately polished man in a white dinner jacket was surrounded by a table of ladies, all of them vying for his attention. Letty's breath almost stopped to think that she was in the same room with *the* Valentine O'Dell, and for a moment she longed to be back in Union so that she could giddily relate this miracle to her sisters. His features were just as straight and glistening as they'd seemed on the movie screen in Defiance, although she had always imagined him to be tall, and in person his stature was rather more like that of a jockey. "It appears that Sophia Ray is not with him tonight. They've been together since they were children on the vaudeville circuit, you know."

"Sophia Ray! What a thing it would be to dine in the same restaurant as *her* . . ."

But perhaps Letty had sounded a little too starry-eyed and provincial, for Amory abruptly changed the subject. "Forgive me—would you like a cigarette?"

The picture of what Letty's older sister would have called "the kind of woman who smokes" rose in her thoughts, and she paused briefly, her lips parted and hesitant. But then she heard herself say, "Yes." The other girls in the apartment teased her for not smoking—especially since she spent most nights hawking the things—and she was just beginning to feel rosy all over, and rather important for sitting where she was sitting, and she didn't want to be gauche now. Besides, that was her old self—it was the Haubstadt in her that objected to smoking, and she wanted to leave that behind. She was Letty Larkspur now.

In fact, the sight of the slender white cylinder between her fingers was emboldening. And though the taste was not so subtle as the champagne she had been drinking, and though it was uncomfortable on her throat, it caused her to be light-headed in two ways now. She smiled calmly and sparklingly, as though to say in a rather deep and sophisticated voice, *Do go on, Mr. Glenn.*

"How do you like the champagne?"

"*Much* better than beer!" she repeated the joke, and it was even funnier this time, and they both laughed loudly.

"Yes, well, theaters"—he paused after the word, giving it emphasis and letting the makings of a smile hover on his lips—"are our business, as I was saying, and before we go any further, I wanted to ask a favor of you."

"A favor?" The word sounded a little tawdry, and for the first time since they had entered the restaurant, she felt a touch skittish. She thought of Grady and the concerned expression he had worn when he saw the limousine, and was glad he was not there to hear the word *favor* on Amory's tongue.

"Yes. You see, I greatly enjoyed seeing you perform the other night. You are far better than their regular singer"—here he bent toward her and let his hand brush hers—"but I suspect you know that already."

Letty blushed and slowly raised her eyes to him over the wide rim of her champagne glass. "Thank you," she whispered.

"You're welcome." He paused to adjust his cuff links and glance around the room. "I think your future on the stage is very bright."

"You really think so?" she asked, in the feathered voice of all ingénues.

"Oh, yes."

Letty straightened in her chair, and glanced at the other women in the room, who reclined rakishly and shot pointed smiles at the men who lingered in the shadow of the bar. Were any of those women current stars of the stage? Did they have any idea that a girl with a future was among them?

"And I know perfectly well that in a year or two, you will not deign to consider a little . . . a proposal like the one I am about to make you."

Letty swallowed. "What's that?"

"I am throwing a party for a good friend of mine, at one of the better establishments—frequented by many show-business types—and I was wondering if you would . . . if you might be willing . . . if you would honor me by considering doing your act there."

"My . . . act?"

"Yes—well, I know I've only heard you sing one song. But whatever songs are in your repertoire. Ten of them, say. And perhaps a little shimmy." He shook his shoulders to demonstrate. "I will pay you thirty-five dollars—"

"Thirty-five dollars!" Her mouth dropped open and her eyelids sunk closed with the thought of all the new dresses and all the jewels she could buy with that. Or she could live sparingly and not work, and begin going to auditions every day.

"Really, you are worth much more, I know that. Naturally. But the people who will get a chance to see you—if I were your manager, for instance, I would advise you to do it, even if it paid nothing at all . . . but I am a humble patron of the arts, and I have only a friendly stake in your future."

Her shoulders danced a little as she closed her eyes, inhaling the warm smokiness of the room and imagining the moment just before stepping onstage, and how many songs she had, and whether she would need to learn a few more before then. "Th-thank you so much, Mr. Glenn!" She had forgotten about the cigarette between her fingers, and when she moved her hand suddenly, a long trail of ash fell onto the table. "Oh!" she giggled, and brushed it away. "Oh, Mr. Glenn, I'm so grateful."

"Good," he said, lighting her another cigarette. "Then you'll do it?"

"Of course! It couldn't be more exciting!"

"Yes, I suppose it couldn't." Amory smiled. A waiter arrived with a large plate of oysters, and her escort wasted no time in dressing them, his fingers moving officiously over the plate of ice and damp, shelled creatures. Then he lifted one up and brought it to her lips.

"Thank you," she managed, swallowing. Letty knew exceptionally little about the sea, but she supposed that was what it tasted like.

"How do you like it?" he asked.

"Well, they're nothing like hot dogs!" she said, using the same joke again and inspiring the same laughter. By then everything in the room had become blurry and golden, and she mused that if Cordelia could see her now, then she would never dare to call her foolish. Letty Larkspur knew how to see to her own interests. The way Amory looked did not even unnerve her so very much anymore, and she had begun to think that, according to the natural order of things, she *should* be accompanied by a man as handsome as he.

By the time his limousine returned her to her door, all her expectations had become gloriously elevated.

"Thank you for a lovely evening, Mr. Glenn," she said as she backed up demurely.

"I will send the car for you tomorrow, before the show," he replied, as he straightened his collar. "Be ready at seven?"

She nodded and waved and turned for her door. The air at that hour was fresh, and the streets were glinting with moisture as though there had been a few episodes of summer rain while she was deep in a restaurant, eating oysters and drinking champagne, just like people in movies did. For Letty Larkspur, New York was brand-new, and so was she.

That night she had learned something that every pretty girl making a go of it in the big city learns at some point or another: In New York there is always something to look at, but it is all infinitely more interesting through a window in the backseat of a limousine.

But Cordelia—who, back in Union, had a year on Letty in school, a few inches in height, and many more forbidden words that she'd taught herself to sound natural saying—was now several steps ahead in understanding how fraught a privileged view can become. She sat on a tapestry spread over the grass on a rise above the white tent on the Dogwood estate, her legs bent upward and covered by the flowing skirt of her black sequined dress, watching the scene before her. Under the glow of the tent's many tiny electric lights, partygoers laughed and swayed to the music, the girls' eyes darting about, the boys making advances.

The young lady of the house was not interested in them,

of course. Her father had already retired, and Charlie was off playing billiards in the house, and Astrid had not shown at all. However, she was not alone. Per her father's instructions, Danny had followed her all night and was standing just behind her, his hand resting on his belt, which Cordelia knew held a gun.

While her mind returned again and again to the dock where she knew Thom was waiting, there was no more restlessness inside her and no more desire to escape. Not since the end of lunch, when she'd practiced shooting with her father. She hadn't felt like saying much—and it seemed that he hadn't, either—and they'd fired off rounds in silence for what felt like hours. When they were through, he showed her how to properly clean a shotgun and then a six-shooter, and when she had brushed and oiled the latter to his satisfaction, he put the pistol in her hands.

"I want you to have that," he'd told her.

"You do?" She'd looked down at the gleaming barrel, the shiny wood grip, the solemn trigger.

"It was my first gun. The first that was really mine, not on loan, not grabbed in a pinch. I bought it from an Italian I used to know, in the old days, when I was just starting to run liquor." He'd given her a serious, intent smile. "You may find it strange, my dear, but I trust you completely. Charlie, too, of course—but his gifts are different than yours. I don't expect you to understand it yet, but in time you'll see."

They had been standing by the pool, in the noonday sun, and she had blinked rapidly several times and wished that she really *were* trustworthy. It was at that moment that she began to regret sneaking off with Thom last night, and as the minutes passed, her regret only grew.

"Oh, don't worry, I know you're sad about that—about the Hale boy," he'd gone on quickly, almost as though he'd read her mind. "I knew him a little as a boy, and there was always something brilliant about him. But this is another thing you'll learn in time: That kind of love is always changing, you can never plant your feet on it. Trust me, there will be others. But those kinds of affairs—you can't ever count on them like blood."

For a brief moment, Cordelia wanted to confess everything she'd done and ask for his forgiveness. But then he smiled at her—wisely, and almost a little sad—and it seemed to her that he knew already and wasn't angry. She felt the weight of the pistol in her hands, and smiled back at him. "Thank you for this. I hope someday I really will make you proud."

By the time the party began, she still wasn't in anything like a festive mood, but she knew that even if she could've slipped away to find Thom, she wouldn't have tried. Darius Grey's first pistol was now tucked away with an old letter he had written for her mother and an even older trench coat—the family relics, her most prized possessions.

Every now and then, a pair of young men would look up at Grey's daughter, whisper something, and smile. But Cordelia would only avert her eyes and turn over the memory of Thom's touch in her mind. She tried to remember what the prettiest thing he'd said to her was, but nothing came right away, and she sighed to think that she'd had all of him she was going to have, and that these meager recollections were going to have to sate her for the rest of her life. *That's the way it has to be,* she reminded herself. The thought was still wrenching, and she closed her eyelids to soften the pain. The girl she had been on the train had had only one hope, she reminded herself: To be reunited with her father. She'd been an orphan then, but she wasn't anymore.

Exhaling sadly, she opened her eyes. The stars were sparser tonight, and she supposed that had something to do with the clouds.

"I'm feeling a little tired, Danny," she said as she stood up.

Once he had deposited her in her suite, she pulled the pins out of her hair so that it fell down over the straps of her dress. She draped a delicate shawl over her shoulders as she crossed to the great open windows, and pressed herself against the back of the white chair that sat just inside the balcony. She was all sighs that evening. For a while she remained very still, listening to the faint music rising up from the tent below, and letting an exquisite melancholy spread through her veins.

Time passed, though it felt like nothing to her, and eventually her eyes drifted shut. In that gentle place, just before sleep, she could feel the way Thom's arms had wrapped around her the night before, and perhaps because of the vividness of her imaginings, she was not immediately surprised by the sound of his voice.

"You're pretty when you're sad, too." He had come through the door and shut it silently behind him.

She raised her head from the cushion of her arms and regarded him. The brim of his hat was tipped down enough to make him unrecognizable, but then he took it off and revealed his smooth, perfect face.

"What are you doing here?" Her voice was half yearning and half angry.

"When you didn't come to the dock . . . I snuck in through the tunnel."

The many sentences she'd told him in her mind over the course of the afternoon—that they would simply have to end it; that she couldn't betray her family; that she was sorry, but it was over—abandoned her now.

"Let's not say anything just yet," she said after a pause.

"All right." He nodded and stepped toward her across the white carpet.

All day she'd been picturing his face, but now she found that her heart was beating too fast, and she had to turn her eyes to the floor. Her knees collapsed together, and she rested her elbows on them heavily, her whole posture bowing with the hopelessness of the situation. Wavy strands of hair obscured her face, and her naked toes turned in toward each other.

"What did they do to you?" Thom asked. He came closer and sunk down on his knees at her side.

She glanced up and then to the place where his gaze was fixed. A great purple bruise had formed on her right shoulder, where the butt of the shotgun had rested, and for the first time she noticed how sore she was there. She had been rather intense about felling grapefruit that afternoon, she realized. With a touch of defensiveness, she replied, "Nothing. *They* wouldn't do that. Dad's been teaching me to shoot."

"Oh."

They were quiet again for a spell, and then his fingers fell onto her thigh. One hand rested there, and the other carefully moved the strands away from where they'd caught on her damp lips. His touch, when it came, melted any convictions. It made her briefly forget everything else she wanted, and all her principles, too.

"Don't say you're going to break it off," he said.

She shook her head, memories of how protective Darius had been that day returning to her in a wave. How like an old man he was in his robe and loafers, his gray hairs poignantly obvious when they lunched on the terrace, his fierce concern when she grew frustrated over missing her targets. There was no bond as strong as blood, he'd told her, and she furiously tried to keep that in the front of her thoughts now.

"Perhaps," she began, but her voice faltered. "Perhaps we should leave it here. Before I get you in any real trouble. Like you said when we met, it was a perfect moment, and maybe neither of us should have wanted anything more than that . . ."

"That was a stupid thing for me to say!" he broke out in a rash tone. Then, in a slower and more serious voice, each word placed carefully after the last: "I didn't know you then."

Cordelia threw back her head, staring at the ceiling and hoping her throat wouldn't get stopped up with emotion. "And what's to say you know me now?"

He stood up suddenly and took a few deliberate steps away from her.

When he turned to meet her gaze, there was a wounded quality in his eyes that her heart leapt to believe in. The sounds of the party below had grown rowdy, and she knew he should go while he could still make his way among them. Who knew what kind of activity there would be in the tunnel on a night like tonight, or what the repercussions would be if, say, Danny was sent to make sure the young lady of the house had gotten to bed all right.

"I'll leave if you want me to," he said eventually.

For a while, she looked at the long, tall stretch of him in a summer suit, his glossy hair neatly in place and those eyes that seemed to know everything. An ache spread across her chest when she thought how awful it would be to sit in this room alone after he had gone.

"Please don't," she whispered.

"I can't promise it'll be pretty," he said after a while. "But I know I can't stand the idea of a day without you."

"It's just that . . . for you to be here . . ."

"Can you meet me tomorrow, on the road? We'll go to the East End, where no one will recognize us, and we can pretend we're other people, and not sit here in fear. I'll be there by dusk . . ."

She nodded and brushed away the tears before he could notice them. "Maybe. I'll try. I don't know now. I don't know anything."

He tried to smile, but only half his mouth cooperated, and in the end the expression conveyed more sadness than joy.

"Till tomorrow?" he said, taking another step back.

Down below, just out of their earshot, was the swagger and wail of a trumpet. There had been a scare about a debutante's twisted ankle that proved nothing to worry about, after which everyone began toasting to her health. Newly formed couples were pledging to stay up for the sunrise, and fresh drinks were being poured.

A peculiar calm was creeping through Cordelia then.

She could see now that her situation was just as simple as all impossible situations. There was only once choice—to meet Thom on the road tomorrow—and yet that was out of the question. The way she had felt, sitting on the rise above the tent, thinking that perhaps all of Thom's kisses were in the past, came back to her now. Suddenly she knew that she couldn't let him leave. Not this way, after only a few restrained brushes of fingertips. If he had to go, she wanted to be sure that they had really known each other, that they had not saved anything for a future date that might never come.

Cordelia stood up and, holding his gaze, drew down the straps of her evening dress. "Don't go," she said.

The light from outside flickered in his eyes, and his lips parted. For a moment they watched each other, and then he moved toward her, lifted her up, and carried her to the bed. As she fell back against the soft pillows, hair fanning out around her head, a smile spread across her lips. She reached up for his face, bringing it down so that his mouth covered hers. All of her began to quicken and soften, and the consequences of their situation dissolved. There was only that room and that warm dark night, and Thom above her, pressing against her, into the sheets.

22

"CORDELIA SEEMS AWFULLY QUIET THIS MORNING," said Astrid, idly using her croquet mallet to scratch her ankle with one hand and pushing her short, lustrous yellow hair away from her forehead with the other. She was wearing a white jersey dress that hung on her lean frame rather like an abbreviated Greek tunic. Beside her was Charlie, in a white V-neck sweater and white slacks, bent over his mallet, concentrating on his shot.

"She wasn't very social at the party last night, either," he said. "Dad was teaching her how to shoot a gun yesterday, and you should have seen how determined she was about it. By the end of the day, she was actually getting kind of good."

"Oh, dear." Astrid looked away from Cordelia, who was

sitting on a wicker chair on the Greys' south lawn—just below the multilevel terrace with its mythical carved stone creatures—wearing a great, flopping, black straw hat and a white boatneck dress with thin navy stripes. "We'll have to talk her out of that."

She paused, squinting at the other party guests—a small gathering of White Cove youth, mostly from families like hers, not families like the Greys—all wearing white, gripping stemmed glasses of grapefruit juice much improved with a few drops of champagne. Apparently they were the stragglers from what must have been a rather epic party last night. Charlie had called her earlier, waking her up, and begged her to come enjoy the morning-after fete, although she could no longer tell why. Despite her flattering dress and her skin—which appeared especially fresh when compared to the faces of the girls who hadn't gotten any sleep—he was paying her no special attention.

There had been a moment, in the kitchen, when Cordelia first came down—they had all been sleepy-eyed and hungry and sweet, and it had seemed to Astrid that they were just like a family of hobos, except with a much nicer house. Many of the people she'd known since she was a child were still there, tired but unwilling to let the party end. *How lovely,* she'd thought. Then she'd grown a little sad, knowing that eventually the summer would have to end, and she'd wondered if she shouldn't just decide to drop out of school now and live like this forever.

And while she wasn't paying attention, Jones had come down and whispered something in Charlie's ear, and after that Charlie was surly, and stopped seeming happy that she'd given in and come. That was just how men were, she was beginning to think. After that she wondered why Jones was whispering unpleasant secrets in Charlie's ear instead of Darius's—it was awfully inconvenient for her, especially when the day was new and had such potential for enjoyment.

"Did your father drink too much and go to bed early?" she asked irritably.

"No." Charlie whacked the ball, which rolled within range of the next wicket. "He's always a little tight in the evenings," he added as he strode forward. "Your turn."

"I'm bored," Astrid declared. She turned toward Emma Cantwell and Cass Beaumont, twenty feet or so behind them, who as of last week had become a couple. "Aren't you bored?"

"No," Emma said cheerily. Then she turned to Cass. "Are you?"

"No." Cass rested his hand against his hip. "Come on, Astrid, finish the game!"

"Sorry," Astrid replied breezily, but perhaps too abruptly to be convincing. "I couldn't possibly! Get Gracie Northrup to play for me."

As she walked back across the lawn, she hoped that Charlie was watching her, yet couldn't help but fear that this wasn't the case. She had no idea what was going on in his mind, but his distraction irked her, and she wasn't about to waste a beautiful day hanging around him while he stewed.

"Are you all right?" she asked as she reached Cordelia.

"I didn't sleep so well last night." She shrugged and an enigmatic half smile played on her lips, though the brim of her hat somewhat obscured the quality in her eyes. "But I'm all right."

"Good." Astrid swung around and looked at Charlie across the vast green, now playing with plump Gracie Northrup, who was laughing loudly in that ungainly snorting way she had. She was a Miss Porter's girl, too, although she had been a senior when Astrid was a freshman. They were four white figures against a great arc of blue sky. "That's the wrong blouse on Gracie," Astrid went on, changing the subject. It was polka-dotted, and the neckline involved a complicated tied-scarf detail that brought too much attention to her large bust. "It makes her look bigger than she is."

"You didn't want to play anymore?"

"Charlie's sore about something." Astrid shielded her eyes and tried to seem not to care. "He's no fun this afternoon. I'm going home, I think. When he's ready to work for me, perhaps then I'll come back. The party is breaking up, anyway. Why don't I get the chauffeur tonight? We can go into the city."

Cordelia tipped back her head, so that the light made her

brown eyes almost translucent. Not for the first time, Astrid noticed how impressive looking she was in the right clothes. On a farm, her features would have been severe, but under the drooping brim of an expensive hat, those high, defined bones were more suggestive of a horsewoman from one of the really old families. "Where do you want to go?" she asked.

"Oh, darling, who cares? We can just drive and invite people to join us."

"Maybe," Cordelia wavered.

Astrid's full lips assumed a pout. "I like it when you say *yes,* Cordelia Grey, but for now I will take *maybe*."

She bent and kissed her friend on either cheek, and then skipped up the stairs without glancing back to see if Charlie marked her exit.

But by the time Astrid had returned to Marsh Hall, she did not feel nearly so carefree. Why wasn't Charlie more interested in her, anyway? Had her beauty faded suddenly, or what was it? As she stepped into her bedroom, the satisfaction of having walked away began to fade, and her eye started to twitch.

In the adjacent dressing room, she sat down heavily on the little upholstered stool in front of the vanity. But there was nothing wrong with her appearance. With agitated fingers, she began to fix her hair, which was cut so that it framed her face girlishly and jauntily at once. In fact, the reflection in the mirror was just as it had been on so many nights, when all the boys had followed her with their eyes and Charlie had seemed in complete thrall to her beauty. And all of a sudden she was thinking of an evening some months ago—it had been cold, and she had worn a white dress like this one, and checked her reflection in this same room, while the smell of hothouse hyacinth wafted in the air . . .

Suddenly, the memory came back to her whole, and she knew she'd made a mistake. She began opening and closing drawers, pushing aside the assortment of things that filled them. Ribbons, hairbrushes, ruined stockings—sad, gaudy earrings that had lost their match. Her big eyes almost welled up at the sight of the black dangling thing, and as she held it in her palm, she forced herself to look up into the mirror, at the kind of girl who would lose an earring in Charlie Grey's bedroom.

No wonder he was so preoccupied and distant, she thought, as she sighed and slumped forward, resting her chin against her fist and giving herself a stern, moody look. How could he not be, when his girlfriend was always chasing phantoms and inventing problems where there were none?

"Ah, me, what's a silly girl like you to do?" she asked her reflection.

Of course, Astrid was not alone in conversing with herself. During those hours when afternoon yields to evening, a city is full of girls in front of mirrors, rotating their faces right and left, finding themselves pretty beyond all conception or else hopelessly inadequate. The scene over their shoulders generally involves one or more of the following: a heap of rejected frocks, a gin drink growing watery with melting ice, a friend or two offering advice while hoping not to be outshone, a neglected sandwich with one lone set of bite marks. Perhaps, if she makes plenty of her own money or has a generous suitor, a phonograph will be blaring out something fast to get her fully in the mood for evening.

In the case of Letty, there was no friend. Fay was executing high kicks and a perfect, frozen smile in the West Forties; Kate was checking coats on the East Side; and Paulette was at Seventh Heaven. Probably she had already told Mr. Cole that Letty wasn't feeling well and wouldn't be coming in tonight. The sandwich had been devoured by Good Egg when she wasn't paying attention. Now Good Egg was running in circles on the small section of floor between the old, rickety vanity and the bed that she and Paulette shared. The quilt was invisible under all the dresses she had tried on and decided against. Most of Paulette's choices had been flashier or more revealing than she felt comfortable in, but now she was alone—or she and Good Egg were, in any event—and she had settled on the dress she'd known since that morning she would wear.

In the mirror, Letty saw a petite girl reflecting light from every point. Her eyelids were coated with iridescent green powder, her lips were the color of garnets and possessed a similar luster, and her dark bob was slicked to a high shine. The dress was a sleeveless sheath with complicated beadwork over the bust and otherwise of a stiff, black fabric. The waist was subtle, and the hemline hovered above her ankles; she had bought it earlier that day after seeing it in a window, where it made the mannequin look like the most sophisticated chanteuse of all time, and it had cost most of the money she had earned as a cigarette girl thus far. But after tonight she would be rich, and anyway all that really mattered was that her appearance was flawless, which as far as Letty could determine, it was.

The full meaning created by the combination of the words *Fifth* and *Avenue* had not completely dawned on Letty, but driving up that fabled street in a polished black limousine, her eyes shining and her head relentlessly rehearsing the words to the songs in her repertoire, she began to take in something of its power.

Her nerves were getting worse, but the genteel rectitude of the passing landscape did calm her some. For a while, she managed to put away entirely her frightened anticipation of that moment just before she was to step onstage. Then her attention was drawn by the face of a large and elegant building of stone, so tall that she could not make out the top from her vantage within the car. Several liveried doormen moved briskly back and forth beneath an overhang of looping wrought iron and white frosted glass. Beyond the ornate exterior, piles of luggage waited on brass dollies inside a lobby of glistening marble and gilt edges. Then the car door opened, ending her reverie.

"Here we are, miss," the chauffeur said.

"Where?" She tried not to appear surprised as she scooted toward him.

"At the St. Regis, miss." He stood back and averted his eyes.

"Oh."

She stepped out of the car tentatively and for a moment stood, unsure and wobbly in her high heels, on the wide sidewalk. She supposed that she had imagined Amory's party would take place in a club, but she tried to look as though this was precisely what she had anticipated. "Thank you," she added, and then, reminding herself to maintain a sophisticated gait, she made her way toward the hotel. She managed this for twenty strides or so, but once she was inside, she realized she had no idea where the dressing room might be or where in this vast hotel Amory was waiting for her, and she began to panic.

"How can I be of assistance to you, mademoiselle?" The voice, coming from over her shoulder, was honeyed and composed.

She turned and found herself looking up at a tall man in a tailored black suit, with a trim, old-fashioned mustache. He was neither friendly nor unwelcoming exactly, and he kept his hands behind his back when he spoke.

"Yes . . . ," she began. "I am here for a party."

"A party, mademoiselle?" He smiled patiently. "Whose party are you attending?"

"Well, I'm not attending, exactly. I'm a singer, you see. I'm performing at a party to be hosted by Mr. Amory Glenn—"

"Ah, Mr. *Glenn's* party."

The man glanced around and quickly placed a hand on her shoulder. He guided her away from the elevator bank, past the grand curving staircase, toward a nondescript door in the corner of the lobby. They walked down a long hall and up a flight of stairs, which opened onto another hall. The lighting there was poor, and she wondered for a moment if she should demand to see Amory immediately—it was all a little shabby, she thought, and not nearly his style. But then, in his businesslike manner, the man led her to a door that opened onto a small but perfect space. Inside was a real dressing room, with an armless, upholstered chair and a mirror ringed with frosted bulbs and a vanity table littered with makeup of all kinds, and she realized that it was only that this hallway was not for public viewing.

This was how the starlets got in.

"Mr. Glenn said he would come visit with you before you go on. In the meantime, is there anything I can fetch you?"

The thing to do, she knew, would be to make a list of

demands. But she couldn't right then figure what they might be; the notion that she was about to enter her own dressing room had buoyed her into new realms of contentedness.

"No, thank you."

"Do ring if you change your mind. My name is Ernest. I am the concierge of this hotel—you can ask the front desk for me."

When he was gone and the door shut behind him, she closed her eyes and did a twirl. The floor was softened by a burgundy-colored Persian carpet, and several beaded and feathered costumes hung on the wall. But that vanity—it was like an altar. Besides makeup brushes and tints, the table before the mirror was occupied by a large polished silver urn filled with ice and a green champagne bottle with gold foil on the neck. There was another door, presumably through to the stage, from which she could hear the faint noises of a gathering—the band playing unobtrusively as people mingled and talked. She could just imagine the vast room, men moving their wives across a dance floor, rumors of various theatrical productions floating in the air.

Some minutes later, the door to the stage opened, and Amory came in wearing a tuxedo, his hair brilliantined and his cheeks ruddy.

"Ah, my dear, how charming you look!" he said before planting a kiss, fragrant and a little wet, on her cheek. She tried not to blush at the intimacy of the gesture. "Now, isn't this tops?

Didn't I say I would give you a start? A real dressing room, in one of New York's swankiest places, and a room of connoisseurs about to learn of your many talents . . ."

"Yes, Mr. Glenn, it's all wonderful!" Letty's big blue eyes darted around. "Only—I'm a little nervous. I didn't practice with the band at all, and I—"

"Have you had any champagne?"

"No . . ." She paused and bit her lower lip. "I'd rather not, before I—"

"Oh, come, we must toast you! You are about to be made a star." And then, with a pop that rattled her down in her core, he opened the bottle and filled two flutes. His dark eyes followed her hawkishly until she sipped. Some of her anxiety *did* ebb with the drink, and she sipped again and gave him a smile. "See, nothing to worry about. After all, had you practiced the night you got up on the stage at Seventh Heaven?"

"Well, *no* . . ." Letty averted her eyes and hoped that revealing her fears that way wasn't too amateurish.

"The band here is very good. They'll follow you. Just improvise, my dear, be spontaneous and free. Listen to your audience, and give them what they want."

He made a broad gesture, and she felt for a moment as though she were in the hands of a very talented director. She nodded trustingly.

"Here." From the wall of costumes, he took a silver

headdress with little shimmering, pearl-encrusted dangles and fixed it so that it sat in the middle of her forehead; she glanced in the mirror at her large, shadowed eyes and the gem of a mouth, and she thought that she did finally look like a girl who could star in her own show. "Now, haven't I gotten you everything you could possibly desire?"

"Oh, yes, Mr. Glenn!" she exclaimed, turning toward him, her eyes round.

"Then how about a kiss?"

The corners of her mouth fell, and her eyebrows rose toward the straight dark line of her bangs. But before she could say anything, he had gripped her with both hands and pressed her to his body as he covered her lips with his. She was too shocked to tell him to stop, but the kiss was over before she really knew what was happening.

He stepped back from her, and in a very different tone, he said, "Now fix your lipstick; it's time to go on."

She turned toward the mirror and did as he said. That kiss was different from how she'd imagined her first kiss would feel—but she tried to let the peculiarity just pass. Instead, she imagined the sensation of being onstage—basking in the gaze of a whole room, under a spotlight, holding their attention with her performance.

"Are you ready?" he said once she'd stepped away from the mirror.

She nodded, though her nerves had grown brittle again.

"Good. Now—I will introduce you, and once you hear applause, you may step out on stage and begin your act."

If she could have managed a smile, she would have given him one, but her face was too paralyzed by nerves to change its expression even slightly.

"Knock, 'em dead," he said, and went out through the door.

She closed her eyes and pressed her face against the door frame. Amory was speaking, though his words were too muffled to make out. By now, her pulse had grown almost feverish. The only two words she understood were the ones spoken loudest: "Letty Larkspur!" Applause followed momentarily, so she filled her lungs with as much air as possible and stepped through a dark, curtained space and onto a blindingly lit stage.

23

THE DAY HAD BEEN THE HOTTEST OF THE SUMMER YET, and at sunset it was still warm enough to swim. Astrid had spent its final blue hours beside the Marsh Hall pool, which was set somewhat beyond the house, between a pair of white stucco bungalows and two rows of tall, thin cypress trees. She had let the sun brown her skin and wondered whether she should explain to Charlie what she had erroneously believed, or just let it go unmentioned and try to be sweet to him all the time. Now, as the sky gave over to the pyrotechnics of dying light, she did a lazy back crawl, listening to the chirping of birds and the gardeners talking somewhere not far off, and watching the pink clouds drift.

"Nice evening, isn't it?"

Surprised, she rolled over, splashing noisily in the water. Billie was sitting on one of the white lounge chairs, wearing a Roman-striped swimming cape and a white turban over her dark hair. She had arrived on the deck without Astrid's noticing and had apparently been there long enough to get comfortable.

"It is," Astrid said, before ducking backward into a somersault. She enjoyed that sensation of being underwater, the outside world muted, and when she came up she decided that if she wasn't alone, then she wasn't going to be able to enjoy swimming anymore, really. By the time she emerged from the pool, Billie had rested her head back against her chair, her eyes closed, with that vague, calm smile of contentment that comes easily in the fine weather.

"All yours, darling," Astrid said as she pulled a white French terry cloth robe with yellow piping over her navy blue tank suit.

Billie remained in a posture of utter relaxation, as she advised, "I wouldn't go up there if I were you."

Astrid, who was trying to get a bothersome amount of water out of her ear, hardly acknowledged Billie. As she walked away across the grass, her damp, bare feet sinking into the blades, she let the comment stray from her consciousness. Discovering that Charlie was not a cad after all had left her feeling pleasantly drained, and she had a heightened sense of the perfection of the day thus far. There was the buzzing of mosquitoes somewhere, and the flash of a firefly now and then.

She was just coming up the hill toward the house when she heard something crashing, followed by an eruption of loud, angry voices. She hurried the rest of the way, through the library with its leaded windows and the big front foyer, and out onto the gravel drive in front. The big cream-colored Studebaker was parked at an angle, as though someone had driven it from the garage in a hurry; its canvas top was down, and the backseats were full of luggage. Midway between the door and the car was a pile of broken glass and what looked to be the shards of a waist-high, blue-and-white Chinese vase that had stood, as long as she could remember, on the second-floor hallway, beside its identical twin.

The driver-side door of the car opened, and Luke stepped out, wearing a rather shamefaced expression. Astrid's lips parted, but before she could react to his presence, the second blue-and-white vase crashed through a glass window above, soared briefly in the air, and then erupted in tiny pieces on the gravel. There was a shriek of feminine fury, followed by a low bellow of male aggression, and she heard her stepfather yell, "Get out!"

Behind her on the stairs were hurried, thudding footsteps, and then her mother appeared, running in a loose-fitting, V-neck apricot chiffon dress, her face taut with rage.

"Oh, good, Astrid—there you are," she said. Without pausing to take in her daughter's expression, she strode outside toward the Studebaker. A few seconds later, Harrison Marsh II came down the stairs, his face boiling and red; like his wife, he did not bother to glance at Astrid as he passed through the threshold.

"Get out!" he screamed again as he dashed onto the lawn.

"You couldn't *pay* me to stay here!" the third Mrs. Marsh spat back.

"Someone will *have* to pay you," he returned, his voice growing crueler as it became quieter. "A woman like her doesn't live cheap, young man," he added, addressing Luke.

"Sir, I—"

"Shut up, Luke," the lady of the house interrupted, hoisting up her shoulders and trying to repin her straw cloche, which had become slightly askew during the fighting. "I always hated those vases," she said to no one in particular. "Astrid, come. We're leaving."

Astrid paused on the front step, the terry cloth robe open—she had not been able to find the tie when she had gotten ready to swim—and her short, damp hair clumping to her neck. She stared at the three people on the drive, each wearing their own wretched expression, and felt a little ill. "Where are you going?" she said eventually.

"To the St. Regis. We'll stay there until I decide what our next move is—Europe or . . . I don't know."

"You don't have to go, Astrid dear," her stepfather said, his voice quieting some as he turned to face her. He was sweating profusely and wiped his forehead with the white-and-green handkerchief he carried. A moment later, Astrid's heart dropped—she realized it was the bandana she'd taken from Luke the day before, and that it must have been the cause of the fight. "Your mother's gone entirely hysterical, I'm afraid. I don't know that you should be under her care. You can stay on here as long as you want."

"Don't be absurd," Astrid's mother snorted. "She'd sooner die than stay in this stuffy old house. Come dear, it will be fun, just like when you were small and we lived at the hotel. Don't you remember?"

Astrid did remember; it had not been fun. At the St. Regis, she had not been allowed to have a pet or run in the halls after an incident that involved waking up one of the Mrs. Astors, whose townhouse was then under renovation, from an afternoon nap. Avoiding all their eyes, she walked forward—the gravel hurt her soft, bare feet, but she didn't think much of that—toward the garage, the great front doors of which Luke had left open.

"Astrid, don't be a headache, now!" she heard her mother yelling. When she didn't turn around, her mother groaned in irritation and started barking orders at Luke.

In the garage—a separate building with a glass roof that seemed large enough to house airplanes—all was quiet. She sighed and pulled her robe around her, turning the small collar up to warm her neck. Astrid opened the door of the red Marmon sports coupe, which her stepfather had given to Billie for her twentieth birthday, and slid into the driver's seat. She had operated an automobile only a few times, with Charlie on the lawn at Dogwood, and she did briefly consider the possibility that now was not the time to test her solo skills. But then she saw that the key was already in the ignition, and her desire to be far away became too great to bear. The part she'd played in the drama made her ill.

"Astrid Donal!" her mother shrieked as she drove past.

But the motor was loud, and she concentrated on staying off the grass. She was not particularly strong and was trying hard to keep a firm grip on the wheel; she stalled out just before she reached the low hedge fence, but by then she knew that stopping would involve a great deal of yelling and that her mother would demand to know what she had been thinking. She managed to restart the engine and to turn onto the drive that ran along the cove.

A mile or so of country lanes separated the entrances of Marsh Hall and Dogwood, and if any local residents had happened to go out for a leisure drive or else been returning early from the city that afternoon, they would have been treated to the sight of one of the more promising socialites of the coming generation, wrapped in a knee-length robe, après-swim, cursing like a galley cook.

The car stalled more than once, and on several occasions

she believed herself destined to land in a ditch. But somehow she managed to stay on the road and eventually arrive at the tall, iron gates of Dogwood.

"Miss Donal!" Danny said, stepping forward from the guardhouse. "Are you all right?"

"Yes, quite," Astrid replied, running her fingers through her hair, so that the strands went straight back from her forehead. She put on a wide smile. "Only, there was such a scene at home, and all I want is to change out of these clothes and have a cup of tea with the magnificent Greys, and maybe not go home for quite a while." She batted her eyelashes. "Won't you let me in?"

Danny grinned and went to push back the gate. She drove the car through the allée of lindens, but it soon proved too much of an incline for her. The Marmon came to a rest just off the drive, on the grass, and she ran up the rest of the lawn and into the house. She was relieved to be here, far from the world where people married to accrue old names and money, at a place where people earned their own keep, whatever that meant.

"Charlie!" she called as she ascended the main stairs, her arms wrapped tight around her waist, her feet moving at a quick jog. She stumbled on the last step, stubbing her toe, but the pain did not then seem relevant to her. "Charlie!"

But no one peeped his head out to see who it might be, so she continued toward Charlie's room. When she pulled back the door, she knew immediately that he was inside. She could smell him. But her relief quickly curdled, for she knew someone else was there with him, too.

"Charlie?" she whispered.

The curtains were pulled, casting the whole room in a rather shabby light. He did not hear her right away, even though she had crept forward and was now standing not far from the big brass bed. He wasn't facing her, and all she could see was his white trousered legs and naked torso bearing down like an animal. The other person was invisible to her, but she knew that it was a girl, by the feminine whimpers she emitted.

"Charlie!" Astrid tried to yell his name, though the sound again more closely resembled a whisper. She glanced down and noticed that her toe was bleeding.

This time he'd heard. His head jerked back, and when he turned his face toward her, his lower jaw dropped in panting chagrin. He lurched upward, his wide-set brown eyes reckless, his chin at a defiant angle. Astrid's eyes flickered from him to the girl he had been on top of; it was Gracie Northrup, lying in a rather compromised position, her stupid polka-dotted blouse undone to reveal the elaborate contraption of her brassiere. The girl's skin was blotchy, and her face, somewhat buried among pillows, held a dumb expression.

"Oh, Charlie, I'm going to be sick," Astrid heard herself

say. Her unpainted lips, which had been smiling mere minutes ago in anticipation of seeing him, were now pickled and tight.

"Astrid," Charlie said, stepping awkwardly off the bed, his belt loop swinging.

"Don't." She inched backward, but he kept coming toward her. "Don't!" she shrieked. "Don't, don't, don't, don't, don't!"

As she ran back down the stairs, she held her arms out for balance and let her robe flap behind her. She could not think about her toe, or the red trail it left. When she emerged from the house, the sky was not yet totally dark, but all the brilliance had gone out of the sunset. As soon as she reached the Marmon, she tried to start it up, but by then she was shaking too much and the engine kept stalling out.

"Ah!" she cried, pounding her hand against the steering wheel in frustration.

"Miss Donal, what are you doing?"

She paused, looked up, and saw Danny, who had hurried over from the guardhouse. Briefly her sense of revulsion eased. Realizing what she had to do made her feel a little cool, almost calm.

"Why, Danny," she said. Then she smiled.

"What are you doing?" he asked again, but this time in a less urgent tone.

"Danny, I need your help." She glanced down shyly, at her rosy thighs on the calfskin seat, visible where her robe was parted. "I don't drive very well, you see, and I need to get into the city right away."

"To Manhattan?" Nervousness had crept into Danny's tone.

"Yes. Won't you drive me?" She could see that he wasn't supposed to—that he was on duty and would be punished for leaving—but she needed to be moving fast, away from this place, so she smiled wider and said, "Danny, this car is really too much trouble for my family just now. Drive me into the city, and then take if off our hands, won't you?"

He closed his eyes, as though calculating the consequences. By the time he'd opened them, he was already walking around to the driver's side. She scooted over to the passenger's seat and folded her legs up girlishly between them.

"Thank you very much, Danny," she said, as they turned onto the main road.

But he was too nervous to meet her gaze. "Where to?" he asked flatly.

Astrid let her eyelids close and twisted her neck so that the wind would hit her face straight on and dry her hair. *What does it matter?* she wanted to say to him. "To the St. Regis," she said instead.

At the St. Regis, at just that moment, Letty stepped into the spotlight, the clunks of her calfskin heels echoing against the stage. She managed a smile, but she could not stop her growing sense of unease. The room was not what she had expected—it was not nearly as large or adorned. There were serious wood beams overhead, and the walls were paneled in masculine dark mahogany. Instead of a great crowd, she made out only twenty or so faces, pointed at her in expectation, several of them chomping cigars. They were all men, every single person in the room, many of them with the added girth of good living beneath their very expensive-looking suits. Amory was seated toward the side, with a few other men his own age.

Trying to keep calm, she twisted and faced the band. They did not fit her expectations, either, for there were only four of them. She had imagined a full orchestra to back her, but she tried to remind herself that the show must always go on, that she was only just starting out, and that perhaps this would allow her voice to shine more anyway.

"Do you know 'I'm Gonna Make You Breakfast in the Morning'?" she asked, screwing up her courage.

The drummer nodded without smiling and tapped the snare drum. The noise did nothing to dispel her unease, but she turned and began to count time with her open palm against the side of her hip. A few smiles grew under mustaches in the audience. She arched an eyebrow and began to rock her shoulders. She lifted her hands, and swayed.

Once she began to sing, she knew that everything was going to be all right. She had the confidence of her voice, and she felt herself lifted by the rhythm of the music. As the song ended, she threw her arms even higher and closed her eyes. She listened to the applause—it wasn't really as enthusiastic as she'd hoped, but it was nice nonetheless, and she knew she'd win them over with the next one.

"Thank you," she purred.

She was just deciding which tune to follow with when the drummer, and then the rest of the band, began to play again. It was slower and more sultry than the previous number. Spinning around, she glanced at each of the men, hoping they might give a clue what she should do, but none of them would meet her gaze. She stood there, her feet wide apart, her back to the audience, her heart thumping. To her surprise, someone behind her whistled.

Slowly, she turned back around. There was a smattering of applause. A few more whistles followed, and then the man sitting beside Amory, whose dark hair was just as slick and whose eyes were glazed, called out, "Show us what you've got under that dress, baby!"

Her chest seized with indignation. Clearly, Amory's friend had had too much to drink, and now he was acting like a boor. She waited for Amory to defend her. But when he didn't, it began to dawn on her that the friend was not the only boor in the room, and not the only man who wanted her to take her clothes off. They were all clapping and whistling.

Letty's eyelids sank shut as she realized what those

thirty-five dollars were really for. What a fool she was. Meanwhile, the band played on, the beat growing louder and more ominous behind her.

"Show us!" the man next to Amory yelled again.

She took a breath and wondered what a real professional would do. *The show must go on*, Mother always said—that's what professionals did. Since she was small, she'd wanted nothing but to be on stage, and now she was, with an audience of show-business men who, after all, might remember her kindly if only she could bring herself to give them what they were calling out for.

Obediently, she put her thumb under the strap of her dress and tugged it down from her shoulder. She was shaking now, but not to the music—in fact, she could not bring herself to do anything remotely like a dance. Her lips had begun to tremble, and when she opened her eyes, she saw that most of the audience was standing up, staring at her like wolves. Ever since she was a young girl, she had been trained to do as she was told, and so the idea of rushing from the stage—however much she wanted to be far, far from those awful leers—seemed wrong. But she knew if she stayed another moment, she would begin to bawl. She let go of the strap and ran.

By some grace of God her tears held until she was offstage, but then they came in a hot, salty torrent. She threw herself down in the chair, draping her body forward over the vanity table, shaking and gasping for air. She cried for the way those men had looked at her, and she cried for the beautiful illusion she had lost. She would have gone on crying—but her solitude was short-lived.

"What's wrong with you?" Amory screamed as he came rushing through the door. His face was redder now, and his eyes had become narrow and mean. "Edmund Laurel, the actor, is getting married tomorrow. This is his bachelor party. This is his last chance to see another woman's natural form before he is tied down forever. Now you've ruined it."

"I thought . . . ," she sobbed. "I thought—"

"That I was going to pay you thirty-five dollars to *sing*?" he spat.

Amory raised his hand and brought it down hard against her face. The line of her left cheekbone, the delicate curve of her eye socket, throbbed. There would be no more tears; the impact of Amory's palm had knocked them out of her. A cold, hard shock stilled her, and she braced for more.

But he had stepped away. She could hear the seething of his breath, but she did not dare look up at him.

"Leave," he ordered with barely contained fury. "Leave now, and don't think you're going to get a single penny for that pathetic tease of a show. You'll never make it in this business!"

Keeping her head down and her eyes averted, she grabbed her jacket from the back of the chair and crept back through that unremarkable hall. If any of the bellhops or guests noticed her flight through the lobby, she was not aware of them. She felt her smallness as she hurried down the darkened avenue, and would have counted it a wonder if anyone had been able to see her at all.

But Astrid did notice Letty, however briefly, as she made her way through the lobby to the subdued, elegant bar, and she wondered why the petite girl with the beaded dress was crying.

"Where's Luke?" she asked, as she took the stool next to her mother. There was a low sepia light in the room, and bouquets of peacock feathers placed strategically here and there, to give some patrons privacy and enable the sightlines of others. Virginia Donal de Gruyter Marsh's slender legs were crossed under her apricot chiffon, and in the dimness it was difficult to make out the wear on her face. She looked up from her cocktail without a hint of surprise in her eyes, and then scanned her daughter from head to toe.

"Whatever are you wearing?" she replied dryly.

Before coming into the hotel, Astrid had opened the glove compartment and found the black scarf that Billie wore around her neck when she was behind the wheel, as well as her brown driving moccasins; the robe was now tied with the scarf, and her wounded toe was hidden by the moccasins. Her hair had dried, but it was still carelessly pushed straight back from her forehead.

"Darling, don't be ridiculous, it's the latest fad."

Her mother smiled wanly at the joke. "He went back to White Cove," she said slowly. "Seems he was rather nervous about losing his job and didn't want to be involved in a big messy divorce story, after all."

"Oh." Astrid caught a glimpse of herself in the mirror and was surprised by how like a child she looked without any makeup on. "Are you getting a divorce?"

"I don't know." The older woman picked up her cocktail and downed the rest of it. Eyes glazed, she went on in a quiet voice, "But I think I'm going to be staying here awhile. How did you get here anyway? What made you change your mind?"

"I was worried about you," Astrid lied. "I realized I was being selfish, and that you shouldn't have to be alone just now," she continued, elaborating her yarn.

At that, her mother smiled again, in the same sad way, and reached for her daughter's hand. Blue veins emerged just below her knuckles. "I'm so glad you're here," she said, with a touch of melodrama.

"Would you like something, mademoiselle?" the bartender asked, placing a napkin in front of the younger lady.

"Yes," the former Mrs. Donal said. "One for her and one for me. Only . . ." She turned on her stool to look at Astrid. "Go change into a dress, will you, darling? I have the old suite we used to stay in, and the maid put all my clothes in the closet. Choose any one you like. We'll make a night of it."

I don't care what we do, Astrid wanted to say. But that would have brought attention to the darkness lurking inside her, and anyway, she wanted right then to feel very pretty, and to have men look at her and ask her to dance. Most important, she wanted not to hear the name *Charlie* or to do anything that might conjure that disgusting image of him in bed, bearing down on Gracie Northrup. So she went upstairs, put on a lavender dress with one shoulder and a skirt that swung out in flounces midcalf, and darkened her lips and eyelids. When she came back down, a handsome British fellow who was probably twice her age was chatting with her mother, but Astrid sat down between them, and winked and flirted until the gentleman's attention was fully devoted to her. She didn't like herself for the way she spent her evening, but soon enough the room was spinning, and after that she couldn't remember very much.

24

IF IN THE LATE AFTERNOON CORDELIA HAD ASSUMED that her wide-brimmed black hat would make her less noticeable, she knew by sundown that this had been a ridiculous assumption. The shadows were long on the country road by then, and she could see, in her exaggerated silhouette, how the wide brim obscured her face while bringing attention to the rest of her. Especially now that it served no practical purpose. The guardhouse was curiously deserted, and anyway by then she had stopped worrying about being spotted. Every time she heard even the most distant noise that might possibly have been created by a car, her hopes bloomed, and every time it proved nothing, she sank further into a state of confused agitation.

For a while she told herself that Thom was not on the road because he was making arrangements for a very special evening. She was still wearing the same blue-and-white-striped shift she'd worn to the croquet party that morning, because she didn't want to appear to be going anywhere particular. Until half an hour ago, she hadn't even made up her mind whether she would meet him or not. She did not consider the possibility that he might have changed his mind.

Her happy thoughts of his impending arrival carried her for a while, but then a black sedan with the top up came hurtling by, seeming briefly to be heading straight toward her before swerving off in the direction of the city. For a few seconds her chest had lifted, thinking it might be Thom. But then the careless speed with which the sedan whooshed by unsettled her, and after that she couldn't help her sense of foreboding.

Thom was never late; it was always he who waited for her. And then she began to wonder if she wasn't the only one who had been warned by her family to stay away. She really had no idea what kind of man Duluth Hale was, except that his son didn't talk of him much and that Darius Grey didn't trust him. After that, her worries morphed—what if she had remembered wrong, and Thom had wanted her to meet on the pier, and when she hadn't shown, he'd walked through to the house? What if Charlie and Darius had him now? Her father had told her he wasn't a violent man—but he *was* an awfully good shot.

Once that thought occurred to her, she found it difficult to shake. She began pacing and eventually found herself back near the main entrance. There was no point in hiding anymore, she thought; something had gone wrong, and one way or another she had to find out what. She walked toward the gate, waiting for some invisible guard to step forth and either chastise her or deliver bad news. None did. She turned back toward the road and the pine forest across the way, cursing under her breath.

That was when she heard the gunshots.

She wheeled around and saw that she was not the only one who'd heard. Six or seven men darted from different points on the property toward the house. She watched, frightened, her hands clinging to the gate. There was shouting, and though her eyes grew wide and her breath short, no one noticed her there. She pictured Thom, who always appeared with not a single hair out of place, who moved with that subtle confidence that suggested he'd never known embarrassment or pain. To think that he might now be hurt—or worse—caused a riot inside her. She had just determined that she must return to the house, whatever the consequences, when she heard wheels on the road.

For a few seconds she allowed herself to hope again, but then she saw that it wasn't him. The car was a hunter green Packard roadster with the cream convertible top down. She knew that car—she had ridden in it before. The man behind the wheel was Charlie. He pulled in the drive and turned the engine off. For a moment, they both regarded each other.

"I hadn't realized you'd left," she said after a pause. The shock of seeing him quieted her frightful imagination, however briefly.

"I had to drive one of our guests from the afternoon home." He blinked at her, his face contorted, though from suspicion or guardedness, she couldn't be sure. It was late for any of the guests to have still been at Dogwood, but she decided not to mention this. "What are you doing here?"

She took off her hat and let her eyes drift toward the house. "There were shots," she said. It seemed the only fact that mattered.

The expression in Charlie's face changed, and he jerked forward. "What kind of shots?"

"I don't know . . ." The desperate feeling had returned to her. "There was shouting after that, and then everything was quiet."

"Where's Danny?" Charlie said as he stepped out of the car and began glancing around frantically. "He was gone when I left. He's not supposed to leave, even for a second."

"I don't know . . . I haven't seen him."

Charlie's big head swung back and forth, his eyes moving between the house and his sister. "Well, come on, help me!"

Following his lead, she stepped forward, and together they pushed back the heavy iron gate.

He had accelerated up the hill before she managed to get the door closed behind her. There were no words between them as he sped toward the house, and seeing how unsettled Charlie was, Cordelia felt her pulse become fast and loud.

"What do you think it was?" she ventured as they came to a halt on the gravel drive in front of the grand steps that led to the house.

By then her brother's face had grown pale, and he only gritted his teeth and shook his head. Without meeting her eyes, he got out of the car, and then they were both running inside. The hall was empty, but they could hear men's voices coming from the enclosed porch. Charlie set off in that direction, and Cordelia followed closely behind him. Perhaps the shots had only been to scare Thom, she told herself. Perhaps he was all in one piece, and once she showed her father that she was still there, and promised never to speak to a Hale again, they would let him go . . .

Twenty or so men were standing on the porch, huddling around one of the floral sofas. Though no one was speaking, the atmosphere was distinctly grim. Many of them were wearing dark suits, and the backs of their jackets formed a wall, which Charlie and Cordelia had to push through to see what they were all looking at.

"Charlie," Elias Jones said, when he saw him. He stepped away from the others and put his arms forward to stop the younger man in his tracks. "Everyone out."

As the wall of men began to break apart, Cordelia noticed the blood on the floor, spreading under the soles of their shoes.

"No!" That was Charlie's voice, but it wasn't like any human utterance she had ever heard. It was the kind of wail of fear and rage that one hears late at night, in very desolate parts of the country, when an animal has lost one of its young.

Then she realized that it wasn't Thom but her father whose blood was spilled all over the white and turquoise tile.

"Oh, no," she heard herself say, as her eyes fell shut and the muscles in the back of her neck grew rigid.

Meanwhile, the men shuffled backward, but they did not leave the room completely. Charlie was pushing against Jones. "Where is the doctor?" he was yelling. "Why hasn't anyone gone for the doctor?"

"He said he didn't want 'im," said Len, the cook. The big fellow's complexion was ashen, and his eyes were rimmed with red. "Said it would be too late when he got here, and a man oughta know when his number's up."

Finally Charlie overpowered Jones and sank down at his father's side. To her surprise, Charlie called out for her. "Cordelia?" he said, without turning to meet her eyes. "Cordelia, come here."

Those thick-bodied men blocking the door watched as she stepped forward and went down on her knees next to Charlie. She had not shaken that sense that he hated her, and was surprised when she felt her brother's arm around her shoulder. He was trying, she realized, to comfort her. For a moment she couldn't tell whether or not her father was still alive. The collared ivory shirt he had been wearing was soaked with dark red blood. But then he opened his eyes, and though they were murky, she knew he saw them, because he said, through labored breathing, "My children."

Charlie took one of Darius's hands, and she took the other. His blood was slick and warm, on his hands and everywhere, and soon theirs were covered in blood, too.

"You are both my heirs," he said. Then his eyes closed, and they did not open again.

For a long time they knelt like that, while the light in the room faded from the burnt oranges and reds of sunset to crepuscular blues. No one switched on the lamps, and the shadows under their burning eyes became pronounced. Once, when she was a girl, she had seen a man pulled under his tractor who later bled to death. This was nothing like that. She could sense that her father was in pain, but he bore it stoically, with none of the wild screaming she remembered on the farm. Both she and Charlie watched him, until she heard Jones say, "He's gone." By then her face was wet with silent tears.

Both Grey siblings were covered in blood. Charlie stood up first, and then Cordelia followed.

"How . . . ?" she whispered.

"We don't know. There was only one man. No one recognized him, though he must have been one of Hale's, and it seems he went out through the—" Jones glanced up at Grey's men, lined up and watching, and then shook his head as if to say that nothing really mattered anymore. "Through the tunnel. Eddie and Wilson chased him, but he had a good start and he was fast, and when they came out the other end, he was already in a motorboat and racing away."

Cordelia buried her face in the crook of her elbow, as she tried to wipe away her tears without getting blood all over her face.

"Both of you go wash up," Jones said. His tone was as even-keeled as ever, except with a faint hint of sorrow. "There's much to decide, but later."

She nodded and glanced at Charlie. But the spirit with which he had put his arm around her was gone. There was a blackness over his irises now, something seething within him, and the ferocity with which he had sped up the hill was now focused entirely on her. It was only in the ensuing silence that she remembered how few people knew of the tunnel. Her mind raced, but she couldn't bring herself to think that Thom could do a thing like this, that she could possibly be in any way to blame. So she passed Charlie, walking out into the hall and toward the stairs.

She took the steps of the first flight slowly, and her weariness and shock briefly crowded out any thought of Thom or Charlie, or how any of it had happened, or why. There was only the stark fact that her father was gone. She thought of him, yesterday afternoon, on the porch, looking somewhat older than usual, telling her that her aim was getting better and what a good shot she'd soon become. It was after she had rounded the first landing and begun ascending the second flight of stairs that she became aware of feet falling behind her. They sounded menacing against the hard wood, and they exactly matched her pace. Her pulse quickened; Charlie was following her. Fear spread through her veins, and though she tried hard to think what to do, she could not begin to imagine how she could help herself if Charlie brought the full brunt of his anger against her.

When she reached the third-floor hall, she turned around and faced him.

"Where did you think you were going, there on the road?" he demanded as he came up behind her.

She stared at him, her face broken by sorrow and trepidation, but could not think of how to answer that question.

"It was Thom, wasn't it?" he continued, circling her. "You're still seeing him, aren't you?"

"What does it matter?" she replied tiredly. "What does any of it matter now?"

"It matters," Charlie returned, yelling now. "It matters because someone has to pay. You *told* him, didn't you? You told him about the tunnel."

Cordelia shook her head and covered her face with her hands.

"Charlie!" It was Jones on the first floor, his voice urgent and demanding. "Charlie, come down now. I need you. You can wash up later."

Though her eyes were still covered, there was no doubt of Charlie's presence as it drew nearer to her. When he spoke, his words were quieter, but in their terse precision, they had become more violent. "He used you. He used you like a whore. He used you to get to Dad, and now Dad is dead. You are useless." His breath by then was hot on her ear. "You are worse than useless. This is your fault."

"No . . . ," she wailed, but he was already walking away, his feet hitting against the polished steps so hard, they echoed up to the ceiling. Anyway, she wasn't sure what she was saying no to anymore. She wanted none of it to be true, but however much it stabbed at her, she knew that to be impossible.

On the first floor, Charlie and Jones were speaking, but she couldn't make out any of their conversation, so she turned and made her leaden feet carry her to her room.

When she opened the door, her maid stood up from the edge of the bed where she had been sitting with her hands folded in her lap.

"What is it? What happened?" Milly asked, her terrified eyes darting back and forth.

"They killed him." Cordelia choked up and brought her fist over her mouth. "Father is . . . dead."

"Oh." Milly shifted, still frightened and now confused, too. "Oh, no."

Cordelia's fist opened, and she spread her palm over her belly. She forced herself to take a long breath and appear somewhat composed. "Don't you fall apart now," she said, and though she had meant to sound kind, she knew that it came out more like a threat. "I need you to draw me a bath."

The maid nodded and went to do as she was told. Once the sound of water rushing into a porcelain tub could be heard in the next room, she returned and pulled Cordelia's dress over her head. She paused, staring at it, as though she were thinking how she would go about cleaning the bloodied garment.

"Just throw the damn dress out," Cordelia said. Then she walked into the bathroom and closed the door.

At first she yearned to know where Thom was and what he was thinking, and hear his explanation, and then afterward to be comforted by him. But as she stepped into the steaming water, the more she felt like the horrible word Charlie had called her. She was an idiot and a whore, and she had been used, in the most obvious way possible. The water felt as if it would scald her skin, but then she became used to it and was relieved that it was that hot, almost as though it might melt away her whole self and the multitude of things she'd done wrong.

For a long while she sat in the bath, and by the time the water had grown cold on her long, goosefleshed limbs, she decided that Thom had never really cared for her. He had never cared for her, and he had taken from her the lone person in her life who had fully embraced and protected her. She began to cry again, her tears streaming down her body into the bathwater. She cried for being so stupid, and she cried for the man who'd lost his life, for the things she'd known about him and the things she would now never know, and she cried for the carefree, privileged world that had been hers for only a few glorious weeks, and she cried for all the years no one had loved her and all the many future years when no one would love her again.

When her tears were gone, she got out of the bath and put on the robe her father had bought her so that she would be warm on cool nights. Everything was very stark within her, and when she went to the French doors and stood on the threshold of the balcony, she saw that the darkness at Dogwood was the same as it was everywhere else.

25

"WHERE'D YOU GET THE FANCY DRESS?"

Letty's eyes were sealed shut, and short strands of dark hair were plastered to her face with sweat. The voice was Fay's, she decided after a moment. So she was home; that was something. But her head was foggy, and the skin around her left eye socket was terribly tender. After a moment, she got up the courage to open her eyes, but this proved to be an error.

"Ohhhh . . . ," Letty moaned. She flinched at the bright light and the sight of her three roommates, standing over her. They were wearing those festively colored robes, and their heads were all cocked at unfriendly angles.

Then the memory of her humiliation at the St. Regis came

back to her, and she had to cover her face. Somewhere along the path home, she had found herself in a second-story speakeasy which looked down on a purple street, where an older gentleman with a well-tailored suit and bad teeth, who claimed to be a Vanderbilt, had bought her drinks. Later on, she had been relieved to find that there was enough gin left over in the icebox to put her to sleep. She was still wearing her new dress, although in its current wrinkled state, it didn't look nearly so glorious.

"Heard any rumors about the midnight gin thief?" Kate seconded. When Letty parted the fingers that covered her eyes, she saw that the brunette was holding up an empty bottle accusatorily.

"What happened to your eye?" Paulette put her hands over her mouth, as though it pained her to see her friend like this, but when she spoke again she, too, had a hostile tone. "Mr. Cole was furious you didn't show at work last night. He said you're not to come back—and he put me on Mondays, and took me off Saturdays, for having wasted his time with you."

Letty rolled over and buried her face in the threadbare sofa's velvet cushions. Her stomach whined and churned. None of her roommates moved, and in the silence, she could hear Good Egg running circles around the couch. An image of Amory's friends staring at her as she stood on the stage at the St. Regis flashed in her memory like a knife.

"Did you make any money last night?" Fay asked.

"No," Letty whimpered.

"Then you'll have to leave," Kate snapped.

"What?" Letty rolled over and her eyes got wide. A cold panic was flowing through her body.

"Oh, honey, don't let the big blues well up, it'll just make it harder for everyone," Fay said, in a not entirely unkind voice.

Letty's eyes shifted to Paulette, who had turned around to sit in a wooden chair by the wood-burning stove. For a while she wouldn't meet her friend's gaze. When she did, she lifted a delicate mauve chiffon evening dress with looping silver beading all over the bodice. In her other hand were a needle and thread, as though she had been trying to repair the garment. "Did Good Egg do this?" she said slowly, holding up the ragged, torn part of the skirt. There was a pile of similarly torn garments in a basket by her feet.

At the sound of her name, Good Egg came racing around again, a thundercloud-colored streak, and began wagging her tail furiously by Letty's legs. "Oh, dear . . . ," Letty said. "Oh, dear. Oh, Good Egg!"

Good Egg threw herself down at Letty's feet and gazed up guiltily with those almond-shaped eyes.

"I'll buy you a new one, I promise!" Letty wailed.

"With what money?" Fay placed a hand on her hip and widened her eyes.

"If Amory Glenn had paid me the thirty-five dollars . . . ," Letty began, but she trailed off when she remembered what the thirty-five dollars had really been for.

"Amory Glenn told you he'd pay you *what*? Just to *sing*?" Fay hooted. "And you believed him," she added, tsk-tsking.

"I'm sorry, Letty," Paulette said. "You have to go. The dog's ruined some of my nicest things, and anyway Clara needs a bed, and I told her she could have your place."

"Clara *Hay*?"

The three roommates nodded. Letty felt as though the Earth was falling away beneath her.

"But I'll pay you back . . . I'll give you all the money I have saved up now, as an advance on rent!" Letty pleaded, grabbing Good Egg's collar gently to make her quiet down. Sensing her mistress's urgency, the dog did pause, letting out a slight whimper, but continuing to wag her tail. "Please, don't put me out. I'll get a job. Good Egg will behave, won't you, baby? Won't you?"

"How much do you have?" Paulette asked.

Letty closed her eyes. After the money she had spent on the dress, that left . . . "Five dollars?" she said, as though it were a question. As the paltry sum hung in the air, she realized that it was too late for her. She didn't deserve to stay.

Fay sighed loudly. "Save your money, honey, and use it for the next train back to Kansas."

"I'm sorry," Paulette said. "Clara's got a job, and you haven't, and I can't stick my neck out for you anymore."

With the troublesome greyhound at her heels, Letty returned to her room and, trying not to cry, began to pack her things into the old duffel she'd carried all the way from Union. The clothes she'd brought from Ohio looked even drabber to her now than they had before. The dresses that Paulette had let her wear had felt like hers, but that had been only a temporary illusion. Friendship, she was beginning to see, could be awfully fleeting.

Before she could help it, she was thinking of Cordelia—but though the memory of her old friend made her sad, she found some strength there, too. She tried to do what Cordelia would have done—she unbuttoned the collar of her old black dress, pressed her straight black hair down over her forehead, and lipsticked her mouth. She bent and looked into Good Egg's eyes and whispered, "We're going to be all right," even though her voice was shaking.

When she came back into the living room, her head was held high. The duffel bag over her shoulder was not, she knew, particularly ladylike, but she found that despite the trouble Good Egg had caused, the greyhound buoyed Letty's spirits and was rather elegant to boot.

"Well, I'll see you around." Letty gave a wave and walked toward the door, with what dignity she could muster.

Fay closed the magazine she had been reading and let her

features assume a mask of sentimental concern. "Don't fall in with any Amory Glenns out there," she said, from the couch.

Without returning her comment, Letty left the apartment behind and stepped, as bravely as she could, onto the sidewalk. The day was clear and new, and she could tell how warm it was going to be once the sun got high in the sky. But that would only shine a cruel light on her hopelessness. There were little pink flowers on the branches of the trees, and people all around, and none of them seemed particularly interested in her or the rough way she'd been treated the night before. They were all just going about their business, as though the girl with the helmet of black hair didn't exist.

"Wait!"

She turned and saw Paulette coming up the three steps to street level, offering her a weak smile with one corner of her mouth.

"Here," she said. The fluttery black dress that Letty had worn the night Amory Glenn took her to the Grotto was scrunched up in her hands, and she quickly folded it into a neat square. "I want you to have this. It doesn't fit me anymore anyway. Really, it looked better on you. And this," Paulette said, handing Letty a ten-dollar bill. She shrugged apologetically. "It's all I can spare right now."

Good Egg sat down beside her on the walk, and looked up inquisitively at the taller of the two girls.

"I couldn't." Letty set her lips together and shook her head. "I've already cost you so much already."

"Who cares?" Paulette said, throwing her arms up. "Anyway, we'll see—maybe someday you'll pay me back with interest."

"Thank you." Letty pushed the dress into her duffel and carefully placed the bill in her pocket.

Paulette bent and kissed Letty on the cheek. "Toughen up, honey," she said with a sigh, and then turned and went back into the apartment.

"Well, Good Egg, where to now?" Her headache was ebbing, and there were still pink flowers on the trees, and Paulette had been kind, even though she probably didn't deserve to be treated nicely anymore. Letty bent on one knee and drew her hand along her dog's slender head. "I'm glad I have you, anyway," she said, and for a moment she shuddered, remembering how narrowly Good Egg had escaped the slaughter, and thinking what might have happened if Grady hadn't been there, with five dollars to give that beastly man.

Grady—she had forgotten about Grady. Suddenly all Letty wanted was to be in Grady's car, going to some special little place he knew, where perhaps they served cocoa. She stood up and began walking fast down the street. He'd told her where he lived as they were driving past it, and though she hadn't been paying much attention, she distinctly remembered him referring to it as his "garret on Bedford."

By the time she rounded the corner to Bedford, she was almost skipping, Good Egg dashing along at her side. Why hadn't she better appreciated that gentlemanly manner with which he treated her before, when it was right in front of her? Surely he would still be willing to help her in any way he could.

As she walked down the street, she craned her neck to look up toward the little hooded windows on the top floors, through the leafy trees, and so she heard Grady's voice before she saw him.

"There you are m'lady!" he called. "How I've missed you."

Letty paused in her tracks, glancing around for him, a smile already blossoming on her lips. At first she couldn't locate him, but then she caught a glimpse, halfway down the block, as he hurried down a stoop and bowed to open the door of a handsome cream-colored car. That was the gesture she most associated him with—that courtly swoop. Suspenders held up his striped slacks, and his collared shirt was rolled to the elbows. She took a few more eager steps in his direction, raising her arm and opening her mouth to call out his name.

But before the sound rose up through her throat, she saw that it was not her he had been addressing. The car door was not being held open in anticipation of her approach. It was being held open, rather, for a woman in a swaying, peacock-colored silk dress coming to stand on the curb in her pretty leather heels. Her lips were painted a very bright pink, and her shoulders were covered with a royal blue shawl as though she were going to the opera. Her red hair had been heated into shiny waves, the way Paulette did hers, except there was something even more fine about the way Grady's lady friend's hair caught the light.

Letty's shoulders went slack, and her heart dropped. She watched Grady gently rest a hand on the woman's forearm and lean in to plant a kiss on the skin of her cheek, just to the right of a cluster of pearls and diamonds that dangled from her earlobe. There was something so smooth and comfortable about him, and she marveled that he had seemed so nervous and boyish whenever they had spoken at the club. But it didn't matter. She had been foolish to think he would want to help her, when she had held herself so preposterously high. She was only glad that he hadn't seen her standing there, pathetic under the weight of that old duffel bag.

But before she managed to slip away, Good Egg recognized him, and let out a friendly bark.

Letty would never know if Grady saw her before she turned round. The surprise and mortification that followed that sound were all she could think about for several blocks, as she fled that pretty redbrick street where her last little embers of hope had burned down to ash and blown away.

26

THE LIGHT ON THE SIXTEENTH FLOOR OF THE ST. REGIS was very good, and Astrid took advantage of it to contemplate the lovely robin's-egg blue wallpaper in their suite. Her thoughts were all over the place, and she began to wonder at the relative simplicity of her name, with its four up-down syllables, especially when compared to her mother's. But perhaps by the time she was her mother's age, she might have a string of surnames, too—that was an unromantic notion, but one she regarded as more or less inevitable, especially that morning, when her head hurt and the whole world seemed rather blah.

Her mother sat only a few feet away from her, on the twin bed next to Astrid's, her dark hair wrapped up in a towel and her shoulders resting against the gold brocade upholstered headboard. In between them stood the room-service cart, laden with breakfast things. Astrid was trying to eat a soft-boiled egg out of an eggcup, but it no longer held any interest for her.

"What a drab breakfast," she said, looking down accusatorily at the half-consumed yolk.

"Eat it," her mother replied, without glancing up from the society column, which she was currently reading. It was Virginia Donal de Gruyter Marsh's standing order, at all the hotels in which she was likely to take occupancy, that the papers arrive for her open to the society pages, folded so that she would not have to read any actual news before her delicate retinas were good and ready. "Who knows when we will be able to buy another," she added darkly.

"I think we should go to the Egyptian section of the Metropolitan," Astrid said, throwing off the covers and standing up barefoot on the soft carpet. She was wearing what looked like red pajamas with the St. Regis name sewn into the breast pocket, but upon closer inspection it proved to be a bellhop's uniform. Although she did try for at least five seconds or so, she could not remember how she had come to wear such a thing. "And then afterward go for watercress sandwiches at the Plaza."

Her mother gave her an unamused look, and Astrid pulled her sleeping mask, which had been high on her forehead, keeping her hair away from her face, down over her eyes, blindfolding herself so that she wouldn't have to see the older woman. Fixing her hands at her waist, Astrid thrust one foot forward and bowed, just like the Little Tramp might have done. When her mother made no response—no spoken one, anyway—Astrid sighed and turned toward the window, ripping her sleeping mask off and dropping it on the floor.

"Pick that up," her mother said.

"No," Astrid replied. They both knew someone else would.

Astrid pursed her lips, and peered over the windowsill at Fifty-fifth Street below. For a moment, she entertained herself by imagining that if she dropped down, the red awning over the front entryway would save her from her fatal fall, and she would be bounced back upward toward her suite, where her mother meanwhile would have been scared into behaving like the lady she had been brought up to be.

"Don't be a headache, darling," her mother said before taking a noisy sip of coffee. "I already have a mean, throbbing one, and it's all I can handle, really."

"Who was that British man?" Astrid diverted the conversation, a touch cruelly, since she knew perfectly well it had smarted when his attention switched from mother to daughter.

"Spencer Gridley," her mother replied blithely. "Though apparently he is no one at all, since the society column has not marked his arrival on these shores, much less in this hotel."

"Have they mentioned *our* arrival?" Astrid asked in her softest, most innocent voice. "In this hotel, I mean."

This time her mother did not respond, except by ruffling the papers, and Astrid, who wasn't sure why she was playing such an absurd game, decided she would go to the Metropolitan by herself. There could be no objection to that, since after all, it was free. She crossed the room and was on the threshold to the adjoining sitting room, when her mother exclaimed, in quite a changed tone, "Oh, my."

"Whatever could it be?" Astrid replied ironically as she turned to face her mother. "Spencer Gridley's a lord, as it turns out, and now he's seen us on our *wuhst* behavior."

But her mother didn't answer her. She only draped the broadsheet across the coverlet so that Astrid could read the headline on the front page: GREY THE BOOTLEGGER ASSASSINATED IN L.I. HOME, it said, and then just below, in slightly smaller type, WHITE COVE NEIGHBOR MRS. DULUTH HALE SAYS SHE WILL PROCEED WITH TONIGHT'S GARDEN SOIREE.

Astrid craned her head back and turned her face at an indifferent angle.

"Well?" her mother went on breathlessly. "Aren't you going to say something? How horrid!"

"He drank too much," Astrid said flippantly.

"I might say the same of you . . . ," her mother replied, bringing the paper closer to her face, her eyes darting over the details. "Well—they say he'll be buried tomorrow. You must go immediately, darling."

"I certainly will not." Astrid lowered her chin and tried not to be interested in the article her mother was now devouring.

"You're right," her mother said, extending an index finger but not glancing up from the paper. "You must have a new black dress. We'll go to Bendel's and charge it to old Harrison. He won't have thought to cancel my account yet. Now that I think of it," she went on, brightening considerably, "we ought to get you a complete little wardrobe, so you won't have to go back to Marsh Hall at all. Nothing extravagant—two day dresses, two for night, a smart little jacket, a cardigan, two sets of heels, two flats, hose, under things, a hat—three at most. Then you can take the train back to White Cove to attend to Charlie, and—"

"No!"

"Astrid, don't be ridiculous!" She slapped her hands against the coverlet in emphasis. "You may think this sort of opportunity will come every month of your young life, but as your mother I am here to tell you, that will sadly *not* be the case. He's about to inherit quite a fortune—and a man never forgets the girl who stands beside him in troubled times."

"Well, I'm afraid I don't like him anymore" was Astrid's haughty reply.

Her mother cleared her throat and took a long time folding up the newspaper. Once she had put it aside, she gave her daughter what was probably intended as a compassionate look. "Who was she?"

"What?"

"Who was the girl?" The third Mrs. Marsh sighed patiently and pushed back the covers, turning so that she was sitting on the edge of the bed with her feet on the floor. "And did you catch him with her, or is it only an intuition?"

Astrid hung her head. A sheaf of blond hair covered her face. "Gracie Northrup."

Her mother groaned. "Gracie Northrup? Her grandfather was a *pea*nut farmer."

"I know," Astrid wailed into her hands. "I mean, I didn't know, but what does that matter? It's only—there he was, on *top* of her!"

"Oh, dear. Oh, there, there," her mother cooed, taking Astrid by the hand and pulling her daughter so that they were sitting side by side on the bed. "He's a lousy cad, dear, but they're all like that. Don't worry—you'll get used to it, and you'll get yours. There. Do cry a little, it will make you feel better, but don't rub your eyes *too* much; they'll get red and leave wrinkles." Astrid's mother sighed and brushed her daughter's hair with her fingers. "Cry a little, and then we'll go to Bendel's, all right? We'll get you the things you need for your wardrobe while we remain in the city, and if you want—*only* if you want—we'll get you a very smart black dress to wear tomorrow, *if* you decide to go . . ."

"I don't *want* to," Astrid blubbered into her mother's satiny shoulder.

"And no one is saying you have to! But come, darling, really, you will feel so much better once you are wearing something feminine and new . . ."

There were a few sobs left in her, and she let them out, punctuating the final one with a hiccup. "All right," Astrid said eventually, wiping the moisture from her wishbone cheeks. "All right, let's go to Bendel's."

"Good girl," her mother replied, clapping her hands.

They dressed and crossed Fifth Avenue, where they were taken to a private room, and over several hours they selected precisely the items that Virginia Donal de Gruyter Marsh had suggested earlier: two dresses for daytime, two for night, a cropped jacket, a long cardigan, two pairs of heels, two pairs of flats, various undergarments, a cloche, a sunhat, and a beret. Plus a black crepe dress with pleated skirt and wide boatneck, and a broad-brimmed black hat with a velvet band and several gleaming black feathers. Astrid's mother had been right; the Marsh account had not been suspended. Afterward, they had lunch at the Colony and charged a bottle of white wine and two orders of lamb chops to Harrison, as well.

When they stepped back onto the street, Astrid felt

a little dizzy but also distinctly refreshed. The afternoon sky had begun to pale, and she caught sight of an afternoon edition hanging from a newsstand. There was a large picture of Darius that was at least a few years old—he was standing on the terrace at Dogwood in a summer-weight white suit, with his hands in his trouser pockets, his eyes squinting in the sun, and a half smile on his face. Below that, there was a smaller picture of Charlie in his green roadster, and beside that was one of Cordelia, unsmiling, stepping out of a limousine in front of the Plaza and looking straight at the photographer. Some irreverence went out of the afternoon for Astrid when she saw that picture of the girl she had begun to think of as her best friend.

"Oh, let's take a cab, don't you think?" her mother said, already moving to hail one.

"Yes," Astrid agreed, though they were only a few blocks from the hotel and she suspected the walking might do her good.

She could scarcely remember her own father—he had still been at West Point when he and her mother had married, and then he had perished somewhere in France during the Great War, although she'd never been told much about it. "He died in a ditch," her mother had said unceremoniously some years after the fact, when a young Astrid had woken up during a cocktail party, having had a dream about him. From photographs, she knew that he was handsome, and blond like her, but that was all. She suspected it was different for Cordelia—Cordelia had dreamed of meeting her father her whole life, but as soon as she had, he'd gone away.

The poor girl must feel like she had no family, which was just how it had always been for Astrid, and suddenly she disliked herself for being such a brat.

"Astrid!" her mother shouted, a little too loudly, as she stepped into a cab.

"I'm going to the funeral, after all," Astrid told her as she climbed in after her mother.

"Oh, that's wonderful, darling." Her mother crinkled her eyes in Astrid's direction, the same way she used to when Astrid was young and had performed well doing jumps with her pony at the White Cove Country Club while Narcissa and Cora Phipps were watching. "Remind me to call the florist's when we get back to the hotel and have a big arrangement sent over!"

27

THE NEWS BEING SHOUTED BY THE NEWSSTAND BARKERS at Pennsylvania Station was all Darius Grey, but after spending the night wandering the streets, Letty was feeling so entirely delirious that the meaning that name might once have held floated over her head and away.

Since she'd seen Grady on the street, she had walked up and down Manhattan, and had arrived here at dawn, as though it were a sign. She was no longer able to think clearly, and though she knew she ought to save what money she had until she had a few things figured out, all she wanted was to sit in a well-lighted place and eat something. Glancing behind her, she caught a glimpse of herself in a mirrored column. The old black sweater she used to wear on winter mornings in Union made her appear even smaller than she was, and the skirt of her old dress peeping out from under it gave her a schoolgirlish aura, albeit one with a puffed and purple eye and a frightened little circle for a mouth.

The cup of English Breakfast she'd ordered was cold now, and there were already innumerable reasons for her to feel sorry for herself without adding the taste of cold tea. Good Egg was demoralized, too. Even her tail was still as she sat under the table, her head on Letty's lap.

"Last call for Montreal!" said the announcer over the loudspeaker, and for a moment she wondered if perhaps that might be a nice place for them to go.

Men and women rushed by, on their way home to the suburbs maybe, or returning from holidays to glamorous locales. Their feet beat out proud *rat-tat-tats* as they passed, and for all Letty could tell, every one of them had someplace very important to be. After a while it made her too sad to look at those people, so she put her head down on the table. The air in the station was hot and stifling, but the marble tabletop was cool against her cheek.

"Train to Chicago arriving at platform seven!" said the voice on the loudspeaker. Letty's eyes had drifted closed. "Stopping at points west: Pennsylvania, Ohio, Illinois . . ."

Ohio. She wondered if her siblings missed her, and if she was a good enough actress to make her time in New York sound like a brilliant adventure when she saw them next.

"Now boarding on track seven, all passengers for Pennsylvania, Ohio, Illinois . . ."

The man at the table next to her stood up, rattling his table against the stone floor before hurrying out of the café. For a few moments, she let her head rest like that, with a sheet of dark hair falling across her face onto the table, and smiled. It wasn't so bad, after all. She *had* had an adventure. However tired and worn down she was at that particular moment, no one could ever tell her she hadn't seen the city.

Outside the café, a sharply dressed blonde in a new black hat swished by, her eyes searching the departure board for the words WHITE COVE. When she saw the track number tick into place, she hurried to board.

"I heard it was a tale of love gone wrong," Astrid heard a middle-aged woman say as she took her seat. The commuter train rumbled alive and headed east out of the city.

"No!" the woman's friend replied. "Really? He *did* have that one special lady friend—that what's-her-name? That—ooo—oooo—"

"Oh, that chorus girl Mona Alexander?" replied the first. "No, no, no—this story goes way back, this story has to do with—"

"That's absurd," interjected the man on the other side of their seats, facing the opposite direction. He was young and wore a dove gray fedora and no wedding ring. "It was business, pure and simple. Duluth Hale arranged it—believe me. Men like Darius Grey don't care enough about love to die for it; that's just some sentimental wash you ladies pick up in your magazines."

"Heavens, what manners!" the first lady said, and then went on noisily expanding on her personal theory of Darius Grey's demise.

"This business about Grey's daughter showing up, not even two weeks before his assassination—well, it doesn't seem coincidental to me," the man grumbled to no one in particular.

Astrid smiled faintly. She could remember the early days when there were agents of the Bureau of Prohibition whose theatrical techniques and bravery made them heroes of the public. But by now, most hearts belonged to their richer and better-dressed antagonists. Average citizens, she supposed, knew a great deal about the various loyalties and grudges of their local gangsters; they followed their alliances and power grabs and killings the way some followed the stars of vaudeville or baseball. All over the city there was talk of what had felled the infamous Grey—who was to blame, who would rise to take his place, whether his gang and various political contacts and purveyors of booze would remain in the hands of his people or be dispersed among rivals.

And those gossips probably knew more about it than Astrid, even though she had spent so much time at Dogwood. But none of them knew Cordelia the way she did.

Astrid had never ridden on a commuter train before. It was shabby, she had to admit, but she rather liked being surrounded by people and hearing all their voices blur acrimoniously together. She liked the names of the places they were passing, too, and she rested her cheek against the window, listening as the conductors informed them that they were in places called Hunters Point, Woodside, Corona . . . At Flushing, the woman who insisted it was all about love got out, and her friend exited at the stop after that. When the conductor made the announcement for White Cove, Astrid was almost surprised; even once she'd stepped out on the platform, it didn't look remotely like the White Cove she knew.

She pressed the wide-brimmed black hat to her head and bent backward to see that the seams of her stockings were straight. Before she could really worry that she might have to walk to her destination, a cab pulled up.

"Where to, miss?" the driver asked, as she climbed into the backseat.

"To Dogwood, please," she said, looking down at her black wrist-length gloves to avoid the stare she knew this would invite. After a minute, he started the engine, and they rolled on through the leafy suburban roads.

As they approached the Greys' place, she saw great, black silk bows dotting the high iron fence. Danny was at the guardhouse, and his face was puffy, and she knew that he'd been up all night drinking and was now in the worst way. A machine gun was slung over his arm, and he did not smile when he saw her approaching.

"No cars allowed," he said to the driver, so Astrid paid the man, thanked him, and got out.

"You missed the service," Danny said coldly once the car had backed up and gone away down the road in the direction from which they'd come.

"Oh, dear." Astrid bit her lip. She had known she was going to be late; one might almost say she had planned to be, because she'd gone on putting herself together even when she knew it would mean missing the 11:31 train from Penn Station. She hadn't really wanted to get there in time to be at Charlie's side. She had, however, hoped to creep up and take Cordelia's hand, just before they lowered her father into the ground. "Where was it?"

"In the ballroom. There'll be a reception after the burial—they made a plot over by the orchard." He paused and pointed. "You got me in a world of trouble, miss," he added, his voice cracking. As he said it, he kept his face directed up the hill and his eyes away from her.

"I'm sorry, Danny," she said softly. "I'll make it up to you later."

She smoothed her skirt and walked up the hill. She cut across the lawn, and when she came over the rise just to the south side of the house, she saw the procession coming down the steps. Charlie was among the pallbearers in black suits who ferried the white coffin. Just behind them Cordelia walked alone, followed by Elias Jones and a herd of people clad in black, some of whom were customers and some of whom were colleagues. Astrid caught up with them right before they entered the allée of elm trees. Cordelia kept her chin up and her gaze steady on the back of her father's coffin, but without saying anything, she reached for her friend. Any outside observer would have said she looked preternaturally calm, but as the girls came side by side, Cordelia put her weight on the latecomer, and Astrid suddenly felt how unsteady she in fact was.

They didn't speak until after the ceremony. Astrid watched in silence as Cordelia and Charlie shoveled dirt over their father's grave. The sunshine was bright—each day was warmer than the one that preceded it now—and the pallbearers' shirts had become soaked with sweat under the armpits. Charlie tried to catch Astrid's eye a few times, but she kept her gaze resolutely on the coffin, and then when the group of mourners turned back toward the house, she put her arm around Cordelia's waist.

"I am so sorry," Astrid said, brushing a few strands of Cordelia's hair behind her ear once they were back in the ballroom, where refreshments were being served and people had begun to talk again. Towering floral arrangements lined the room, many of them from the city's finest hotels and oldest families. The largest had been sent by Mr. and Mrs. Harrison Marsh II.

Cordelia glanced at her. She had those washed-out eyes that are the product of many tears, and her chapped lips twitched at the corners, as though she were trying to smile but couldn't. "Oh, Astrid, you have no idea how awful . . ."

"I know, baby." Astrid sighed and puffed out her pink lips. "I know, I know."

The French doors of the ballroom were thrown open so that the mourners could gaze out on Dogwood's gorgeous vistas, those vast, exquisite grounds that Grey's illegal dealings had reaped. Women in slim black dresses glanced about, seeing who else was there, and men talked with one another quietly but still with more verve than was really appropriate for a funeral. Some of them did not seem particularly bereaved, Astrid realized; they had come because it was a curiosity and a local event of much interest, and she couldn't help but feel a little bad for Charlie, who was accepting condolences on the other side of the room. Meanwhile, she huddled with Cordelia by the grand piano, and whenever anyone glided too close to the girls, Astrid shot an uninviting look their way.

"I think I need to lie down," Cordelia said after a while. "Could you walk me up to my room?"

"Yes," Astrid said immediately.

As they crossed the waxed floor of the ballroom through the mingling guests, she let her gaze rise from her shoes and dart backward, to the place where Charlie stood surrounded by men in dark suits. His eyes were sad and tired, and they followed her as she passed through the double doors, his brows drawing tenderly together and his lips parting as though he wanted to call out to her. But she looked away quickly and let Cordelia lean on her as they went up the stairs.

"Can I get you anything?" Astrid asked once they stood on the threshold of Cordelia's room.

"No, nothing. I'm just so very, very tired." Cordelia walked slowly to the bed, unpinning her hair and sinking down into the pillows. "Go take care of Charlie," she said after a moment, without opening her eyes.

Backing out of the room, Astrid nodded, as though this was exactly what she had planned to do, when in fact she was already considering various routes out of the house that might save her from coming face-to-face with Cordelia's brother. Quietly, she pulled the door into its frame, and then with a sigh, turned around. There, down the hall near the stairwell, stood Charlie, his legs wide apart and his back slightly hunched, waiting for her. Neither said anything for a moment, and she lifted her chin and walked straight for the stairs, as though she didn't see him at all.

Just as she was about to pass, he reached for her arm, and while she did make an effort to brush off his grip, she didn't struggle. "Astrid . . . ," he said in a low, broken voice.

"I am very sorry for your loss," she replied with prim formality, holding her head so that her profile was to him. "But I cannot feel pity for you just now, so I think it's better not to speak at all."

"Astrid, don't give me any trouble," he pleaded, sinking onto his knees and wrapping his arms around her legs and laying his face against her stomach. "Not now."

From above, she contemplated his head of polished hair, rested like a naughty child's against her middle section and probably ruining her brand-new dress. He was so helpless and harmless like that, and no matter how she tried, she could not maintain the disgust she'd felt for him a few seconds before. Already, it was slipping.

"Oh, Charlie," she said in a weary, hopeless way, thinking of the tragedy that had befallen him, and the betrayal he had committed against her, and the sad story of the girl in the room at the end of the hall. "Come on," she urged, and helped pull him back up to his feet.

Silently they walked together to his room. For a moment she did feel sick again, the way she had the last time she'd stood on that spot, but there was something purifying about seeing his brass bed neatly made and empty of any strange girls, almost as though there had never been one there. She walked over to it and lay down on her back. He wavered in the doorway a minute, his big body framed by the afternoon light falling from the high windows of the front facade. Then, with a few long strides, he crossed the room, fell down beside her, and began to weep. He buried his head against her breast and wrapped his arm tight around her waist, so that she felt his shaking as he soaked her dress with tears.

"Don't ever leave again," he said, when he was done crying. "Promise me you won't ever leave again."

"Charlie!" she exclaimed. "The last time I saw you—"

"I didn't mean it. That was nothing. That was a real moron thing to do, and I'll never do anything like that again," he replied in a quick burst. "I'm sorry—can't you see I'm sorry?" he went on, almost shouting. "Don't you believe me?"

Astrid rolled her big eyes toward the windows, which framed a green-and-blue slice of the landscape. She didn't know if she believed him or not—it did not suddenly seem like a very interesting question—and her thoughts returned to the night before, and how she and her mother had danced with two sailors on the St. Regis rooftop and afterward gone down in the elevator, shrieking, to hail them a cab. Whose idea that was or how long it had taken, she couldn't remember, although she had a distinct memory of standing on a pier somewhat later, in a shell pink evening gown, and waving up toward someone on the deck of a very high ship.

"Astrid?"

Charlie was staring up at her with pleading eyes. He pushed himself up and took her face in his hands, and began to press his lips against hers. At first she didn't want him to, but then something in her stirred and she began to taste the sweetness of his kisses.

"Charlie," she said, pushing him back. "You don't—you don't think she's prettier than me, do you?"

"Gracie?" For the first time that day, Charlie let out something like a laugh, albeit a brutal one. "She's a dog. You—you—you're the most beautiful girl I know!"

Tears had begun to collect at the corners of Astrid's eyes, but she tried not to look like the last of her fury was dissolving as quickly as in fact it was. "Swear it," she commanded.

A pause followed, during which Charlie remained motionless, blinking at her, his large palm resting against her hip. Then he stood up, hovering over her in shirtsleeves—he must have left his jacket down in the ballroom—looking very broad and very serious and, despite the solemnity of the occasion and all the many things he had done wrong, very handsome.

Then he sank to one knee and picked up her small, gloved hand. "Astrid Donal, will you marry me?"

Her bottom lip fell, and her black lashes batted back and forth in confusion. "*Marry* you?"

"Yes. I don't have a ring or anything yet, but I'll get you a big one, whatever kind you want. Only, don't ever leave. I want you to be mine. Forever. Okay?" He bent, so that his head was resting over her hand. "Just say you will."

She drew her fingers along the back of his thick neck. Suddenly she knew she couldn't go back to living in hotels or traveling around Europe where divorcées with high standards of living could get by cheaply. The thing to do, she knew, was to draw her answer out, let him get nervous, punish him a little for what he'd done. But already she was picturing the big ring he was going to get her, and her lips had spread into a soft smile, so there was no point in saying anything but yes. He *did* love her, despite his actions to the contrary.

"Yes," she said.

"Yes?" He stood and picked her up, holding her close at the chest and swinging her feet off the ground. She was just seventeen, and he was twenty, and she was going to spend the rest of her life with him.

Perhaps there was still bitterness in the remote chambers of Astrid's heart. But she had never felt so safe as she did held up in those big arms, and anyway, despite the sadness of the day, the air was warm and alive, and her body was light and comfortable. If she had wanted to, she could have gone on making trouble. But she didn't want to. She was relieved that she could stay here, in this house, and be Charlie's, and never have to worry about anything ever again.

28

"IT'S NOT YOUR FAULT, DANNY," CORDELIA SAID FROM the driver's seat of the Marmon coupe he had somehow or other secured for her, in a voice that made her sound entirely sure and controlled, even though her heart was like a butterfly trapped in a jar. Danny was standing by the guardhouse, his hat tipped down over his face, as though he wanted to hide from the world. Instead of responding, he glanced back up the hill crested by the roof of Dogwood, where the wake was still being held despite the encroaching velvety darkness.

"What've you talked me into?" he muttered.

She ignored him. "Whatever you do, don't tell them you've seen me, all right?"

He nodded and said, "Take care of yourself, Miss Grey."

When she had gone a little ways up the road, she turned the headlights on and picked up speed. She had learned to drive when she was twelve—her uncle had not been precious about it—but she'd never been behind the wheel in clothes like these. Her long hair was slick against her skull and tied back in a hard bun, and her body was covered in a dress of champagne-colored silk, cut in the preferred style of young women who frequented nightclubs: A long, fitted torso was suspended by thin straps, but the skirt flowed out below the hips, with enough frothy volume that no one would notice a flask or two hidden in a garter belt.

Now that she was driving faster, the breeze chilled her bare shoulders. She was thankful for this, for it numbed some of the sadness and self-loathing. She had always had a fine sense of geography, and had picked up the lay of the land in White Cove just from driving around with Charlie and Thom. But it was different to be in control of the car herself, navigating the narrow roads, and that calmed her.

The sign for Avalon, the Duluth Hale residence, came up sooner than she had anticipated. Already she could smell the sound over on the other side of the property and hear the voices rising up from the party Thom's mother had thrown, despite—or maybe because of—the tragedy at Dogwood. This thought caused a bitter twist in her stomach, but she put on a smile as she left the car on the lawn and went through the gated opening in the high stone wall.

"Do you have an invitation, little lady?"

She held the gaze of the guard. "I'm a guest of Thom Hale's."

He looked over his shoulder at a second guard. "Escort her up, and ask Thom if she's okay."

As they walked across a manicured stretch of green, she contemplated the house, all lit up for the occasion. The white shingled structure was perhaps not as castle-like as the Greys' place, but its wings and satellite buildings spread out like great, encompassing arms.

There was much noise inside. A band was playing, and there were conversations from every corner. Heads turned toward Cordelia as she glided through a grand ballroom that was obviously in more frequent use than the one at Dogwood. Perhaps that was because Duluth Hale's wife was still around, and she did not run her household like a sleepaway camp for a gang of boys. Some of the faces were familiar to Cordelia; they were people who had been just as happy to drink Darius Grey's liquor whenever he opened his property to them. But she did not dwell on this, and only followed the guard down a sweeping flight of limestone steps onto a grand patio that faced the water.

Avalon had its own pier, from which small vessels came and went, ferrying guests to shore, illuminated in the darkness by tiny electric bulbs strung up their masts. There was a second band playing on the patio, although the mood near the lapping water, under a bridal arch of stars, was more languid and romantic. The dancing was less frenetic here, and couples swayed together in the subdued shadow of the house.

"Mr. Hale!" the guard called out, and then a tall figure, who'd been facing the black water with his hands stuffed in his pants pockets, turned around. His patrician lips parted, and his eyes became soft at the edges, in a show of sorrow that some foolish, feminine part of her believed in. "She says she's yours."

"Yes—she's mine." Thom nodded and the man left.

For a moment the two stood there, a yard of air and all the things they'd never told each other between them. She let her brash mouth spread and lengthen. It was a smile that said, despite everything, *I know you*.

"Aren't you going to ask me to dance?"

"Would you like to dance?" he replied, in a gradual, concerned way.

The touch of his hand, subtle and familiar at the small of her back, caused a flutter in her chest. She bent her elbow and rested her hand just below his neck, letting him lead her forward onto the floor. People had noticed the couple by then, and they were inclining toward each other to say, "Isn't that Grey's daughter?" and "What's she doing here, after all that's happened?"

Thom's cheek was inches away from hers, and she could feel the smooth warmth of his skin when it occasionally brushed her own. "Are you cold?"

"No, not at all."

"I'm sorry I couldn't call," he went on, lowering his voice to a whisper. "I wanted to know if you were all right. I wanted to tell you how sorry I was. I wanted to tell you that no matter what rumors you hear, I had no part in—"

"Oh, Thom!" she interrupted him, and gave a sad, sparkling laugh. "I know all that. *You* couldn't be responsible for such an awful thing." And she added, as an afterthought, "I hadn't known him very long, you know."

They had turned with the dance, and she became aware of a man, thick in the waist and wearing a pale pink suit, on the steps up to the house. He had a scarred platter of a face and the kind of eyes that are never moved, and she knew somehow that he was Duluth Hale. Then they turned again, and a few seconds later she felt Thom's shoulders go rigid. But his voice, when he spoke next, had his characteristic smoothness.

"I'm so glad you came. I thought you wouldn't want to see me anymore, after everything that happened . . ."

"I'm very happy to be someplace like this, where everything is gay." She paused, as though realizing something. She was lying a little more than necessary to confuse him and perhaps catch him fumbling in his story; but really just to exact a small revenge. To lie to him in some miniature, petty version of the gargantuan way he'd lied to her.

"Did you wait very long for me on the road?" he asked.

A pause followed, and when she turned her face to look at him, she could see that he was thinking about something else. "Yes—but that's all right."

She closed her eyes and pretended to be enjoying the music, trying to swallow the fury this deception stirred in her. She would like to slap his pretty face and tell him how stupidly she'd worried over him on the road.

They had come to the edge of the dance floor, and suddenly he stepped off.

"Will you follow me?" he asked. "I'd like to be alone with you."

So—her moment would come sooner than she had imagined. "Yes." She tried to twist her face flirtatiously.

They walked quickly across the grounds, past the house. He picked up her hand, and she matched his pace as he began to run between trees. They had gone far enough to not be seen, and she realized he must be searching for some specific location. Soon they reached the stone wall, and they moved along it until they came to a spot where the wall had been broken and worn down, dipping to a low point about four feet high.

Thom put his hands on it, testing its strength. When he turned toward her, his eyes had become uncharacteristically wild. Both his hands sought her waist; he took hold and pulled her closer, putting his mouth to hers. She draped her arms over his shoulders, playing along, mimicking his passion. Their lips parted, and he glanced over her shoulder in the direction of the party. "How did you get here?"

That was not a question she had anticipated. "In a Marmon coupe," she answered before she could consider the best reply.

"Good," he said. Then he climbed up, so that he was sitting on the wall, and offered her his hand. She grabbed hold and, pressing her foot against a stone, let him pull her upward. In a matter of seconds, they were on the other side. The darkness here was more complete, and she could just make out his features by the golden glow at the edges of his face. He leaned against the wall again, glancing back to see if anyone had noticed. That was all the time she needed to bend down and remove the six-shooter from the garter between her thighs.

There was a noise when she cocked the gun, and Thom revolved, slowly, to face her. All that bright-eyed sweetness of the past quarter hour went out of her face, and she allowed herself to look at Thom and see him for what he was: a cold deceiver, who even now, after having made her complicit in the murder of her father, was willing to take advantage of her for his own personal gratification.

"Cord," he whispered.

He had never called her that before, and the memory

of her father using the nickname the day he'd taught her how to shoot caused a pain that seized up her throat and spread toward her jaw. "Don't you dare," she said. "Don't—we both know what you did."

"I can imagine what you must think, but you must let me—let me explain," he said, stepping toward her and reaching out in his usual smooth manner.

"Stay where you are!" She moved backward, keeping the gun steady and pointed at his head, but he kept coming, and as the seconds passed, a panic overtook her. She lifted the gun over his head and fired.

The noise a gun makes was louder than she had remembered, and it shocked both of them. Her hands stung—she had forgotten how heavy and hot the gun was after it went off. Her eyes grew wide. Thom was contained and watchful, yet he was frightened, too—though he held his body motionless, the veins along his neck were alert. She remembered how terrified she'd been about the possibility of her father and Charlie hurting him, when she thought they'd been holding him at Dogwood. She imagined him like her father: his pristine suit ruined, his fine torso torn up in three different places. For a moment she was sure she was going to be sick. The gun fell out of her hands, landing faintly between them.

She became aware of shouting, from over where the rest of the revelers were. One of her eyebrows quivered, but neither she nor Thom said anything, and before he could try, she had turned and started to run. Really running this time, kicking off her shoes as she went and hurtling forward through the trees as fast as she could. If there were stones or needles underfoot, she did not feel them. She looped outward, making her way back around near the entrance, where the lawn was filled with guests' cars.

There were still two guards at the gate, talking in a hushed, agitated way, but they apparently thought the gunman would be coming from the other direction, because their backs were to her and they were pointing their rifles inward toward the property. Thom had not followed her, and she was able to tiptoe, very quietly, between the vehicles. Once she found the Marmon, she slipped over the closed door, so as not to make a sound, and crouched with her head down by the wheel. As soon as she got the engine going, she stepped on the gas pedal as hard as she could and careened away from Duluth Hale's place without daring to look back.

The guards must have heard, but by then she was gone. She headed inland at a reckless speed, glancing over her shoulder, indifferent to her hair as it came down and blew back across her face. It was late, and she hadn't yet passed anyone on the road, but she barreled on wildly, praying that the Hales weren't on her trail.

Around the time a small sign told her she had passed

out of White Cove and into the town of Nashitogue, she realized she had told Thom what make of car she was driving. It would be easy for them to spot her, even if she pulled over and crouched in the back, or put a hat on and returned through White Cove at a respectable speed. Surely they were fanning out now, all over the town and probably all over Long Island, looking for her. They had had little trouble killing her father, with all his connections. Why would they hesitate when it came to Cordelia, who was just a girl from Ohio whom nobody had heard of two weeks ago?

That thought haunted her a while, and then she careened off the road, crashing through a decrepit split-rail fence. The Marmon made a red streak across an open field, until her erratic driving caused the car to stall out as she was trying to go up a rise. It rocked to a stop. She twisted around, checking for pursuers over her shoulder. The cloud of dust she'd raised was sinking slowly back toward the purple earth, and besides a few cicadas, there was only a vast silence. She sank back in her seat and tried to feel relieved—she had escaped, after all.

But the quiet worsened her fear. That was when her heart began to assume a ragged beat, and a true sense of hysteria settled in.

For where could she go to now? All her life she'd saved pennies and borne indignities with a prideful shrug of her shoulders, buoyed up by the idea that someday she would meet her father, that he would be a great man and that he would take her in. Well, she'd had that, only to ruin it with her own heedlessness. And in her failed attempt to avenge the old man, she had now made herself a fugitive, too. The enormity of her trouble dawned on her, and with that, her breath became short. She had nowhere left to go.

She would never know how long she sat out there in the field, or how it would have ended had something extraordinary not happened: There was a roar just behind her, unlike any sound she'd ever heard, and a great flying object came speeding by, so low and close to her that she felt its extreme heat. For a moment, she thought it might have been a comet, but then she realized that was absurd. After she heard the crash and saw the flames rise up down the field, she knew it was an airplane and that someone was in it.

Though she drove fast, she was more controlled than she had been before. In a few minutes she arrived at the wreck. The nose was in the dirt and the left wing was on fire, but she did not make out the pilot until she had stopped the car and rushed forward on foot. He was hanging half out of the cockpit, his flying goggles still on his face. Perhaps he'd hit his head, because he didn't appear to be trying to escape the burning biplane. Placing her body under his and bracing herself, she undid the strap that held him. The weight knocked them both over, and for a moment she feared she was trapped. But in the next moment he said, almost matter-of-factly, "You'd better get us out of here, before the fire spreads to the gasoline tank."

Wincing, he managed to push himself up enough so that she could roll over, and then, wedging herself under his shoulder, she helped lift him upright. They walked like that together to the car. He was young, and he wore a white cotton undershirt tucked into brown pants that his black boots laced over. He was not much taller than she was, and though he was slender, there was a compact strength to every inch of him.

"Are you all right?" she asked, as they hobbled forward.

"Fine." His voice was deep and calm—almost perversely, considering the smoke now blowing over them and the fall from the sky he must have just experienced. "I hope you don't drive like a woman," he said as she helped him into the front seat.

"I beg your pardon?" She was almost too shocked by his lack of gratitude to fully respond to what he'd said.

But he only stared back at her, with wide-set, pale blue eyes that were somehow out of place against his sun-darkened olive skin. His hair was deep brown and cut close to his scalp, and he had full, unsmiling lips. She blinked and slammed the passenger-side door, and then didn't look at him again until they were headed toward the road and she heard the explosion behind them.

"Oh, God," she whispered.

The calm drained briefly from his face, and it seemed as

though something might actually have hurt him. But he only asked her if she knew where the hospital was.

"No," she answered truthfully, and though she felt she ought to be insulted by his terse manner, she was mostly awed by the coolness he maintained despite the pain that his bruised and broken body was surely causing him. If she'd had that kind of toughness, she thought, she could have taken care of Thom Hale, or better yet, not fallen prey to his advances in the first place. "Do you?"

"Where are we?"

"Nashitogue." They were racing down a road between two farms now. "I think so, anyway."

"Good." He tried to adjust his leg, which was obviously badly wounded. "Take this road all the way down, and then a left at Willow Lane. That will bring us to the Catholic Hospital in Rye Haven. You can drop me there."

Her body felt almost weightless with adrenaline, and both their breathing was audible as they hurtled through the darkness. It must have been very late, and though she supposed she might have asked him what he was doing up in the air in the middle of the night, she never did. There was only an ever-lightening sky and the thought of getting the stranger to a place where they would declare him okay.

Cordelia brought the Marmon to a shrieking halt in front of a stern, redbrick building with yellow light pooling from the high windows, and came around to help him out. The lobby was deserted, and so for a minute or two they stood alone in the plain white hall. Just as she was about to ask him what he thought they ought to do, a nun in a black habit came walking down the hall, and then several more appeared from other directions.

"Oh, dear," said the first.

"Is it really him?" asked another.

"I've had an accident," he said in that plain, clear voice. Turning toward Cordelia, he said, "By the way—you don't drive like a woman."

"Thank you," she replied with a raised eyebrow, "although I'm not sure that's a compliment. And anyway, shouldn't you be thanking me?"

"Yes," he said, and smiled. His face, so symmetrical with its big, serious features, had not previously seemed capable of smiling. But in that moment she realized how false most smiles were, and what a tremendous waste of time. His was rare and incomparable, and she was glad that he had been gruff before and saved that happy expression for now, so that she could truly appreciate it. "Thank you."

"It was nothing," she answered lightly.

"On the contrary; I could have died." The nurses flocked around him and were excitedly talking among themselves and calling out to others down the hall. Someone produced a wheelchair and urged him off Cordelia's shoulder and down into it. "I will make it up to you, I promise."

He reached out for her hand. She was surprised by how reassuring it was to feel a human palm against her own, and took in a sudden breath.

"What's your name?"

"Cordelia Grey," she said. She wanted to know his, but she paused too long, lingering in the curious glow of that simple touch, and by the time she realized that she ought to ask, he was being wheeled away. Then she glanced down and realized how ridiculous she looked—she was barefoot and wearing a dress that wasn't good for anything except drinking and dancing in, and her hair was falling down over her shoulders, and she no doubt had black makeup smudged around her eyes.

"Are you all right, dear?" one of the younger nuns asked.

"Oh—yes. It was him that was in the accident."

"Ah." The young nun crossed herself. "Thank *God,* he didn't die."

"Do you know him?" Cordelia asked.

The young woman giggled, and then realized she wasn't joking. "Of course! That's Max Darby, the famous pilot."

"Oh!" Cordelia started. Her head dropped back, and she heard herself laugh. "Of course it is!"

"Well, what do you mean, of course? He's a very good

pilot; he's never had a crash!"

"Oh, yes, I'm sure he is. Only—he's been following me, I think, without knowing it."

The young woman let out a dreamy sigh and said, "Lucky you. He's an *angel*."

"Yes." Cordelia turned to leave that cold, hygienic light. "I guess he is."

The fear and urgency that had driven Cordelia to that field had dissipated by the time she settled back into the car. It seemed a long time ago that she had pointed a gun toward Thom Hale's head, and longer still that she had wanted him so badly, she'd thought of giving up everything. Dawn was already brightening the sky, but she did not feel tired. The last bedroom she'd called her own was in a house full of bootleggers who probably had little interest in her survival anymore. But she wasn't afraid. By chance, she had been handed a finer sense of her powers. Her life had taken a wonderful turn, and then an awful one, but there would be a great deal more of it yet. She started the engine and turned the car in the direction she was always heading for—toward White Cove.

"They're waiting for you in the library," said Anthony, the night guard, when Cordelia pulled up to the gates of Dogwood.

In fact, they met her on the front steps. Charlie and Astrid were both still wearing their black funeral clothes and carrying a woolen blanket, which they wrapped around Cordelia's shoulders.

For a moment she could do nothing but glance from one to the other.

Charlie put an arm around her, squeezing her shoulder with his big palm. "We'll get 'em, don't worry."

Astrid stepped forward and took Cordelia's face in her hands. "You look like hell, darling. But we'll make you all better tomorrow."

"I can stay here, really?" Cordelia said.

" 'Course." Charlie managed to give her something like a smile. "Dad would kill me if I didn't look after you."

"Can I go to bed now, then?" she asked. "I've never been so tired."

"Yes, but—"

"There's someone here for you," Astrid finished his sentence. "In your bedroom."

Cordelia pulled the woolen blanket around her shoulders as she climbed the stairs. Her legs ached, and it took her longer than usual to rise to the third floor. By the time she entered her room, her lids were heavy, and she had almost forgotten there was a guest.

But then she opened the door and saw Letty sitting on one of the stuffed white sofas by the window. She appeared more petite than Cordelia remembered, in the old black dress, with her slick dark hair framing her tiny white face. One of her eyes was swollen and bruised, and there was a rather scrawny greyhound lying at her feet. She appeared fragile and exhausted.

"What happened to you?" Cordelia asked.

For a moment Letty didn't reply, and Cordelia remembered that the last time they had seen each other, they had been angry. But then the younger girl giggled and said, "What happened to *you*?"

Turning, Cordelia caught a glimpse of herself in the mirror and laughed outright. "I guess neither of us are at our best," she said after a while. "Do you hate me?"

Letty lowered her eyes and shook her head. "No."

"Are you going to stay awhile?"

Letty lifted her head, and her blue eyes rose under the line of black bangs. "I don't have anywhere else to go," she said. Perhaps she feared that sounded insufficiently grateful, because she quickly added, "I mean, I'd love to, if that's all right with you."

Cordelia smiled and went over to her friend, sinking down on the carpet beside her and laying her head on the other girl's lap. The white curtains fluttered open, and she could see a mandarin light just beginning to shine through the tops of the trees. There were many things she wanted to say to Letty, but she wasn't sure she had the energy, and anyway there was lots of time. They had traveled a great distance, and now they knew what a big city was, and they were both worn down. But all that could be discussed tomorrow. Tonight they'd sleep well, at Dogwood, whatever that meant.

It means home, she thought, and closed her eyes.

ACKNOWLEDGMENTS

I am so incredibly grateful to have such good friends and editors in Sara Shandler and Farrin Jacobs, without whom this book would have been a sad shadow of itself. I owe many, many thanks to Joelle Hobeika, Josh Bank, Les Morgenstein, Elise Howard, Kari Sutherland, Kristin Marang, Cristina Gilbert, Melissa Bruno, Sasha Illingworth, Beth Clark, Liz Dresner, Andrea C. Uva, KB Mello, Melinda Weigel, and Laura Lutz. And a giant thank-you also to Ryan Shawhughes and family for lending me a desk with a view on Long Island to write at.